"The Greatest Place on Earth"

Personal Note: A Work of Absurdity?

by Jeff Weisman

Journal of Experimental Fiction 91

JEF Books/Depth Charge Publishing

Aurora, Illinois

Cover Art and Design by Norman Conquest

ISBN 1-884097-91-X

ISBN-13 978-1-884097-91-1

ISSN 1084-547X

This volume is volume 91 of

The Journal of Experimental Fiction

JEF Books/Depth Charge Publishing

The Foremost in Innovative Fiction

Experimentalfiction.com

JEF Books are distributed to the book trade by

SPD: Small Press Distribution and to the

academic journal market by EBSCO

Dear Reader:

This is my attempt to capture what it felt like to live during the first two years of the Trump Administration. I'm not trying to explain anything. I'm not trying to overly judge anything. I'm simply trying to claim how absurd it really was.

I hope you can grant me that much leeway.

Yours,

Jeff Weisman
Fall 2018

All a man can betray is his conscience.

—Joseph Conrad

For my brother

Dear Shelley:

I found this in the attic when I was cleaning out the house. I'm not exactly sure what you'd call it, but your great-grandfather referred to it as his "unifying treatise," so this must be his manuscript he completed years ago regarding a pivotal assignment he was sent on while teaching at the university. I know you will find it a little disturbing, but I still thought you should see it. He is your great-grandfather.

Love you,

Dad

And PS: Please remember your great-grandfather was a real kook. He was a great man, yes. But he was also a real kook.

And PPS: Don't forget that.

The Acts

Act One

A Ticket to the Spectacle

FIRST RELEVANT JOURNAL ENTRY

A man stopped by my office today seeking my services for a research opportunity he would like me to embark upon concerning the inexplicable behavior of the residents from the tourist Town known as "The Greatest Place on Earth." Apparently, the residents have recently taken to exhibiting odd sociological and psychological behaviors that defy clear understanding. Some of the behaviors he mentioned were as follows:

- Randomly assembling and reassembling roadside attractions
- Worshipping a giant man-made shoe they call "The Sole of Truth"
- Mindlessly rambling on about impending dooms about to befall upon them
- Engaging in blatantly pathological public demonstrations
- Offering genuinely contradictory explanations for said exhibitions
- Consistently disregarding their own previous convictions
- Routinely stressing the fact that "Everything is just grand"

(Again, this is only a partial list of the examples he provided me with)

When I asked the man why he was asking me to serve in this capacity instead of one of my colleagues, he responded, "You come highly recommended. In fact, by all accounts, you are perhaps the most esteemed person in your field." Now, I certainly appreciated the compliment, but I also found his response highly suspect (one should never trust flattery from a stranger), yet still, the sincerity and conviction in his voice were unmistakable.

So then, after a brief discussion, he said he would return "the following day" (his exact words) to hear my answer. In the meantime, he asked that I consider an appropriate budget for my "expedition", as he took to calling it. And that I understand that The Bureau (which was all he would tell me regarding his, and my potential, employer) would provide me with an assistant.

A Side Note: The man wore an expensive suit, an elaborate tie, and had a unique coiffure.

(The closest approximation I can think of)

So I decided to at least consider this request (although, at this time, I will refrain from telling Ginny and the kids about it. I don't want to involve them with this until there is a need to).

SECOND RELEVANT JOURNAL ENTRY

While discussing Hegel's theory of madness (the alienation complex, more specifically) with one of my first-year graduate students, the man from yesterday showed up again.

This is my recollection of our conversation—

"Have you considered my opportunity?" the man asked, leaning against my bookcase (once my student left, to clarify), the man donning the same outfit from yesterday only this time wearing an enormous black top hat.

"I have," I replied, sitting up in my chair. "And I have some questions and concerns."

"Yes, yes, I expected as much. So what are they?"

"Alright then," I said, looking over at the man. "First, why do you even care about this Town?"

"I don't," the man answered, leafing through several of my books concerning dementia. "Not in the least, quite honestly. But The Bureau insists that I have this situation investigated. Hence, my inquiry regarding your services."

"Okay," I replied, hesitating slightly, while realizing I needed to re-word my question. "But why does The Bureau care about this matter then?"

"I'm not sure," the man answered, looking at me, his eyes disconcertedly fixed on me. "Some of the board members say it has to do with their values, they are worried about The Town, while others say it has to do with the legitimacy of their proprietorship, they are the benefactors of The Town, you know, while others contend it has to do with reinforcing their narrative. But regardless, I don't know."

"Reinforcing their narrative?" I repeated, opening up my notebook in order to write down some of my thoughts in real time.

"Yes," the man said, turning again to examining several of my books.

And then he told me this: The Town makes its money on selling its story. It is "The Greatest Place on Earth," you know. People come far and wide to experience this Town. However, the current behavior apparently questions that narrative. In fact, The Bureau's even concerned about the long-term viability of The Town. Hence, again, my inquiry regarding your services.

"So," I said, looking over at him, his top hat partially obscuring his face from me. "They want me to explain why this is occurring?"

"In a sense," the man answered, picking up Combe's book on phrenology. "But it would seem more accurate to me to say that they want to know about the residents. Should they be worried about them or not?"

"About their behavior, you mean?"

"Yes well, to the degree that it threatens theirs," the man answered, putting down the book. "To the degree that it threatens theirs."

"Their wellbeing then?" I asked.

"Their stability," he answered, turning and glaring at me, his face suddenly blanketed by an obviously forced smile.

My First Real-Time Thought: This man is rather oblique.

"And how long do you expect my services to be needed for?" I then asked.

My Second Real-Time Thought: And disturbing.

"As long as your expedition requires," he answered, before turning and looking out the window of my office, the morning sunshine slightly muted by a thin layer of cirrus clouds, and then he added, "Although, I'm sure you would want to finish up your work as soon as possible."

(What the word expedition makes me think of)

"I do have a wife and two children to be concerned about," I added.

"We both do," he replied, pushing his top hat up slightly further over his forehead, better revealing his lightly greying greasy hair and his bushy eyebrows. "Which is why I'm hoping we can get on with this. So what other questions do you have?"

And then, to focus things to the main particulars, my questions went like this—

How do you want me to do this?

Answer: Like any field research assignment, embed yourself with the "indigenous population" (his specific term), study their behavior, formulate your hypotheses, test your theories, and provide us with your conclusions.

Will the townspeople know I've been asked to conduct this research?

Answer: Some of them, perhaps. But I'm not sure. However, either way, feel free to conduct yourself as you see fit since what we want is a true verdict on their behavior.

And why me again?

Answer: Because your character is unassailable. Or at least, The Bureau makes that claim.

A Second Side Note: This man is clearly keeping something from me.

And their behavior has not been seen as overly dangerous or alarming?

Answer: No, it has. (He then laughed for several seconds, in a genuinely disconcerting fashion, to specify, before continuing.) But that is not our concern.

And how do you want me to update you on my findings?

Answer: Through frequent dispatches regarding your work. Also, if need be, various Bureau Operators will contact you. In fact, you should expect that.

And I can have a staff?

Answer: You will be provided with an assistant upon your arrival. But all those details will be worked out upon your acceptance of this offer.

And I will be compensated appropriately.

Answer: Money is no object. But much more importantly, you have the opportunity to be involved with one of the most significant research studies ever conducted. In fact, if you are able to accomplish this task, your name will most certainly go down in the annals of history.

So I will be able to publish my results?

Answer: Yes, well, that has not been decided yet. Not at all.

A Third Real-Time Thought: That is unfortunate.

And what do you expect from my dispatches?

A Fourth Real-Time Thought: And he is clearly hiding something from me.

Answer: As much information as you can provide—notes, drawings, pictures, anecdotal evidence, secondary ruminations, anything and everything that will help support and explain your conclusions.

(Why I will avoid drawings)

And have any other researchers been asked to do this?

Answer: Yes, several, in fact. But they have all quit on us, or more accurately, perhaps, disappeared on us, although we did fire several people and we even lost someone. But that is no worry, no worry at all. And you will have their work to build off of, of course.

A Fifth Real-Time Thought: That is also distressing.

And when do you want me to start this?

Answer: Yesterday, of course.

"Alright," I then said. "I am interested. But I need to talk this over with my family first. It is not easy for me to leave them at this time."

"Good," he replied, again adjusting his top hat on his head. "And of course. Talk with your family."

"They are my primary concern. However, thankfully, the university will clearly support my research if I should choose to embark upon this opportunity. That should not be a concern. Dean Littlefield's always looking for breakthroughs in our work to sell to the alumni."

"Of course. And when you have made your decision, please stop by my office. I will be expecting you shortly."

He then handed me this card—

The Bureau Clerk
Office 4114RU12
111 Carnival Street

A Personal Note: I don't know why I am considering this. I don't trust this man. I don't know what to make of this Bureau. I've only heard questionable things about this Town. And it's a terrible time to leave my family—and to some little two-buck hickville place too. But still, there is something intriguing about this opportunity. Why would this Town effectively be going nuts?

"Fine. I will stop by your office and tell you either way first thing tomorrow morning. You have my word."

A Second Personal Note: And the extra money would be nice.

"Good. We await your response."

THIRD RELEVANT JOURNAL ENTRY

"But dad, you said you were going to take me to visit some colleges this summer. And I still need you to help me with my admissions essay," Aaron whined, half-heartedly dropping his fork onto his plate, his thin face nearly covered in acne and his brown hair slicked back with gel.

"I know," I responded, cutting into my piece of meatloaf with my knife and fork, while considering one of the many images the man from that morning left me with from our conversation—

The Distracted Talkers

They

Transmit

In Gibberish

Quite frequently,

Like a disjointed wire,

No less

He stressed.

"And you were going to spend more time with me this summer dad," Evelyn added, before I could even respond to Aaron. "You promised me that you were going to do that. You've been gone so much lately. Isn't that what you said?"

"I know. But this is a really good opportunity for me. And I still should be able to get you that internship with Professor Dolton," I said to Evelyn, the ceiling light shrouding the dining room in a soft yellowish-white hue, while I slid my piece of meatloaf through the brown gravy on the side of my plate. "I will contact him again for you. And we can still work on your designs together later this summer. I don't think it will take that long. It really shouldn't."

"Let's be supportive of your dad kids. I know this is going to be tough on us, but this sounds like a good opportunity for him," Ginny interrupted, her shoulder-length brown hair, slightly greying, pulled back into a bun, fully revealing her attractive face, and suddenly reminding me of when we first met my junior year of college.

"I'm Robert," I had said, sitting down next to her in the cafeteria at our Mount Prospect College, my dorm mates Charles and Arnie staring over at me from the other table.

"I know," she answered, looking up at me, her face almost glowing in the large hall. "You're in my Intro to Ethics class. And I'm Ginny."

"And you're going to marry me someday," I said, only half in jest.

"It really is," I added, looking at Ginny, before scooping up a forkful of peas and carrots from my plate. "But I don't want to go if you don't support it."

"None of us like you being away for so long, especially not now. And right after that last research trip you were just on. But what do you say kids?" Ginny asked, looking over at Aaron and Evelyn, the thought of the two of them sitting in the same seats that they'd been sitting in since they were little suddenly reminding me of another image from earlier that morning.

The Bigger People

They

Seem

To

GROW,

The man had said.

"Fine," Evelyn replied. "And now I'm thinking after high school I want to go college somewhere on the east coast because you know they have the best engineering schools."

"And you Aaron?" Ginny added, looking over at Aaron. "Can we do this for your dad?"

"If that's what you want mom," Aaron answered, his voice an odd mixture of a metallic baritone and a raspy shudder.

A Side Note: Why am I doing this exactly?

"It's settled then," I said, looking at Ginny, while stabbing my fork into my mound of mashed potatoes. "I will tell the man tomorrow."

"It sounds like an opportunity you just can't pass up," Ginny continued.

A Personal Confession: Part of me is looking forward to being away from Ginny right now.

"I know," I replied, suddenly smiling, before setting my forkful of mashed potatoes on the edge of my plate. "The research possibilities seem quite intriguing. But it's going to be real tough to be away from all of you again."

FOURTH RELEVANT JOURNAL ENTRY

Given the fact that the man's room was located on the far side of the city, I decided to hail a driver for the ride over there. And on the way in the carriage, I had one of the more disconcerting conversations I'd had in a while.

A Personal Note: I still don't know why I am doing this.

START OF TRIP SYNOPSIS

Driver (turning onto Rodham Avenue from Donner Street): Did you hear about them Russians?

No, I responded. I've been so busy with my work lately I haven't paid much attention to the news. And I've been out of the country for a little while too.

Driver: Yeah well, they're trying to take over everything.

They are? I said.

Driver: Yeah, just like everyone else.

Is that so? I replied, not sure what this man was talking about.

Driver: That sure is. And I tell you, this whole world's going to hell in a handbasket.

Right, I said, seeing the man from The Bureau's building come into view at the end of the street. And it truly was one of the odder sights I'd seen in a while.

(What the thing looked like really)

Driver: And you can take that to the bank.

END OF TRIP SYNOPSIS

And then I paid the man, got out of the carriage, and walked up the stairs, which seemed more like a warehouse passageway, to be more accurate about it, before finding the man sitting at a desk at the end of the corridor, clearly waiting for me.

"Ahh," the man said, now wearing a bright red jacket, "I've been expecting you."

"Yes," I answered, looking around the corridor, the walls covered in various billboards and sign advertisements for lemonade and peanuts, while wondering if I should ask where exactly we were, before adding, "I had to attend to a few things first this morning."

"Of course, of course," the man replied, "But no matter. We've been expecting you."

"We?" I said, looking over the man's shoulder to see if I could see anyone else around.

"We, no me," he immediately stammered, smiling at me. "Sorry. I have a tendency to do that. I just meant me. That is all."

Another Side Note: I really don't trust this man.

"Okay."

"But sit, sit," the man said, gesturing with his hand for me for sit down at the chair in front of his desk. "I want to hear your decision. I've been hoping for some pleasant news. We all have actually."

"Thanks," I replied, pulling out the chair, the corridor barely illuminated by a single light bulb dangling precariously overhead. "And yes, I've agreed to your offer. But I still have some concerns."

"Wonderful, wonderful," the man said, suddenly opening his drawer and pulling out a huge file of paperwork. "That's wonderful news. We are most excited to hear that."

"But I want to be able to terminate my services at any time," I added, sitting down in the chair, the corridor faintly smelling of roasted corn and cotton candy.

"Here," the man simply replied, sliding the huge file of paperwork over towards me. "This will answer all your questions. And that is truly wonderful news."

"And if I ever have any cause for concern, I will simply leave," I continued, repositioning myself on my chair.

"Of course, of course, whatever you say," the man said, glancing over at me, his eyes simply shining like an iridescent ball. "But where can we go, you see? Isn't that the question?"

"I don't know. But those are my concerns," I answered, flipping open the file cover and seeing this written across the first page—

--WARNING--

TOP SECRET

Yet Another Side Note: What have I gotten myself into?

"No matter. No matter at all," the man said, suddenly getting up and starting to walk through the door behind him, before pausing for a moment, looking back at me, and adding, "It is all in your file."

And then the door clanked shut.

FIFTH RELEVANT JOURNAL ENTRY

"And you need to leave right now?" Ginny asked again, looking at me from the doorway, her reading glasses dangling over the front of her white blouse, her blue eyes glaring at me. "But it's Saturday? And that station you mentioned's on the other side of the city."

"I know, but my train ticket's for this afternoon," I answered, stuffing the last of my supplies into my bag. "They want me to get started as soon as possible. And I've worked everything out with Dean Littlefield already. Professor Weinstein will cover my classes."

"But the kids are out too. Don't you want to say goodbye to them?"

"I spoke with them this morning," I replied, shoving my file into my bag (the thing nearly two inches thick). "They'll be fine. And I will write."

My morning conversations—

Aaron: I'll be fine dad. It's not like you haven't been away before.
Me: But I need you to keep an eye on things while I'm gone.
Aaron: I know. Don't worry. I always do.

**

Evelyn: I'm fine dad. Like you said, we can work on my designs when you get back.

21

Me: We will. And I'll look into that internship for you too. Promise. But I feel bad.

Evelyn: Don't. I know how important your work is. And I can do it on my own too.

"But I'm going to miss you," Ginny said, leaning against the doorway. "And I was hoping we could work on things. You know we said that that's what we were going to do now that you were back. I wanted to start this weekend too. We really need to do that Bob."

A Personal Note: I know she's right.

"We will," I replied, zipping my bag shut, before stopping for a moment, and seeing my reflection in our bedroom wall mirror—my slightly thin build, pale white skin, oversized ears, brown eyes, chrome wire eyeglasses, brown mustache, short greyish brown hair, white dress shirt, black tie, black suit jacket, black dress pants, and my five foot eleven stature suiting my forty-nine-year-old disposition—before parting my hair again with my pocket comb, and then walking over to Ginny. "Trust me. We will," I then said, putting my hand against her check, her skin soft like a warm sheet of silk. "I know we need to."

"I hope so," Ginny said, kissing my hand, her brown hair bobbing against her shoulders. "It's just that everything's been unraveling lately."

"You know what I said," I responded, looking at her, her face suddenly belying her age. "It'll be alright. And I care about you Ginny. More than I can even say. And you know that I love you."

"I love you too," Ginny replied. "But sometimes that isn't enough."

"Sure it is," I said, before walking back over and picking up my bag. "And I'll write frequently. We can work on things that way."

A Second Note: Perhaps I can earn another award for this.

"Be safe," Ginny then said, stepping over to our dresser, the hustle and bustle from the city street below our window suddenly filling our room. "Okay. Because I'll worry about you."

"And look under your pillow," I added, starting to walk down the stairs, before stopping for a moment and kissing her.

A Brief Reflection: And what did that man mean by "we even lost one"?

"And take this," Ginny said, handing me the silver framed picture of our family from our dresser—the kids twelve and fifteen at the time, standing in their Sunday best, and Ginny and me standing next to them outside the Lincoln Cathedral, smiling proudly.

"I left you something," I continued, taking the picture frame from her and putting it in my bag.

A COPY OF MY FIRST LETTER

```
Dear Ginny:
    I know I haven't been perfect lately.
I've been so busy with my work. And that's
been a real strain on us. And you've been
wanting more out of life too, like going back
to graduate school and getting a better job.
And I know that's probably what lead to what
you did. At least I think that's what lead to
what you did. But I just need some time to
work things out. We have built so much
together. I need to know what we should do.
    Love, Bob
```

And then I took off down the stairs, enthusiastically.

Act Two

All Aboard! All Aboard!

"Enjoy the ride," the ticket agent said pointing me towards the train at the back of the station, the train completely inappropriate given the nature of my journey once I turned around and saw it.

(The closest thing it reminded me of)

But nonetheless, I was excited to find my seat and have a chance to finally peruse through my file. However, that was nowhere near as simple as it sounded.

BIZARRE MOMENT NUMBER ONE

"Excuse me, excuse me," I said, pushing my way through one of the many train cars. "Excuse me, I need to get through. Excuse me."

"Watch it," this man, standing in the middle of the aisle, barked, turning and looking at me, as I tried to squeeze past him. "Can't you see that I'm standing here?"

"Sorry," I replied, suddenly noticing the man's face was all bruised and bloody. "I'm just trying to find my seat."

"We all are," the man said, continuing to stare at me, while grabbing the hand bar above him. "But just because you have a ticket doesn't mean you have a seat," he then added. "Don't you know that?"

"What does that mean?" I answered, fumbling with the strap of my bag, while the fifty or so other passengers all seemed to ignore us. "A ticket means you have a seat. That's what a ticket means."

"Not exactly," the man said, turning slightly so that I could pass him. "That's what they want you to believe. But not every ticket's the same. Even if they were issued by the station. And it's not always easy to tell them apart."

Personal Note: What does that mean?

"You can say that again," an older man, sitting on a bench next to us, suddenly huffed. "Almost half the people on this train don't belong here."

"Absolutely," the bloodied man said, continuing to stare at me, his breath smelling faintly of whiskey. "And I'm just waiting for them to clean this place out."

"Right, of course," I responded, not at all sure what to make of this conversation, before continuing on towards my seat, the train suddenly starting to move. "Excuse me."

BIZARRE MOMENT NUMBER TWO

Then, while pushing my way through the next car, I suddenly glanced up and saw what looked like a monkey, or at least what I believed was a monkey, dressed in a blue suit, sitting on the overhead luggage rack, smoking a cigarette and drinking a glass of vodka.

"Quite a train," the monkey then said, exhaling a huge cloud of smoke.

"Yes," I responded, fumbling with my bag down the aisle of the train car, while wondering if I was actually seeing a monkey sitting on the overhead luggage rack dressed in a blue suit smoking a cigarette and drinking a glass of vodka talking to me.

"Almost unmatched," the monkey continued, before taking a sip of his vodka.

And then the monkey simply disappeared, the whole thing undoubtedly some kind of optical illusion, I concluded.

BIZARRE MOMENT NUMBER THREE

"Ticket sir," the attendant said the moment I stepped into the next car, the train rocking back and forth as it continued to speed up down the track. "Can I have your ticket please?"

"Yes," I answered, looking over at him and immediately realizing that he looked like some sort of clown more than anything else.

(What he truly reminded me of)

"I need to see your ticket sir."

"Yes, yes," I answered, taking my ticket out from inside my jacket pocket and handing it to him. "It's right here."

Another brief thought about what the man from The Bureau had said—

Have

They

Thoughts

Uneasy

"Interesting," the attendant replied, pausing for a moment to look at my ticket. "You have one of those ones. Well good for you. Your seat is right behind you."

"What does that mean?" I asked, turning and seeing a seat in the back corner of the car, a man in a bright blue suit sitting in the seat next to the window.

Personal Note: What did that mean?

"But of course," the attendant continued, his whole expression seeming somewhat forlorn, while pointing to the seat. "Sit down."

"I'm glad I found it," I added, straining to hold my bag over my shoulder. "It was very unclear from the markings."

"It shouldn't have been," the attendant said, before starting to walk down the aisle of the car. "Ticket."

BIZARRE MOMENT NUMBER FOUR

"Are you on vacation?" the man sitting next to me asked, before I could even get fully comfortable, my seat at the back of the car seeming more like a bench at a park than a seat on a train.

"No," I answered, looking over at him and suddenly realizing that the man's face was covered in a thin layer of paste. "I'm actually on a business trip."

"A business trip?" the man repeated, genuinely taken aback by my response. "But don't you know where you're headed?'

"Yes, of course," I replied, trying not to stare at his face too much. "Although I've never actually been there. But I've heard some great things about it."

One of the things I heard: Everyone has an equal opportunity to win the prizes there.

"It is an awesome place," the man stammered, pulling out a pocket watch from his inside coat pocket and checking the time. "The Greatest Place on Earth. And rightfully so. I'm meeting my family there, in fact. We all are so excited too. They left yesterday."

"Good for you," I said, looking out the window over his shoulder and suddenly seeing an enormous storm approaching.

(My best approximation)

"But what kind of business do you have there?" the man asked, obviously bothered by my disclosure.

"Research," I answered, steadying myself against the side of my seat as the train rocked back and forth down the track, the sky continuing to darken outside the window. "I'm a Professor of Psychology at the City University. And I've been asked to study the people there. Apparently, they've been engaged in some potentially concerning behavior lately."

"There's nothing wrong with the people there," the man immediately barked, again pulling out his watch and checking the time. "What kind of nonsense is that?"

"I've just been asked to research the people there," I repeated. "That's all. I hope that storm doesn't get any closer to us."

Another thing I heard: They have entertainment available for every interest and persuasion.

"But that's ludicrous," the man said, completely ignoring my concern about the weather. "I was just there a few weeks ago. There's nothing wrong with the place."

"I don't know what to tell you," I replied, noticing that the man's face seemed more like a mask than actual skin covered by paste. "That's why I'm heading there."

"Now sure," the man interrupted, continuing to hold his watch in his hand. "The Mayor seems a little reckless at times. He has a way of operating that's a little hard to get a grasp of. And the

Shopkeepers can be a little unique. And the Cabinet at Large, as it were, seems rather ineffectual. But that's no worry."

Another thought I just remembered from the man at The Bureau—

Some

Have

Been

Shrinking

Lately

He said.

"I really hope that storm doesn't get any closer," I repeated, continuing to watch the sky darken out the window.

"And the Welcoming Committee might be a little unwelcoming by the usual standards," the man continued, clearly ignoring my concerns about the weather. "And of course, by and large, the townspeople might be a little violent."

"The clouds are something else."

"Perhaps even a little more than a little violent at times," the man simply continued. "But that is the way it's always been. Don't you understand?" the man then asked, staring right at me, his face clearly a mask, I suddenly realized.

"That's what I'm there to discover," I answered, shifting in my seat slightly. "It seemed like an interesting research opportunity for me."

"And you better not mess with things," the man suddenly barked, putting away his watch. "It's The Greatest Place on Earth for a reason."

"Of course," I replied, wondering why the man seemed so concerned about my inquiry. "I just want to learn the truth."

"I've told you what's going on," the man then barked again. "Didn't you hear me? There's nothing to worry about."

"Then that is what I will find out," I replied, suddenly noticing the clouds vanish right before my eyes. "I'm just interested in learning what's actually going on out there."

"And look," the man continued, pulling out a piece of paper from his inside coat pocket. "I was given this the last time I was there."

MEMORANDUM OF STATUS REGARDING THE GREATEST PLACE ON EARTH

Dear Everyone:

This memorandum hereby establishes that everything is perfectly grand at the Greatest Place on Earth. There are no concerns to be had. There are no worries to be bothered with. There are no issues to be dealt with. The people are just grand. The managers are just grand. Honestly, everything is just grand.

Signed,

The Mayor

"Interesting," I said, once the man finished reading the note. "And can you believe that storm? It just vanished."

"So see," the man continued, carefully folding the piece of paper and putting it back into his coat pocket. "And I have proof."

"Certainly," I said, looking out the window, the train continuing to rock back and forth down the track. "I understand what you're saying."

(What I then saw out the window)

"Good," the man replied, leaning back in his seat, his short black hair seeming oddly fake. "And don't you forget that."

"No, of course not," I added, thinking I could finally start looking through my file. But then we heard this announced over the train's newfangled intercom system—

Friends and neighbors, strangers and alike, thank you for riding The Most Magnificent Wonderland Adventure Train. We are truly pleased that you've chosen to spend your time with us. And we will do everything that we can to entertain you. However, like all things riveting, we ask that you engage in a profound suspension of disbelief.

One other thing I heard: For the right price, you can buy anything you want there.

So, friends and neighbors, strangers and alike, please sit back, relax, and enjoy the ride.

And then two women suddenly appeared at the back of the car, both dressed in swimsuits, hula hooping down the aisle.

Yes, enjoy the ride.

"Now, let me get some rest," the man sitting next to me said, surprisingly unconcerned about anything else going on around him.

And then the two women disappeared into the next train car, truly as fast as they arrived.

"Okay," I mumbled, not really sure what to think.

But regardless, I figured I better take advantage of the time and start to read through my file, so I pulled it out, set it on my lap, and opened it up to the first page.

CONFIDENTIAL/SENSITIVE MATERIAL

TIERCIARY INTELLIGENCE REPORT
ACTIVITIES AND BEHAVIORS OBSERVED AND NOTED
REGARDING RELEVANT AND POSSIBLY IRRELEVANT

CONDUCT OF POTENTIAL CONCERN INVOLVING TOWN RESIDENTS OF THE GREATEST PLACE ON EARTH

Summary

—Lately, RESIDENTS have been assembling in large numbers at the airship hangar and coliseum in Town in order to rant and rave about various perceived gripes. Some recent examples: "We need to change the name of The Town to the Greatest Greatest Greatest Place on Earth." "Only three-legged birds deserve our respect." "Flood the pond." "Oxygen should be the color yellow." This is only a small sampling.

—A former JANITOR from the town recycling center confirms that several RESIDENTS have engaged in recent sexual behaviors deemed almost too offensive for description. The behaviors mentioned were as follows: Bestiality with a flock of pigeons, prolonged paddling sessions with septuagenarians wearing pink nightgowns, autocoprophagy (eating of one's own feces). This is also only a small sampling of said behaviors.

—Multiple examples provided involving instances where otherwise rational PEOPLE have been caught behaving in truly irrational manners. Some examples of recent irrational behavior include attempting to talk out of one's anus, looking to literally cut a baby in half, proclaiming that the right way to walk is by cartwheeling backwards. Whittling with bayonets. All of these examples are attributed to either current or former MEMBERS of The Town's citizenry.

—Repeated claims by various DAY LABORERS that their jobs are being replaced by unspecified WORKERS from a neighboring Town. However, these claims remain largely unsubstantiated at this time.

—Routine statements by various HOMELESS RESIDENTS regarding unspecified instances of a potential coup.

—At least fourteen RESIDENTS have been caught making repeated visits to The Town archives in order to replace undisclosed documents with apparent exact copies of said documents. Intentions regarding this behavior remain unclear.

"What you must remember," this lady, topless, her breasts voluptuous and glistening, perhaps twenty-nine-years-old, standing beside me suddenly said, "Is that everything is as it seems."

"What," I stammered, not sure where this lady came from, her face partially shrouded behind a long green veil. "What does that mean?"

"Exactly what I said," the lady answered, pulling her veil completely back to reveal her stunningly attractive face, her face immediately reminding me of an old-time vaudeville performer's. "It's all right in front of you. Nothing's in hiding."

"I don't understand," I said, failing to force myself to not stare at her breasts. "What's not in hiding?"

Personal Note: That is one to not tell Ginny about.

"What you're seeking," the lady said, smiling at me. "We have no need to hide anything from anyone. Why would we?"

"You don't?" I asked, suddenly noticing that one of her eyes seemed to be made of stained glass.

Then, inexplicably, three giraffes, wearing pink jump suits, tap danced down the aisle of the train car.

"No," the lady said, before suddenly vanishing into thin air, literally disappearing right before my eyes.

And then the giraffes vanished into thin air too.

Of course, I didn't know what to make of any of that, and quite honestly, I still think it was nothing but a dream, because when I looked down at my lap, I saw my file was turned to this page—

Jeff Weisman

"The Seductress"

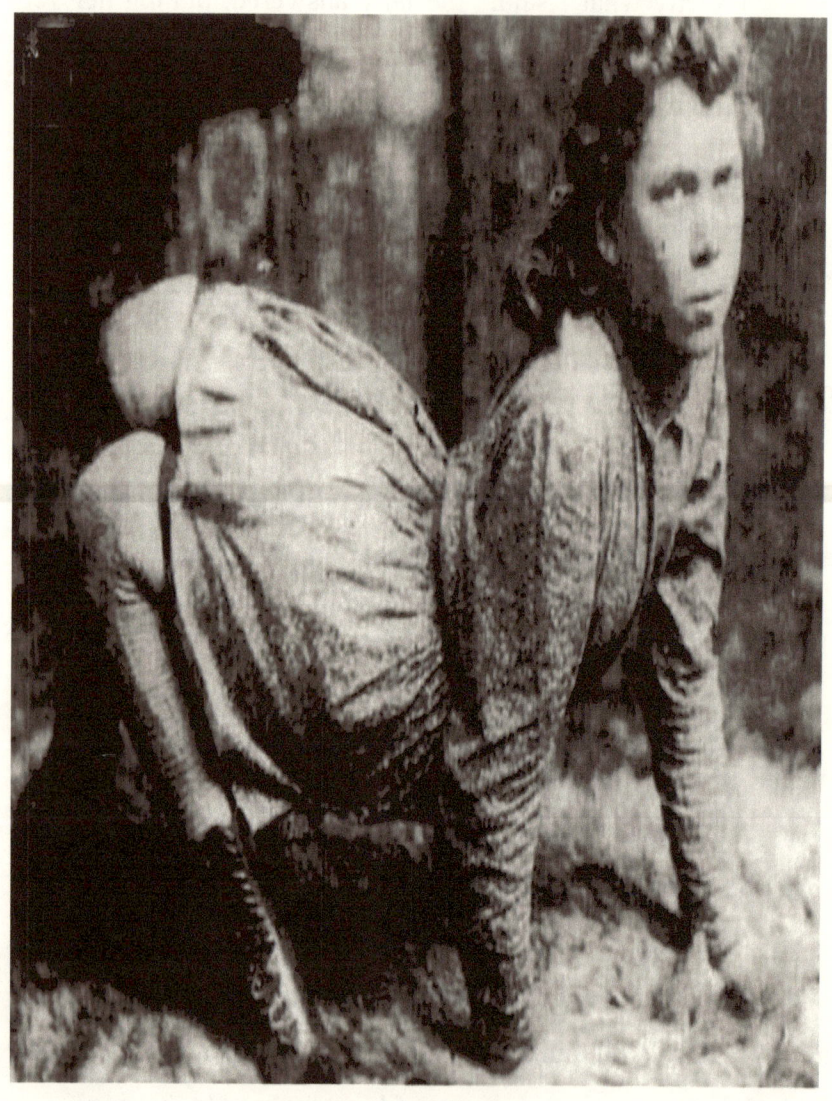

But still, I found the whole exchange utterly unnerving. And then, before I even had a chance to really think about it, let alone process the point of that last file, a train attendant entered the car, announcing: "Next stop, The Greatest Place on Earth."

"Good," the man in the bright blue suit sitting next to me said, reaching down and grabbing a football shaped black satchel. "I thought we'd never arrive."

"Me neither," I replied, hastily closing my file and putting it back into my bag. "I have much to get to."

"Right, business," the man sneered, heaving his satchel onto his lap. "But remember what I said. You got it?"

"Yes, of course," I answered, largely trying to ignore him, while looking out the train window over the man's shoulder.

(What I saw out the window)

"Because I meant business too," the man then huffed.

"I know," I added, thinking about how I needed to locate my assistant, while suddenly seeing this out the window—

(What I then basically saw)

"And don't you forget it," the man continued. "Do you hear me?"

"Yes," I replied, continuing to try to ignore him, while suddenly seeing this out the window—

(What I saw basically then)

"Good," the man said, getting up from his seat. "And have a nice day."

Act Three

Welcome to the Big One

Stepping off the train, I was immediately overwhelmed by the crush and throng of people racing about the platform, looking for friends or family, lugging enormous travel bags, pulling carts, clutching onto children, tugging miniature dogs, hauling oversized coat boxes, carrying large trunks, while smoking cigars, sipping wine, slurping coffee, and muttering seemingly nonsensical statements like, "save the bedazzled" and "embody the penultimate" as I searched about for my assistant who I was told by the man from The Bureau would be waiting for me upon my arrival.

Personal Note: What does "tag the moon" mean?

Then, as I made my way down the platform, the planks cracking and nearly breaking under my feet, I suddenly saw a large caravan of people wandering past in the distance and heard some man grunt behind me, "Damn, it's the crusaders again."

(Basically what I saw)

"Who?" I mumbled, almost instinctually, watching the caravan slowly disappear behind a row of buildings.

"Out of my way you fool," some other man suddenly barked, pushing me aside. "I've got business to attend to."

"Yeah," another man grumbled, bumping along past me. "Hurry it up."

And then before I could even think about it too long, a man suddenly grabbed me by my arm and pulled me down the platform, simply rushing me along.

Second Personal Note: Why is everyone in such a hurry around here?

"You have to keep moving," the man said, quickly leading me off behind the main station house. "No one has the time to focus on things around here."

"What's that?" I said, still trying to get my bearings, while noticing the man was wearing a cheap brown jacket and slacks, a yellow construction helmet plopped on top of his head, his build thin and lanky like a wooden board, his white skin slightly discolored and splotchy, his mustache wispy, his whole face reminding me of a poorly-drawn cartoon character. "But that was quite a sight," I added, racing along with the man. "I'd never seen anything like that before."

"What are you talking about," the man huffed, stopping at the back of the building, several people rushing along in front of us, while the man looked at me. "I know you just got here. But even you're not that stupid. Please. Keep things straight."

And then the man proceeded to tell me a whole litany of rules: Don't stare at anything too long; don't believe what you hear; don't trust anyone; don't worry about anyone else; let everyone know what you think; keep to yourself; spout your disdain frequently; shut up; pick a side and stick to it; trust everyone; play along the best you can; don't rock the boat; aggrieve openly; adamantly hold your convictions; let everything go; embrace the discontentment.

"But that doesn't make any sense," I said, looking at the man, his whole being seeming to project a kind of unsettled energy. "And half of what you just said contradicts something else."

"Good," the man replied, pulling me by the arm again. "You were listening. Now let's get going. We have to keep moving."

"But why?" I asked, as we hurried along the back of the station. "What's the rush? And aren't you the assistant anyways? So we're fine."

"Of course, I'm the assistant," the man answered, continuing to pull me along. "Who else would I be? But we need to get going. We still need to get you through the station. And there's no guarantee of that. So let's go."

"What are you talking about," I said, rushing along with my assistant, genuinely confused by his inexplicable concern. "We're fine. It's just a station. But can I ask you a question?"

"If you must," my assistant answered, glancing over at me. "But hurry it up. And remember to keep your head down. You don't want to be cornered by one of the guards."

"What?" I stammered, looking over at my assistant. "Why would that matter?"

"Right," my assistant responded, staring at me. "You want to play dumb."

"I just got into Town," I said, noticing everyone hurrying along with their heads down. "This whole place is new to me. So what are you talking about?"

And then my assistant just stared at me for a moment, doing a double take, in fact, before simply erupting into laughter. "It's not new to you," my assistant then said, clearly struggling to contain his laughter. "And you never left The Town."

"What are you talking about?" I replied, staring at him. "I've never been here before."

Personal Note: What was he talking about?

"I see," my assistant then said, looking at me curiously. "That's what you want to think. But no matter. What was your question anyways?"

"My question," I stammered, completely caught off guard by my assistant's strange response. "Right. How long have you been with The Bureau?"

"Quiet," my assistant then said, pointing over towards the far side of the train platform. "We're too late."

And then, before I even had a chance to process what my assistant said, two guards, at least that's what it seemed like, stepped out in front of us and ordered us to halt.

Personal Admission: I need to tell Ginny I'm sorry about what I said right after I got back.

"Affiliation," one of the guards then barked, the man seemingly wearing a tattered police uniform and holding some old-fashioned rifle.

"Here," my assistant quickly replied, handing him his billfold from inside his jacket pocket, his whole demeanor continuing to exhibit a kind of unease that was painfully unsettling. "You'll see my registration's there. And you'll see that everything's in perfect order."

"Good," the second guard said, looking at me. "And yours?"

"What are you talking about?" I replied, utterly befuddled by his gruff command.

"Quiet," my assistant immediately said, twisting his head toward me. "Do as they say."

"And look, you can just see it on his face," the second guard barked, staring at me. "He's one of them."

And then, before I could even formulate a response, let alone a thought, the first guard belted me across the face with the barrel of his rifle, knocking me out cold.

TIME SERVED

"You alright," I suddenly heard, as I looked around, my vision uneven and blurry, while seeing a middle-aged black man, a little older than me, sitting on a concrete bench next to me, reaching out to grab my shoulder. "You alright?"

"What?" I responded, immediately pulling away from the man.

"You," he said again, continuing to stare at me. "You okay?"

"Where am I?" I answered, reaching up and grabbing my cheek, a large welt clearly pronounced on the side of my face.

"The same place as all of us," the man replied, leaning back on the bench, his head resting against the brick wall. "Jail. You've been out for several hours now."

"Jail," I repeated, standing up and quickly noticing a metal door lined with bars to my right, the whole ten by twelve concrete block cell suddenly becoming clear to me.

"But where's my assistant? And how did I get here?" I asked, half to myself and half to the man, while walking over to the metal door and glancing down the hall, a seemingly endless number of jail cells suddenly visible to me. "We were just on our way to Town."

"Oh, you're in Town," the man replied, sitting upright again and laughing momentarily.

"But what is this place?" I then said, straining to see if I could make anything else out around me. "It seems mammoth."

"I told you," the man answered, continuing to chuckle slightly. "Jail. And it's quite the place too, huh?"

"But I didn't do anything," I said, turning and looking at the man, his face taunt and strong looking and his eyes piercingly focused. "How could I? I just got here. I've been invited here for business, in fact."

"That's what everyone says," the man replied, before wiping a little sweat from his brow. "Innocent as charged."

Personal Note: What does that mean?

"But this place is huge," I said reaching up and feeling the welt on the side of my face again. "How many people are here?"

"I don't know," the man answered, shaking his head at me. "A battalion's worth. Maybe even more. It's hard to say."

(What the word battalion makes me think of)

"But that's ridiculous," I replied, turning and looking at the man. "This is a tourist Town. And I don't see anyone else."

"They're here," the man said, almost laughing at me again. "Don't worry about it. You'll see them in the mess hall. And you'll hear them cry at night too."

"But what did you do? Why are you here?"

"I didn't do anything," the man answered, taking a rag out from his from pants pocket and wiping his brow. "Like everyone else, I'm innocent as charged. We're all innocent here."

"But people have to be here for some reason," I then said, walking back over to the door and straining again to peer down the corridor.

"Why?" the man replied, snickering briefly. "Now sure, some say they probably did something, although I've never met anyone yet who knows exactly what."

"But that doesn't make any sense."

"So," the man said, getting up and walking over to the metal sink in the corner of the room. "What did you do?"

"Nothing," I answered, shaking the doors. "Guard," I then yelled. "Guard."

"See," the man said, twisting the faucet on. "Innocent as charged."

"Guard."

"And I wouldn't bother with that," the man simply added, looking back over at me. "It won't do you any good."

Personal Note: What does that mean?

And then, after a few disconcerting minutes (my cellmate simply sitting against the wall counting the cracks in the ceiling), I reached into my shirt pocket and pulled out a letter from Aaron I somehow forgot I brought with me.

Dad: (It said)

I've been thinking a lot about what I want to do after I graduate from high school this year. Of course, I want to go to college. But I don't know what I want to do after that.

My friend Deon, he wants to be a dentist.

And my friend Butch, he wants to be a banker.

```
And Evelyn, she says she wants to be an
architect. But she's always wanted to do that.
      And Kristine, she wants to be a
veterinarian.
      But I don't know. I really don't.
      And so dad, how do you know what you want
to do anyways?
Your son, Aaron
```

"And keep your head down," my cellmate suddenly said. "Especially when you see a guard. You won't know what they will do next."

"But we're not doing anything," I replied, putting the letter back in my pocket.

"You're funny," the man simply said, before chuckling softly. "Really, just too much."

JAIL BREAK

"Where did you go?" I half-yelled, suddenly seeing my assistant walking down the corridor with a guard, before jumping up from my concrete seat.

"Finally," my assistant huffed, approaching the door, the clank of his boots on the concrete floor reverberating around my cell. "We've been walking for hours and hours around here. I almost didn't think we were going to find you. Let's get out of here."

"But what happened?" I stammered, standing in front of my assistant.

"Is this your friend?" my cellmate asked, getting up from his seat and starting to walk towards the door. "Can he get me out too? Remember, I didn't do anything either."

"You didn't tell them what they needed to hear," my assistant answered.

"Stand back," the guard suddenly barked, standing outside my cell, his baton clutched in his hand.

"But I want to leave too," my cellmate said, looking over at me. "I didn't ask for any of this."

"I said stand back," the guard repeated, before unlocking the door and suddenly rushing my cellmate.

"Let's go," my assistant said, pulling me out of my cell and hurrying me off down the corridor. "We've got to get out of here. Now."

"But what about my cellmate?" I asked, hearing my cellmate start to scream in pain behind us, the guard clearly pummeling him repeatedly.

"No time," my assistant repeated. "And do you want to get killed yourself."

"We'll come back for you," I yelled, racing over towards the far door.

"You promise," my cellmate screamed over the obvious kicks and punches and baton belts, his voice thundering down the hall. "Because we're going to hold you to that."

"Shut up," my assistant barked, literally pushing me through the door. "I told you the rules."

"But we can't just leave him there," I said, nearly bounding up the stairwell. "And why did they arrest me? I didn't do anything."

"I told you," my assistant repeated, racing up the stairs with me. "Because you didn't tell them what they needed to hear. So from now on show them this," he then said, foisting a card on me—

A BUREAU EMPLOYEE
BIG WIG ENTERTAINMENT
(Not redeemable for cash)

"Alright," I answered, stuffing the card in my pocket, while stepping out of the building, the bright red sunset almost burning my eyes, before doing a near double take at the sight of his newfangled automobile.

(A pretty close representation)

"Come on," my assistant said, rushing out the door. "We've got to get going."

"That's your motorcar," I immediately replied, leaving the building with my assistant. "And we really should go back and help that man. He didn't seem like a criminal to me."

"You don't know that," my assistant said. "You're not in charge around here. And besides, you've got your work to do. You should focus on that."

"But he said he was innocent."

"Everyone does," my assistant responded. "What else can they say?"

"And why have so many people in jail?" I asked. "It's a tourist Town."

"I'm here to help you," my assistant answered. "Not to answer your questions."

Note: What did that mean?

"And you're staying with us at our place on the edge of Town," my assistant continued, driving us down the bumpy road. "It's where we keep all of the main Bureau representatives. I'm there too. So you'll be right in the thick of it all."

"Good," I replied, noticing several houses in the distance with odd signs in front of them like "Barns for Farms" and "Peals need Squeals" and "Bolts do Colts", before adding, "But I still don't get what happened."

"I told you," my assistant said, turning onto a side road. "You need to follow the rules."

"I didn't do anything though," I repeated, holding on to the door handle, the automobile rocking back and forth. "And those guards didn't even let me respond."

Personal Note: What did "you're not one of us" even mean?

"Perhaps," my assistant interrupted. "Perhaps. But you need to listen to me."

And then my assistant proceeded to tell me several more rules: Don't expect anything from anyone; don't expect anything to proceed smoothly; expect the unexpected; anticipate the disturbed; relish the shocking; embody the appalling; stay unfocused.

"Right," I answered, turning and looking at my assistant clutching onto the steering wheel, his yellow construction helmet pressed down tightly over his scrawny head. "And why did we have to stop here again?"

"Because we do," my assistant answered. "The Bureau mandates it."

"Why would they do that?" I replied, shaking my head at my assistant, while seeing a large warehouse building in front of us. "And this is where I'm going to get my checkup?"

"It is," my assistant responded, pulling into the parking lot.

"But this doesn't seem like a place you'd find a doctor."

"It doesn't, does it," my assistant simply said, looking at me. "But that's what they want."

"What does that mean?" I asked, getting out of the motorcar. "And it's getting late too."

"I don't really know," my assistant answered. "But evidently you can find all the real professionals here."

Personal Note: What did that mean?

"Fine," I simply replied, walking along beside him. "This place looks ridiculous though."

THE DOCTOR

Staring at the doctor, I suddenly remembered where I saw him from. "My file," I thought to myself, suddenly picturing the page—

Jeff Weisman

"The Practitioner"

"Yes, of course, please," the doctor said, sitting down in his chair in the corner of the small examination room, his white coat flanking his thin build. "Have a seat. We need to see how you're doing."

"But I'm only here to work on my research. I really don't see why I need a physical to do anything like that."

"Yes, of course, of course, but think of it as a necessary formality," the doctor replied, picking up his clipboard, his hair frizzing wildly all about him. "Because everyone must undergo a thorough evaluation in order to work for The Bureau. That's simply the way it is."

"Alright," I said, scooting back a little further on the examination table, the paper mat crinkling beneath me. "If you insist."

"I do, I do," the doctor stammered, casually sitting back in his chair. "And you're saying you're in fine health."

"Yes," I answered, looking at the doctor, his hair admittedly distracting me.

"Honestly," my assistant suddenly interrupted. "In fact, he's in the greatest condition ever known to man. All other human specimens are based on him."

"Of course," the doctor said, taking his pen out from his front coat pocket and clicking it open, the pop sound reminding me of an old water gun trigger being pulled, before repeating, while writing on his clipboard, "In fact, he's in the greatest physical and mental condition ever known to man. All other human specimens are based on him."

"Health itself is envious," my assistant continued.

"Health itself is envious," the doctor repeated, leaning forward in his chair and obviously writing that down on the piece of paper on his clipboard too.

"Projected lifespan is ten thousand, two hundred, and twelve years."

"Projected lifespan is ten thousand, two hundred, and twelve years," the doctor again repeated, continuing to write on his clipboard.

"A simply stupendously stupendous human specimen," my assistant added, smirking at me slightly.

"A simply stupendously stupendous human specimen," the doctor repeated.

"I am," I said, not sure what to think of what was going on.

"See," my assistant interrupted, looking over at me, his yellow construction helmet sitting half-sideways on his head. "Right from the horses' mouth."

And then my doctor handed me this typed letter—

To Whom My Concern:

I have been the personal physician for Mr. Williams since (put requested date here). Over that time period, I am proud to report that Mr. Williams has remained in excellent health. In fact, he's in the greatest physical and mental condition known to man. All other human specimens are based on him. Health itself is envious. Projected lifespan is ten thousand, two hundred, and twelve years. He is a simply stupendously stupendous human specimen.

Additionally, over the last (put requested timeframe here), his weight has remained excellent, his virility is magnificent, his stamina is unrivaled, and his genitals are truly remarkable. (Add additional points as needed.)

If employment entertained, I can state unquestionably that Mr. Williams will be the single most healthiest individual ever employed by The Bureau.

Yours truly, MQ. DDC. DDQ. RS. TQ. DBR. NDDWA. FESE. CQUR. PPR. PPASL. MT.

"What's this?" I said, looking at the letter, wondering what I was supposed to say to that.

"It's perfect," my assistant simply replied. "The Bureau will love it."

"Obviously," the doctor chuckled, putting down his clipboard and pen on the table next to him. "We all will."

"We all will," I repeated, continuing to stare down at the letter. "But this is my note."

"Of course," the doctor chuckled again, running his hands through his hair.

And then we simply left for our quarters on the edge of Town.

THE INN

"Enjoy your stay," The Innkeeper, an older woman, said, staring at me, her mouth oddly shaped like some kind of pipe cone, while opening my door to my room, my room as small and dirty as it was providing a kind of profound relief nevertheless.

"Thank you," I replied, tossing my bag onto my bed, the wallpaper a dull brown and the dresser some kind of weird hand-carved monstrosity. "That's my intent."

"Of course," The Innkeeper said, staring at me for a moment, her face oddly ashen and thin and her hair seemingly dyed a silver-grey hue. "What else could you say?"

"I don't know," I replied, not sure what the point of her response was there.

"But remember this, this is The Mayor's Town. And don't you forget it," The Innkeeper then added, before walking off down the hall and muttering, "We won it fair and square."

Personal Observation: Everyone seems to be uneasy about something around here.

Then, unpacking my belongings and placing them in my dresser, the small room in the inn barely lit by a single bulb pulsing overhead, I noticed a piece of paper, haphazardly taped to the underside of the top drawer, so I pulled it out and read it—

THE ROSETTA CODEX

Postulate=Parameter=Squared

Contradicted by Variables

Plus Apparent

Therefore

Known=Unknown

And I had no idea what it meant, or who wrote it or even put it there, for that matter. But somehow it seemed important.

Personal Note: Why did it seem important?

So then, I simply finished packing my belongings (placing my family picture on the nightstand next to my bed) before lying down to sleep, knowing that tomorrow I had to get to work.

Act Four

Step Right Up, Step Right Up

Sitting down at the typewriter at my desk in the corner of the room that next morning right after I woke up, I immediately wrote this—

Dear Ginny:

Lately, I've been thinking a lot about what you did. I know you didn't mean it. And I know you didn't mean to hurt me. But I'm still struggling with letting it all go. It's just so hard to think of you with another man. And it's just so hard to think of how I can trust you again. I know you've told me repeatedly that you will never do it again. And I know you've said you were sorry a hundred times already. And I do believe you. I really do. But I just don't know what to make of it all.

Perhaps, this research opportunity right away like this after my last trip is actually a blessing in disguise. You know? It will give us both a chance to work through things.

I do love you. I do. I just need more time. Love, Bob

Then, I put my letter in my pocket, pushed my chair back, and headed downstairs.

Personal Confession: I skipped something about the previous night's events that I now feel compelled to reveal in order to remain true to this chronicle. So, here it goes—

"Sir," I heard, while watching my door open slightly and then seeing a young woman, perhaps twenty-five, stick her head around the edge of my door, before knocking again and saying. "Sir, can I come in? Maid service?"

"What's that?" I answered, lying in bed, the quilt pushed to my side, the faint moonlight filling my room.

TEN SHEEP

"Maid service," the young woman repeated, strolling into my room, her dress barely covering her voluptuous body.

"But it's the middle of the night," I replied, continuing to lie back in bed, my sleepwear suddenly gone, and my penis erect. "And who are you?"

"The Innkeeper's Daughter," she answered, swaying in front of me. "Of course."

NINETEEN SHEEP

"Oh, that's right," I panted, feeling her warm body press against mine, her breasts cupped in my hands. "Yes."

"Deeper," she groaned, staring down at me. "Give it to me good."

FORTY-ONE SHEEP

"Yes," I repeated, before quickly sitting up in bed and staring out my window, The Town lights visible in the distance, while rubbing my head, sweat covering my brow, The Innkeeper's Daughter gone—this whole episode seeming unreal to me, but still, it was highly disturbing, because I'd been having these bad dreams lately. And I knew my marriage was tenuous at best.

Personal Note: Freud would have a field day with me.

So then, I walked through the front parlor and into the kitchen (suddenly realizing I hadn't eaten in a day), and was immediately taken aback by what I saw.

(A rough approximation)

But it wasn't only nine people, and (and I hope I don't offend anyone here) it wasn't your average assortment of people either, because it seemed like somehow every possible freak (and again, I really hope my terminology doesn't offend anyone here), but every possible freak that could be amassed together in one place was all sitting at the table in the inn playing different games and having breakfast. Just a few examples of the guests—

THE SKYWALKER

He was a truly a strange man, perhaps fifty or so, white, with a conflicted and tortured energy, who kept blabbering on and on about how "everyone's out to get him" and "only a gold throne will keep me from the heathen" while insisting on things like being able to live in a glass case, wearing a helmet with a siren built into it, hourly being able to visit exotic places, meandering around with an armed guard detail of twelve hundred men, staying at the inn for free, and all the while working to poison the drinking well. It was truly unsettling.

THE PROCTOR

She was a plain woman, maybe sixty, also white, with a strange aura of entitlement about her that oddly didn't seem deserved or earned, who constantly mumbled things about how we needed to save the children and give them choices and improve their lives and get them better opportunities. Yet, she didn't seem to know any children. Nor would she go near them. And she certainly didn't seem to like them for that matter. But apparently all of that was irrelevant regarding her endless ramblings. Or concerns, to specify.

THE CONSTRUCTOR

He was a peculiar man because he was a former world-renowned coroner who insisted on spending all of his time building elaborate dioramas of tenement houses. And he would outfit these things in truly amazing ways too: million dollar bedroom sets, two million dollar hand-carved kitchen cabinets, priceless Tupperware. Truly, no expense was spared. And he was black too, which for whatever reason, just didn't seem right.

THE HUMAN KOW-TOW

He was something else too, because not only did he seem to fundamentally contradict himself by refusing to ever acknowledge any wrong of his own, but he seemed to literally relish in that contradiction. For example, he would routinely be overheard muttering things like, "the further I am away from everyone the better I understand them," and "give them nothing to show them care." And yes, all of this seemed utterly bewildering. And yes, all of this was horribly and painfully confounding too. But given the fact that it was coming from one of the more foppish and facile people to ever live, it somehow seemed fitting.

THE HORSEMASTER

He was nothing short of miraculous since everywhere he went he would ride a large white horse. If he needed to brush his teeth, he would ride a large white horse. If he needed to go to the bathroom, he would ride a large white horse. If he needed to masturbate, he would ride a large white horse. Yet, inexplicably, he couldn't stand horses. Or fresh air, for that matter. And, just to specify, he kept wanting to put price tags on things too, which no one could quite figure out. And yes, he was white too.

THE SHILL

He was a truly unsettling, spindly figure, more akin to a waif actually than an actual adult male, who literally spent all his time hawking the wares of someone else. And he would say anything too: No picture has ever been greater than that, what you're saying isn't what you're saying, what we did yesterday wasn't what we did yesterday, of course, we can be everywhere at once. And those are just a few of the rantings that immediately come to mind.

THE SLEEPTALKER

He was probably one of the weirdest of them all, because he would simply fall asleep in the middle of doing almost anything, walking around, sitting at the table, trying to stand up, defecating, and no matter where he was, awake or not, he would only talk in half statements, saying things like, "we need to recalibrate the aforementioned" and "the prologue was nothing short of." And yes, he was white too. And yes, he was nearly insufferable.

THE ESCAPOLOGIST

Bluntly, he was actually quite infuriating because every time you thought you had him pinned down, he would vanish right in front of your eyes and then reappear somewhere else. On top of a building, and then on a dollar bill. In a helicopter, and then at a schoolyard. And on top of all of that, he was always caught wandering around with this woman he called his wife. But honestly, no one really believed she was married to him. And that included her too. And yes, he was white too, of course.

Personal Note: Why did it seem appropriate to say "he was white too, of course"?

Nevertheless, there I was, standing in the doorway to the kitchen, clearly knocked off guard, taking in the scene, when I finally saw my assistant.

"There you are," I said, walking over to him, sitting at the far end of the table.

"Yes, yes," he replied, looking up at me, a large plate of scrambled eggs in front of him, his yellow construction helmet plunked down tightly on his head. "I heard you had quite the time last night too. Good for you."

"You did?" I said, pulling out a chair, the legs scraping loudly against the hardwood floor, as the multitude of guests crowded around the table muttered away imperceptibly, a plate of eggs in front of my seat. "But I don't know what happened last night."

"Don't worry," he chuckled. "Your secret is safe with me."

And then, before I could even respond, The Innkeeper, again an older woman with obviously fake silver-grey hair and an overall disjointed disposition, walked into the room and announced: "Plans everyone. What's on the agenda today?"

And then we heard this—

The Tightrope Walker: Headed somewhere, mam. Still not sure where though.

The Lion Tamer: Lounging around, mam.

The Belly Dancer: Me too, mam.

The Trapeze Artist: Same as yesterday for me, mam.

The Contortionist: Ditto here, mam. Looking to infuriate someone today.

The Snake Charmer: Yep, same with me, mam.

The Glass Eater: That goes for me too, mam. Divide to conquer.

"Sounds good everyone," The Innkeeper said, before suddenly holding up a picture of The Mayor and proclaiming, "All hail the chief."

"All hail the chief," everyone responded, including my assistant, who quickly nudged me on the shoulder, clearly indicating to me that I should follow suit.

"All hail the chief," I added, not exactly sure why, but understanding I had to.

"And other news?" The Innkeeper then asked while putting away her picture of The Mayor, and then several people quickly started talking.

"Harry was running his mouth off about our plans for the courthouse again," The Shill said, as I suddenly noticed a picture on the wall above him.

(Basically what I saw)

"And Martha was blabbering about our intentions for the airfield," The Lion Tamer said.

"And I caught Jack talking with Melony again," The Trapeze Artist added. "And he wasn't even hiding or anything."

"And the Greenhorn here," my assistant said, looking at me. "Was busy with the maid last night."

"What?" I stammered, dropping my fork onto my plate of eggs.

"You were," everyone replied, staring at me, before I could even respond. "Well, good for you," everyone then added.

"Definitely," The Innkeeper said, and then everyone proceeded to rate her looks.

The Proctor: A six.

The Contortionist: A five.

The Snake Charmer: A four.

The Belly Dancer: A nine.

The Shill: A two.

"A two," The Sleeptalker said, looking up from his plate of eggs, "But that's," and then he simply zonked out.

"No matter," The Innkeeper continued. "We know that numbers aren't really his thing."

And then The Noble Preacher, or at least that was what he called himself, because he was holding a Bible and wearing a green suit and smoking a cigar, and clearly looked like he didn't belong there, said: "Blessed be our Father, please watch over us, and guide us as we leave here today to do your bidding, for it is in your name that we endeavor to proceed. Amen."

"Amen," everyone answered, before quickly getting up from the table and hurrying off.

Another Personal Thought: What did I do last night?

"Tell me, what did you do that for?" I immediately asked, looking at my assistant, still sitting at the table, holding his cup of coffee in his hand.

"What did I do what for?" my assistant repeated, before taking another sip of his coffee.

"But you said my secret was safe with you," I replied, shaking my head at him. "And I didn't even do anything. I wouldn't do anything. I'm a married man."

"No matter," my assistant responded, looking at me. "It's no matter at all." And then he pulled out a piece of paper from his pocket and handed it to me.

DISPATCH NUMBER ONE: The Researcher is conspiring AGAINST me. The Researcher is conspiring against you. This is the greatest TRAVESTY known to man. We cannot stand for this. We cannot allow our Town to be stolen like this. Stand up for what is right. Stand down for what is left. Stand strong for what is weak. Don't cave. CORN FARMERS!

"What does this mean?" I asked my assistant.

"We don't really know," my assistant answered, putting down his cup of coffee. "We almost never know. But it certainly is important."

"And why did you give this to me? And am I the researcher being referred to here?"

"I don't know," my assistant answered, shaking his head at me. "But it seemed relevant to your work."

"Right," I said, looking at him completely perplexed. "And that's what we need to get to."

And then we got up and left for Town.

A Personal Note: I find myself worrying about Evelyn a lot more lately. She's so hard headed and convinced at times that she's right about everything that I don't know what to do with her. She's like her mother in that way. But I don't know how to get her to see that we need to be able to accept the fact that we're wrong at times, that we're all wrong at times. She's so different from Aaron in that way. He wants to question everything. And she doesn't seem to want to question a thing. Really, what am I supposed to do?

"Where are we going now?" I asked my assistant, as we drove down the road again, the motorcar bumping and squeaking along.

"To the Town Hall," my assistant answered, clutching onto the steering wheel. "We need to check in."

"Check in?" I repeated, quickly glancing over at him, his mustache suddenly reminding me of a thin line of mascara drawn onto his face.

"Well, more like follow-up," he responded. "Don't worry. You'll see."

Second Personal Note: I don't trust my assistant either. And what does that even mean?

"Okay," I said, looking out the window and suddenly seeing an airship take off from the field in the distance.

(A decent representation)

"And you know, we're real lucky," my assistant suddenly said, continuing to drive down the road, breaking my train of thought. "The weather seems fantastic today."

"We are," I stammered, wondering what to make of that sight. "But do you see that? I've never seen an airship like that before. And what's it doing out here?"

"Oh, that's just The Mayor," my assistant responded, looking over at me. "He knows we're stopping by. So he wants to make a grand entrance. Don't worry. But the weather really does seem nice today."

"Yes," I replied, not quite sure what to make of his response, before deciding to ask him something that had been on my mind since we first met. "So, how long have you been working for The Bureau?"

"The Bureau?" my assistant answered, turning down a side road. "Twelve years, exactly. It's been the true honor of my life."

"I see," I said. And then I decided to ask him something that had been on my mind ever since the first man from The Bureau contacted me: "And why do you think they want me to do this?"

And then he proceeded to tell me this: Well, some think it's because there's a true concern regarding what's happening out here. They're worried about the stability of the residents. And they're troubled with their behavior. In fact, they're concerned that The Town itself is in jeopardy. That what's guiding the residents, so to speak, is illegitimate and therefore must be nullified. Yes, yes, that is certainly what some think.

"Is that right?" I said, looking over at my assistant, his face suddenly stern and oddly decisive. "And that's similar to what I was first told when I was offered this job."

"I'm sure it is," my assistant answered, turning down an even smaller side road. "Of course, that's not what everyone thinks."

And then he proceeded to tell me this: While some others think that the whole thing is simply a bunch of baloney concocted in order to cede control of their Town. They are convinced that there is a conspiracy at play to delegitimize their duly elected officials and thereby strip them of their sovereign authority. And they are concerned that The Town itself is in jeopardy from this threat. That is certainly what some think.

"Really," I replied, again looking over at my assistant. "And what do you think?"

"Me," my assistant answered, turning onto an even smaller road still. "It doesn't matter what I think. But I will say this, you better get this squared away, because everyone's counting on you."

"What does that mean?" I asked, suddenly seeing a building come into view.

"Exactly what I said," my assistant answered, slowing down. "It's truly a matter of life and death. Believe me, it's not a game."

And then I had a brief recollection from that morning: The Punishment Game.

MATCH YOUR CRIME WITH YOUR PENALTY

CRIME	PENALTY
1. Extortion	1. Life
2. Aggravated Assault	2. Probation
3. Money Laundering	3. Three Months
4. Sexual Assault	4. Six Months
5. Fraud	5. 1 ½ years
6. Bribery	6. Six Weeks
7. Rape	7. None
8. Insider Trading	8. Twenty years
9. Racketeering	9. Thirty to life
10. Embezzlement	10. 500 years
11. Tax Evasion	11. Seven years
12. Treason	12. A fine only
13. Perjury	13. Pardon (if desired)
14. Blackmail	14. Not even a word

Note: Please consider economic status, race, gender, religion, and any other relevant extenuating circumstances when making your selection. Also, you can pick the same penalty more than once.

And then we watched the airship land in front of us and The Mayor step out, who I immediately recognized as The Prospector from my file—

"The Prospector"

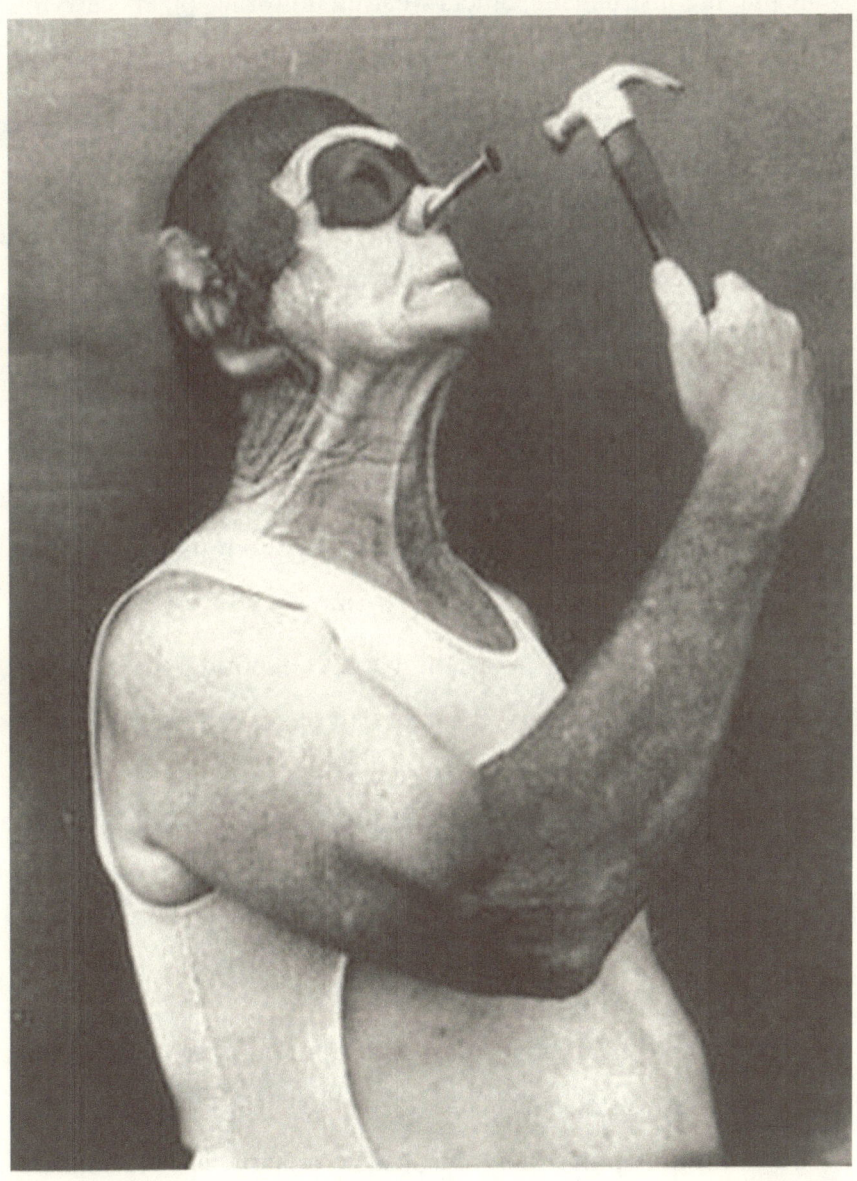

Also, I must clarify, walking beside The Mayor was an odd looking man (who I quickly learned was The Mayor's Deputy), while following behind them was an enormous parade of people, some playing instruments, others wearing uniforms, others carrying odd signs and banners proclaiming things like "Freedom is a dessert best left unfed", and yet still others were walking along looking as serious as I'd ever seen anyone look in my life.

"Come on," my assistant said, parking the automobile in the field next to the building. "We don't want to be late."

"Alright," I replied, opening the door and suddenly noticing a woman, wearing an elaborate dress and an oversized hat, wandering along beside the man (The Mayor's Deputy, to clarify), carrying the exact same monkey I saw on the train in her arm, or at least what seemed like the exact same monkey. "But that's," I then stammered, completely confused. "That's."

"Hurry up," my assistant barked, ignoring my obvious confusion, as I sat there with the door half open, still trying to make sense of what I was seeing. "They're waiting."

"I am, I am," I then continued, getting out of the motorcar and walking over to the steps outside the building.

And then I saw the following:

1. Hundreds and hundreds of people (although, later, this number was disputed)
2. A military procession of tanks and transporters and soldiers
3. Dignitaries from seemingly every corner of The Town

4. Thousands of paramours and girlfriends (although this remains a point of contention)

  (Granted, this is only a partial picture of what I saw)

"Here ye, here ye," the odd looking man standing beside The Mayor suddenly announced, before blowing into a twisted looking trumpet. "Let me introduce The Mayor."

"BooooOOOOOOOOOOOOOOOOOO," the crowd then groaned, obviously disappointed in having to wait for The Mayor to speak.

Personal Note: I found all of this utterly bewildering.

"Citizens, residents, friends, enemies, lovers, and varied transients, we have summoned you here today in order to help me welcome our newest member to The Town," The Mayor's Deputy (who I now understood was the odd looking man) declared, standing on a large dais.

Then someone behind me roared: "What are you doing?"

"That's right," The Mayor's Deputy continued. "A most revered and esteemed individual."

Then someone else behind me boomed: "Why are you talking to us?"

"Who has been selected, after great diligence, to serve on our behalf."

Then another person behind me screamed: "What are you talking about?"

And when I looked at my assistant, hoping he could clarify what exactly was going on and who these people were shouting at, he simply shook his head at me and muttered, "Just keep your mouth shut. Do you hear me?"

"For victory is our only vice."

And then the crowd suddenly roared: "YeeeeeaaaAAAHHHHHHHHHHHHHHHHH."

Personal Note: Why does my assistant seem to be trembling? And why does The Mayor's Deputy seem to be winking at someone behind him constantly?

And then The Mayor stepped up to the microphone, motioned for me to walk onto the dais next to him, put his right hand in the air, without bothering to wait for me to do so, I must clarify, and then said: "Do you swear to follow every order I ever give you?"

"What?" I answered, looking at him. "What was that?"

Yet Another Personal Note: An audible gasp could be heard when I paused there.

"I need your blind allegiance," The Mayor continued, taking out a handkerchief and partially tying it over my eyes. "So, do you swear to follow every order I ever give you?"

"You can have my blindness," I replied, almost despite myself, if I'm being truly honest.

"Good, I have your allegiant blindness," The Mayor said, stepping back from me and putting his hands in the air.

The crowd then roared:

"YeeeaaaaaaAAAAHHHHHHHHHHHH," again.

Yet Another Personal Note: Or was he (my assistant) smiling?

And then I took off the blindfold and looked out at the crowd of people, all clapping vigorously, as The Mayor stepped over to the side of the stage and grabbed a sheet of paper from a nearby table, a smoke bomb suddenly going off a little ways behind me.

"How wonderful," one of the people behind me suddenly muttered. "The Mayor's always looking out for us. What an amazing man."

And then The Mayor gave me this—

THE TOWN CHARTER

We, the residents of "The Greatest Place on Earth," hereby declare the following:

1. **Up is down**
2. **Down is up**
3. **Right is left**
4. **Left is right**
5. **Off is on**
6. **On is off**
7. **Out is in**
8. **In is out**

"So I now officially ascribe you the title of, My Loyal Servant," The Mayor then proclaimed, raising his hands in the air triumphantly, and exclaiming further: "Thank you. Thank you. Thank you. I am the greatest."

"YeeeaAAAAAHHHHHHHHHHH," again everyone roared.

(What I saw to my right)

"What's going on?" I whispered to my assistant, just as I had a sudden recollection from my file—

Preliminary Analysis of Mayor (a previous researcher wrote): The Mayor seems to be suffering from a bizarre strain of narcissism, mixed with an overly inflated ego, delusions of grandeur, potential paranoia, and tendencies of self-loathing and hatred, all intermixed with early signs of dementia. However, further analysis is necessary in order to form any final judgment.

"Just be quiet," my assistant simply barked, clapping profusely. "I told you already."

And then when I looked behind me, I suddenly realized several people, all seemingly key members of The Town, were standing on their copies of the paper I had just been given, the monkey I had seen on the train earlier suddenly visible on the shoulder of one of the key Town members (or at least that's what I thought I saw).

Regardless, I pocketed my Charter, and waited for my assistant to tell me what to do next, while noticing that both The Mayor and The Mayor's Deputy were standing on their copies of the Charter too, smoke from the smoke bomb still lingering in the air.

Personal Reflection: Why was that lady crying behind me the whole time?

And then we watched everyone leave, as a strange looking person to my immediate right (a newspaper reporter, perhaps) was mumbling out loud to himself while writing this down on a piece of paper: "The single most memorable moment in the history of our Town just took place."

"Come on," my assistant said, looking at me. "It's time to go."

Act Five

Children of All Ages

And then, after walking for a little bit, we approached an odd looking building on the far side of Town and started to head toward the door, before noticing an older mother scolding her young son in the street, the sidewalks bustling with people all around us.

(What the building looked like)

"You're a worthless loser," the mother suddenly yelled.

"But I," the boy stammered.

"Don't but I me," the mother continued. "You never should have even been born."

"But mom," the boy stammered again, clearly on the verge of crying.

"If only I could get rid of you."

Yes, yes, yes, several people around us suddenly started chanting.

"Mom," the boy stammered yet again. "You don't mean that."

"Don't tempt me," the mother yelled again, yanking on the boy's arm.

Yes, yes, yes, the several people around us continued chanting.

Personal Note: There's clearly a cruelty under the surface around here that's alarming.

"But mom," the boy then pleaded again, unquestionably in pain.

"You know I only say what I mean," the mother screamed, continuing to yank on the boy's arm.

Personal Note Continued: It's almost palpable.

"Should we do something?" I said, turning to my assistant.

"Yes," my assistant answered. "Keep your head down. And come on. You need to see this."

And then we walked into the building, and I was immediately struck by the sight of all these people sitting around a massive round table talking away in the middle of a huge room.

A Man: We really need to get along better.

Another Man: Sure, if you listened to me.

A Woman: You're just trying to undermine everything.

The First Man: That's not true.

Another Woman: You shouldn't speak like that.

Yet Another Man: I can speak any damn way I want.

The Second Man: The hell you can.

A Second Woman: Please everyone, we are better than this.

The First Woman: You don't know what you're talking about.

Yet Another Woman: Let's be civilized everyone.

A New Man: Don't tell me what to do.

The Original Man: Cooperation people, that's the operative word.

The Second Man Again: The hell it is.

The Second Woman Again: You're going to be the death of us.

The New Man Again: No, you are.

The First Woman Again: No, you are.

The First Man: No, you are.

The Second Woman: No you.

And then everyone got up in the middle of talking to each other, suddenly moved to a different seat in the room, and proceeded on with their conversation as if nothing happened.

Personal Note: Why didn't I do something to help that boy?

The First Man: Really, we need to get along better.

The Second Man: If you listened to me.

The Second Woman: You're just trying to undermine everything.

Another Man: That's not true.

Yet Another Woman: You shouldn't speak like that.

Yet Another Man: I can speak any damn way I want.

The Second Man Again: The hell you can.

The Second Woman Again: Please everyone, we are better than this.

The First Woman Again: You don't know what you're talking about.

Yet Another Man: Let's be civilized everyone.

A New Woman: Don't tell me what to do.

The Original Man: Cooperation people, that's the operative term.

The Second Woman Again: The hell it is.

The First Woman: You're going to be the death of us.

A New Man: No, you are.

The First Woman Again: No, you are.

The Original Man: No, you are.

The Second Woman Again: No you.

And then my assistant just looked at me, got up, and quickly started to leave the huge room.

Initial Thought: I can't tell if they are confused or if they are trying to confuse me. However, either way, I must admit—I am confused.

"Come on," my assistant then said, turning and looking back at me, everyone still sitting at their seats around the massive table. "We've got to get going."

"We're leaving," I huffed, racing to catch up with my assistant, who was already walking out the door. "But how was that supposed to help me?"

"I don't know," my assistant answered, stepping into the street. "But that's how everyone's supposed to start their research. So let's go. There's someone else we still need to see today."

(What I saw ride past me)

"Alright," I replied, continuing to hurry along next to my assistant, the bright late afternoon sunshine nearly blinding me.

A Sudden Memory: It was a beautiful spring day, in the early afternoon, quite a few years back, with the sun out, and a soft breeze blowing, as Ginny and I sat on the edge of Lake Sandalwood, picnicking.

"Can you believe it's been ten years already?" she said, handing me a pickle and mustard sandwich (my favorite, just to say).

"I can't," I replied, smiling at her, her face looking slightly older than I pictured it. "We've been through so much."

"And the kids are growing faster than I could have ever imagined," she added, motioning to see if I needed a napkin, her blue eyes sparkling in the sunlight.

"They sure are," I then said, while nodding no. "And I want so much for them. I want them both to be able to pursue what will make them happy. And I want them to get good jobs and have families. I want them to dream big. They sky's the limit. That's what I always say."

"Me too," she added, brushing her shoulder against mine. "And I know it's been tough at times to be married to me. Alright, more than tough at times. And I know I'm probably not who you really thought I was when we first met back in college."

"I'm tough too," I interjected, watching several ducks land on the water near the far edge of the lake.

"We're both tough," Ginny continued. "And the kids make it tough too. They always seem to want something different than us. But they're certainly worth fighting for."

"They sure are," I replied, smiling at her. "Even though they sure have their own spirits."

"And I'm glad we stuck it out," Ginny then said, turning and facing me, the lines on her face clearly evident. "Through the good and bad times."

"More good than bad," I responded, looking at her.

"True, and at least we've always been able to trust each other," she then continued. "Because we know we're trying to do what's best for our family."

"Agreed," I said. "That is our bedrock."

"And here," my assistant suddenly said as we approached a small diner just down the street from the building we were just at, while handing me this—

DISPATCH NUMBER TWO: The word is there's a TRAITOR among us. So if you see anyone snooping around, or asking questions, or simply LOOKING suspicious, report that person to the proper authorities immediately. Our TRUST is in ME.

Which, in all honesty, I didn't even know what to do with (although it concerned me some, especially since my job was about asking people questions and looking around at things) but regardless, before I had a chance to even think about it too much, my assistant handed me this—

DISPATCH NUMBER THREE: Furthermore, any DOUBT as to my assertions or validity of my claims shall heretofore be construed as THE biggest SCANDAL in all of history! EVER.

Personal Note: What is the point of these dispatches?

And then I stopped for a moment, the door to the diner a few feet in front of me, and I tried to get a grasp on what was going on.

However, before I could even think about that too much, my assistant handed me this—

DISPATCH NUMBER FOUR: Glitch spackle!!

And I had no idea what to make of it, so I simply walked into the diner (my head honestly spinning from these dispatches) before suddenly overhearing two women near the front of the restaurant having one of the strangest conversations I'd heard since I'd arrived at this Town.

"Me," the first woman said, an attractive lady with bright green hair and large lips, "I just grab them by the balls whenever I want to."

"I hear that," the second woman replied, also an attractive lady, but with curly yellow hair and small eyes. "Especially if I'm feeling nice and randy that day."

"And they just let you fondle the hell out of them too," the first woman continued. "It's like they don't even care."

"You can say that again," the second woman chuckled. "Hell, I remember this one time when I was just standing at the trolley station. And I simply reached over to this man, some unsuspecting chap, donning some cheap business suit, but with an ass on him, I tell you, that would make any woman squirm, and I just reached down into his pants, grabbed ahold of him and just started going wild."

"Yeah baby," the other woman said. "I hope you gave it to him good because they sure deserve it. And it's amazing how they just stand there and take it. It's like they're nothing but our playthings. Seriously, just our little squirt toys lollygagging around for our delight."

And then, seemingly out of nowhere, two other women, also whom I hadn't seen yet, stood up at the front of the diner and started commenting on their conversation—

First Woman: Us women and our locker room talk.

Second Woman: Oh, you know how we are.

First Woman: I've heard worse talk in a church choir.

Second Woman: Me too.

First Woman: And you should hear me go on about my neighbor.

Second Woman: I do the same with mine.

First Woman: But I just can't help myself.

Second Woman: Me neither.

First Woman: Hell, even my kids can't believe it.

Second Woman: But girls will be girls.

First Woman: You can say that again.

Second Woman: And besides, everyone talks like that.

And truly, I didn't know what to make of any of that, but before I could even think about that too much, my assistant simply grabbed me by the arm and said, "Come on. We've got to keep moving along. He's waiting for us."

One Personal Thought: Does everyone really talk like that?

"Alright," I replied, looking around the diner and suddenly being struck by the sight on the wall in front of me.

(My closest approximation)

And of course, I had no idea what to make of it, but again, before I could even think about it too much, I was suddenly accosted by a large man wearing an expensive pink suit simply jabbering nonsense in my face.

"The bull moon sprocket," the man said, literally spitting in my face. "Spills triplets in quadrilateral elliptical fountains like orphans near the abundant glockenspiel with unspecified mortal posting updates and opulent turpentine."

"What?" I stammered, truly caught off guard by this man.

"For refraction inoculations occur over translucent confetti," the man simply continued.

"What?" I repeated, staring at this man.

"Come on," my assistant barked again, suddenly pulling me away from the man. "Let's go. I told you, he's waiting."

"Alright, alright," I stammered, looking at my assistant, genuinely pleased to be away from that man. "But who was that?"

"The Town Accountant," my assistant answered, continuing to pull me along. "And don't worry. He always talks like that."

"The Town Accountant," I repeated (unconsciously, mind you), before suddenly noticing another man from my file sitting at a table in the far corner of the diner—

Jeff Weisman

"The Magistrate"

And then we approached the man, and he immediately proceeded to tell me this (before I even sat down, mind you): "Good, good," the man said, looking at me. "I understand you've been hired on by The Bureau to be the new researcher for The Town."

Personal Note: Why didn't he wait for me to sit down?

"Yes," I answered, sliding into the booth. "I got here yesterday."

"I know, I know," the man continued, suddenly glancing around the room. "Everyone's been talking about you."

"They have," I answered, sitting down at my desk.

"Of course, you're the talk of The Town."

"Really," I replied. "I didn't know anyone cared."

"Oh, I wouldn't say they care, per say," he then said, pulling out a cigarette and lighting it. "It's more like you're a curiosity. Something akin to one of our more appealing attractions. And they're certainly talking about you. But I didn't come here to talk about that."

"You didn't," I said, waving my hands in front of my face in order to dissipate his cigarette smoke. "Then what did you want to talk to me about?"

"I wanted to warn you about the last researcher."

"But I've heard there's been several researchers. And there's even a few others here now."

"True, true," he said, again glancing around the room, before taking another drag from his cigarette. "That's all true. But there's one researcher in particular you should be aware of."

"And who's that?"

"Oh, we don't like to mention his name exactly," the man said, after giving me a brief description of him. "But here." And then he took out a marker and wrote this on his hand—

SHADY DAVEY

"I see," I said, wondering why he had to write it so big (and weirdly, too).

But before I could even think about it too much, the man simply continued on. "And you should know what happened to him."

Research Note: And how come this man seems so antsy about everything?

"Why?" I asked, again waving his cigarette smoke away from my face. "What happened to him?"

"Well, it depends on your perspective I suppose," the man answered, taking another drag from his cigarette.

And then he proceeded to tell me this:

A. He was considered the most vile and repulsive human being on the planet. He literally embodied all that was evil in the world. Honestly, many people thought he was simply a traitor to the very Town itself. For he conspired against all that was good and decent and proper in the world. In fact, people even changed their children's names if they had his.

B. He was truly considered something of an enigma. For somehow, he simultaneously seemed to be both a worthy and revered man while also being a despicable and unprincipled sop. And yes, this confused most everyone, including those who held this belief too.

C. He was considered something of a saint. However, there was plenty of caveats to that. For he did apparently undermine the integrity of the institution he embodied. And he certainly played a key part in the trajectory of The Town itself. But regardless, he was considered an amazing person, willing and able to speak truth to power in a way that was utterly humbling.

D. He was not even considered. In fact, he was not even known to be a person, let alone known to exist. Which was miraculous to everyone involved, honestly.

(What the word miraculous makes me think of)

"But regardless," the man continued, again taking another long drag of his cigarette. "He met a most ignominious fate around here."

"He did," I replied, truly confused. "But what does that mean?"

"Simply put, he was scolded away into millions of dollars."

Which bluntly, both confused and impressed me, but either way, again, before I could completely finish my thought, the man got up and started to leave.

"That's all," I said, looking at him, the man already standing over the table.

"Oh yeah, here," he then said, turning around and handing me a piece of paper. "I almost forgot to give you this."

And then he simply left the diner, while I read the note—

Yo Dude:

It's me, Reg. The guy from jail yesterday. I'm still in here, by the way. And I still need your help. So please, help me out. I don't know how much more of this I can take. I'm counting on you.

Thanks man.

Personal Note: And what did the man mean by "your perspective" anyways?

And then I suddenly had an odd memory from my file, while I sat there befuddled—

Research Insight Notation: There seems to be a conflicting relationship the townspeople have with this Town. For at any given time, there seems to be nearly as many of the townspeople in favor of its current trajectory as opposed to it. This is a consistent point too. However, what this exactly means continues to allude me.

"Well, I hope that helped," my assistant said, sitting in the booth across from me, his yellow helmet oddly shining under the artificial light of the restaurant.

"But why did I have to meet that man?" I replied, not actually sure what to think.

"It was a prerequisite," my assistant responded, almost without thinking about it.

"A prerequisite," I repeated, looking at my assistant. "For what?"

"Your research, of course," my assistant answered. "So you're good now I take it?"

"I don't know," I responded. "I don't know what to think."

"Yep, you're good," my assistant said, leaning back in the booth. "That's the reaction everyone has."

Personal Note: What did that mean?

"So I can start my research?" I asked, rubbing my hands through my hair. "That's what you mean by me being good?"

"You can start, yes," my assistant answered. "But I wouldn't ever say you're good."

And then we got up to leave for my assistant's automobile just down the street from us, it somehow nearly nighttime out already (which struck me as being most peculiar, quite honestly).

Another Personal Note: What did he exactly mean by a "prerequisite" anyways?

And then, when I stepped outside, I looked in front of me, and it seemed like everything changed—the world, the universe, the sky, the very nature of eternity itself.

And then I looked down, shook my head, and looked back up again, and then it seemed like nothing changed.

And I didn't know what to do.

Another Personal Note: What did that mean?

So then I looked back down again, shook my head, and quickly looked back up, and then it seemed like everything changed—the world, the universe, the sky, everyone in it.

And then I looked back down, shook my head, and looked back up again, and it seemed like nothing changed.

And then I looked back down again, shook my head, and looked back up, and then it seemed like everything changed.

And then I looked back down, shook my head, and looked back up again, and it seemed like nothing changed.

And then I looked back down again, shook my head, and looked back up, and then it seemed like everything changed.

And I really didn't know what to do. Or think.

Yet Another Personal Note: What is going on around here?

And then we went back to the inn, (myself, at least) utterly ready to crash out.

Act Six

Indulge in the Concessions

And that next morning, when I got up, I immediately sat down at my desk, opened my file, and read this—

PRELIMINARY ANALYSIS SUMMATION OF THE GREATEST PLACE ON EARTH

There appears to be a fundamental disconnect between the core values and standards established in their various codices and historical beliefs and the literal practices of said values and standards established in their various codices and historical beliefs.

Possible explanations for this behavior—

One: These values and standards never actually existed.

Two: These values and standards are essentially fungible.

Three: These values and standards are meant to be alluded to only.

Four: These values and standards are fundamentally meaningless.

Five: These values and standards are illusory by design.

Six: These values and standards are inherently duplicitous.

Seven: These values and standards are simply theoretical constructs.

However, more analysis is needed in order to draw a final conclusion as to the nature of this observation.

And this somewhat confused me (and disturbed me too, for the record), but regardless, I put my file away and wrote this in my notebook—

First Insight Observation: There seems to be a peculiar tendency to accept the implausible as probable, the impossible as hopeful, and the impractical as rational around here.

And then, I left my room and went downstairs and immediately saw nearly all of the inn residents playing a game that can only be described as this: The Construction Draw.

PICK UP A DART AND THROW IT AT THE BOARD TO WIN
THE PRIZE

Roads

                                       Dams

           Bridges

                         Power Plants

                Electric Grid

Wind Turbines

                         Railways

                                 Buses

Airfields

Interstates

Ports

Alternative Energy

Schools

Parks

Note: Empty spaces denote that nothing will be done. Also, all board prizes are meant to be merely hypothetical in nature only and should not be construed as meaning to be accomplished.

And yes, the sight of that seemed beyond odd to me, but regardless I was excited to get going, so I looked around the front parlor and found my assistant talking to a man I immediately recognized from my file—

Jeff Weisman

"The Pugilist"

But then, before I could even get all the way up to my assistant, I was immediately caught off guard by the nature of their conversation, because honestly, it seemed like the man my assistant was talking to was carrying on out of both sides of his mouth (so to speak). Seriously, it was like this—

Clearly,	Clearly
It's	It's
Appropriate	Inappropriate
That	That
He	He
Talks	Talks
With	With
Him.	Him.
And	And
We	We
Certainly	Certainly
Shouldn't	Should
Be	Be
Concerned	Conerned
About	About
It.	It.

And honestly, it was that confounding, but like I said before, I was so excited to simply get going on my research that I just ignored it.

"Let's go," I said, standing over my assistant. "I want to get to things right away today."

"I know," my assistant replied, getting up from the couch. "And I've got our first stop already set up. I've been waiting for you."

"You were? And you do?" I said, honestly surprised by my assistant's response. "I didn't know you had something specific in mind."

"The Bureau ordered it," he answered, picking up his yellow construction helmet and putting it back on his head. "Didn't you see the dispatch?"

"No."

And then he handed me a piece of paper.

DISPATCH NUMBER FIVE: Everyone should spend some of their time today at the TOWN center worshipping the "Sole of Truth." You have been TOLD. Stand proud. THANK ME!

"So let's go."

Personal Note: Who exactly is sending out these dispatches?

"Alright," I replied, waiting for my assistant to get up from the couch. But then, before I could even turn around to head to the door, the Tongue Twister started ranting away.

THE TONGUE TWISTER

Now, she was an almost unimaginable figure because she was both simultaneously seductive and repulsive to everyone who saw her. In fact, many argued that she really should have been called Lady Medusa. Nevertheless, she would spend hours at a time simply spewing the most amazing things out to everyone she met. Some of her most memorable lines: "dates are alternative," "time is irrelevant" "inventions are conventions" "the heart is words" "Buy the Mayor's daughter's wares." And these are only a few of her greatest hits, so to speak.

Anyways, there I was, standing in the parlor, waiting for my assistant to get up from the couch, as the Tongue Twister (who I suddenly realized was The Seductress from my file) started going off to everyone in the room: "Listen everyone, we will all thank our lucky stars for the very day he (and I swear she was talking about this dog she was clutching in her arms) was born. For on that day, the seven oceans of the world were formed. And on that day, the conception of a deity was made real. And on that day, your very life was saved."

"And it's because of him that we get to breathe?" the Gorilla-Faced Man (this guy who seemed to never leave the couch) asked.

THE GORILLA-FACED MAN

He was something else too because not only did he seem to have no interest in his own act ("Really, I have to don this getup

127

again?" he was routinely overheard saying), but he had no idea what his act was supposed to be ("you mean, a gorilla is part of the ape family?" "And, you mean, gorillas are bipedal animals"), were just two of the more glaring examples that immediately come to mind. But he was sure infamous for them. And honestly, his whole deal was almost a farce onto itself.

"Only," the Tongue Twister answered.

Another Personal Note: I don't miss Aaron and Evelyn fighting all of the time.

However, before she could even finish her rant (and I never could figure out who she was talking about, although everyone was certainly captivated by her every word), my assistant simply rushed me out of the inn.

Personal Note: Why was everyone so fixated on her?

And then, sitting in the car, bopping and rolling along, I suddenly felt compelled to ask my assistant about his life: "Do you have a family?" I asked.

"Me," my assistant replied, obviously surprised by my question. "I do. And I love them more than anything."

And then he proceeded to tell me this: Of course, I really worry about my daughter Regina. See, my wife, Olivia, she's not from here. And so my daughter's a mixed-breed, so to speak. Which obviously isn't a problem for me. But that makes things hard on her because people just don't want to accept her sometimes. And so they'll say the meanest and cruelest things to her. They'll tell her things like she's an animal and that she's no good and that she's worthless. And that scares me because she's a human being. And she has feelings. And no matter how much I tell her that it doesn't matter what other people say, it still hurts her. I know it does. And I don't know what to do about it, because so many people just don't seem to care. Or they don't know that it's a real person that they're talking about. And it doesn't have to be like that. If they just got to know her, they would see that she's an amazing person. She loves like no one I've ever known before. But people don't want to see that. They don't want to see who see is.

"Oh," I said, looking at him, honestly taken back by his sudden disclosure.

And then, before I could even think about it too much, he continued: And my wife's the most amazing person I know in this world. Honestly, I couldn't even have survived half of what she's been through. Probably not even a quarter. See, she came here when she was ten years old. And it was something else too. Nothing like my family. We took a boat. Sure, we were fleeing a war and the trip killed my great-uncle, but still that seems easy in comparison. She literally had to escape her village in the middle of the night, and pay someone to smuggler her out of her own country, and then she had to walk for hundreds and hundreds of miles just to get here, and she was a girl, you know, and she was hurt really badly, but she got here, and she made a life for herself, and she did it all with nothing but what she could carry on her back. Leaving her mother and father behind. It's almost unimaginable. And she made me promise her that no matter what I did I would try to make a better life for our daughter, because as she put it: "I didn't sacrifice my life for nothing."

"That's incredible," I said, again looking at him, nearly speechless still.

"And everything I do's for them," he added, as we pulled up to quite the sight.

(A rough approximation)

"Of course," I said, still not quite sure what to say. "I know what you mean."

"Absolutely everything."

Personal Note: Do I really know what he means?

And then we got out of the car, the crowd of people gathered around the "Sole of Truth" numbering in the thousands, and I immediately set about trying to learn about the nature of their behavior.

AN OLDER WHITE WOMAN

Why do you come here?

Because I can.

A MIDDLE-AGED BLACK MALE

And you?

Because I must.

A YOUNGER WHITE WOMAN

And you?

Because I should.

A MIDDLE-AGED WHITE MALE

And you?

Because I want to.

A YOUNGER ASIAN MALE

> And you?
>
> Because I better, damn.

ANOTHER MIDDLE-AGED WHITE MALE

> Exactly.

A YOUNGER WHITE MALE

> And you?
>
> I don't know.

ANOTHER OLDER WHITE WOMAN

> And do you come here often?
>
> Only every chance I get.

A TEENAGE WHITE MALE

> Me too.

A NATIVE AMERICAN MALE

> And you?
>
> Same here.

A MIDDLE-AGED HISPANIC MAN

> Ditto for me.

ANOTHER MIDDLE-AGED WHITE MALE

> Ditto for me too.

ANOTHER TEENAGE WHITE MALE

> And what brought you here?
> Obedience, of course.

A YOUNGER BLACK MAN

> Freedom, and nothing else.

AN OLDER WHITE MALE

> Equity.

ANOTHER OLDER WHITE MALE

> Excitement, pure and simple.

(What the word excitement makes me think of)

A MIDDLE-AGED BLACK MALE

> Straight up hatred.

A MIDDLE-AGED WHITE MALE

Love.

ANOTHER MIDDLE-AGED BLACK MALE

Righteousness.

ANOTHER MIDDLE-AGED WHITE MALE

Nothing less than verification.

ANOTHER OLDER BLACK MALE

Revenge.

A YOUNG WHITE GIRL

And what does the "Sole of Truth" mean to you?
Everything.

A YOUNGER WHITE MAN

Same with me.

AN OLDER ASIAN MALE

And you?
Same here.

YET ANOTHER MIDDLE-AGED WHITE WOMAN

And you?
Me too.

YET ANOTHER MIDDLE-AGED WHITE WOMAN

You took the words right out of my mouth.

And of course, after nearly an hour of that, continuing to hear contradictory and even completely disparate responses to questions like: "Do you seem to be getting what you were hoping for here? And do you feel let down at all? And is this what you wanted?" I didn't know what to make of it, because I was honestly more confused than when I started, so I was actually relieved when my assistant grabbed me by the arm and told me we needed to go to lunch.

"It's required," he said.

First Reflection: There seems to be no driving reason for their allegiance to this practice.

And then, over a pastrami and cheese sandwich, I decided to ask my assistant what he thought was going on there: "So, what do you think's bringing people here?"

"The Bureau, of course," he responded, without even pausing. "Don't you know that already? I gave you the dispatch. And please, I told you about the questions."

"So it's that simple then?" I batted back.

"Yes," he answered, looking at me. "And fine I'll answer your questions this one time."

"But The Bureau doesn't run this The Town," I then said. "The Mayor does."

"Right," he answered, chuckling briefly, while looking at me curiously. "You're a funny man. And I thought you were some renowned researcher."

"I am," I replied, picking up my sandwich. "But none of this is making sense to me yet."

"Why does it have to make sense?" he then asked, continuing to stare at me curiously.

"Because human behavior makes sense," I answered back, dropping my sandwich down on my plate. "We do things for specific reasons. That's why."

"We do?" he replied, before taking a sip of his chocolate milk.

"Yes," I answered, starting to get annoyed with him. "That's my field of expertise."

"Then what's the point of self-sacrifice?" he then asked me, obviously not agreeing with my point. "Or self-immolation?" he then added.

"Hope," I answered back, without even skipping a beat. "And belief. In both cases the point is about being part of a larger cause. Even suicide's driven by discernable reasoning."

"Really?" he replied, almost bewildered by my response.

"Yes," I responded, defiantly. "And I see the symptoms around here, but I don't see the cause," I continued, largely ignoring him.

"They're the same thing," he said, while chuckling again. "Don't you see that? Why do you think you were brought here?"

"To find the cause," I immediately answered back. "Of course."

"Right," he answered again, before again chuckling briefly while staring at me curiously. "You really are a funny man."

Second Reflection: There seems to be a kind of willful acceptance to the nature of things around here that I simply can't explain yet.

So then I decided to explore more about the idea of this Bureau.

Question: And what's the point of The Bureau then?
Answer: Oh, I don't know. I suppose gain.
Question: Gain, gain for what?
Answer: Itself, of course. I mean, look at it around here.

(My basic view out the window)

Question: That's all then?

Answer: Isn't that enough? And The Mayor provides that too.

And then we went through a whole question and response ordeal about The Mayor not unlike the sequence that I had with the initial man I encountered from The Bureau.

"So what is it that people find appealing about The Mayor?"

Response: He's an outsider. And he's reckless, I suppose it's that. And he's got hutzpah too.

"That's all?"

Response: No, his successes too. He's a wealthy person you know. And we're all attracted to that. And he has a good life. And he's brash. He'll say what we all want to say.

"What we all want to say?"

Response: Perhaps not all. But either way, he's a hard worker, and he's a family man, and he focuses on the people around here. And that's important. And he knows who to look out for.

"But who exactly does he look out for?"

Response: The Bureau, of course.

"So he doesn't look out for the people then?"

Response: The Bureau is the people.

"What does that mean?"

And then my assistant just looked at me for a minute, I swear like I was from Jupiter or something, and then simply said, "You really are a funny man."

Personal Note: I simply don't trust him.

And then we finished lunch, paid (my assistant picking up the bill and handling the tip, "Bureau policy," he stressed), got back in the motorcar and returned to the Town Square. Of course, when we got there, I was even more confused than before, because now I simply saw hundreds of people running up to the "Sole of Truth", spouting all sorts of random things at it—

"Absolution," one person yelled.
"Blessedness," another person yelled.
"Exaltation," another person roared.
"Consecration," another person screamed.
"Adoration," another person wailed.

"Glorification," another person roared.

"Veneration," another person hollered.

"See," my assistant said, standing next to me in the Town Square. "They're the same thing."

And then I turned around and saw quite the unexpected sight.

(A rough gist of things)

And I didn't know what to make of it, so I turned back to my assistant and asked, "Who is that?"

"The opposition," my assistant answered, affixing his yellow construction helmet down tighter onto his head. "They're everywhere we go."

"They are?"

"Yep."

"And what are they opposing?"

"Everything," my assistant answered, looking at me.

And then he simply proceeded to list a whole litany of things: The color of algae, the names of birds, the nature of hippodromes, the purpose of placards, the size of puzzle pieces, the length of muskrats, the shape of twigs, the temperature of tap water, the diameter of theater signs, the height of rainbows, the texture of granite, the viscosity of milk.

"Really," I interrupted, utterly confounded by his response.

"Of course," my assistant said, staring at me. "It's the cause."

Another Observational Note: What does that mean?

And then everyone simply left.

Yet Another Personal Note: And I do miss Ginny's goofy way of saying "periwinkle."

"Where are they all going?" I asked, watching everyone rush away.

"Home," my assistant said, turning around and starting to walk back to his automobile. "They've had enough for the day. So let's go too. We still need to stop by their headquarters tonight anyways. You need to see that in order to know anything about this Town."

"Fine," I replied, truly confused by how things operated around here.

And then we went back to the inn, and I wrote this—

Third Observation Notation: It seems that there's some sort of external phobia or collective paranoia driving the behavior around here that's utterly bewildering to me because the townspeople seem to have a true willingness to suspend all matter of common sense and personal rectitude in order to believe that their actions can justifiably result in an outcome they deem desirable. For, no amount of common sense or objective analysis could seemingly explain their genuine belief in this blatant idolatry otherwise. Additionally, this near blind worship of the impossible seems to have gained a foothold in all elements of this Town. Moreover, there seems to be a reciprocal relationship at play here that simply alludes me at this time. For the townspeople seem to be both driving and reaping the perceived benefits of this partnership as much as The Bureau itself.

And then I paused for a moment, my pen cupped in my hand, and looked at my picture of Ginny and the kids on the dresser next to my bed, before continuing—

All of this seems to most closely align with some other examples of collective group behavior that are found in the record of human activity. But I don't want to draw that kind of unfortunate conclusion yet. That would be so tragic.

So tragic.

So tragic.

So tragic.

And then I suddenly realized I was repeating myself. Not unlike history, I thought. Not unlike history, at all.

Act Seven

Partake in the Midway

And then, after resting at the inn for a little bit, I opened my file back up and immediately came across this page—

XOXOXOXOOXOXXXOOOXOXOXOXOXOXOXOXO
XOXOXOXOXOXOXOOXOXOXOXOXOXOXOXOXOXOXOOO
OOOOOOOOOOXXXXXXXXXXXXXXOOOOOOOOOXOX
OXOOOXXXXXXXXXXXXXOOOOOOOOOOOOOOOOOO
OOOOOOOOOOOOOOOOOOXOXOXOXOXOOOOOOOO
OOOOOOOOOOOXOXOOXOXOOOOOOOOOOOOOOOO
OOOOOOOOOOOOOOOOOXOXXXXXXXXXXXXXXXX
XXXXXXXXXXXXXXXXXXXXXXXXXXOOOOOOOOOO
OOOOOOOOOXOXOXOXOXOXOXOXOXOOXOOOOOOOOO
OOOOOOXOXOXOOOOOOOOOXXXXXXXXXXXXXXOO
OOOOOOOOOOXOXOXOOOOOOOOOOOOOOOOOOOOO
OOOOOOOOOOOXOXOXOXOXOXOXOXOXOXOOOOOOO
OOOOOOOOOOOOOOOOOOOOOOOOOOOOOOOOOOOO
OOOOOOOOOOOOOOOOOOOOOOOOOOOOOOOOOOOO
XXXXXXXXXXXXXXXXXXXXXXXXXXXXXXOOOOOOOO
OOOOOOOOOOXOXOXOXOXOXOXOOXOXOXXXXXXXX
XXXXXXOOOOOOOOOOOOOOXOOOOOOOOOOOOOOO
OOOOOOOOOXOOOOOOOOOOOOOOXXXXXXXXXXX
XXXXXXXXXXXXXXXXXXXXXXXXXXXXOXOXOXOX
OXOXOOOOOOOOOOOOOOOOOOOOOOOOOOOOOOOO
OOOOOOOOOOOOOOOOOOOOOOOOOOOOOOOOOOOO
OOOOOOOOOOOOOOOOOOOOOOOOOOOOOOOOOOOO
OOOOOOOOOOOOOOOOOOOOOXOXOXOXOXOXOXO

147

And I had no idea what it meant. So then I decided to go back downstairs and see if I couldn't find my assistant (figuring that maybe he could tell me a little bit more about what was going on in this Town).

Personal Note: Why can't I forgive Ginny?

But then, when I left my room, I noticed a door at the end of the hall (somehow I hadn't seen it before, which definitely seemed odd to me, and it almost seemed like it just materialized out of nowhere to be honest), but regardless, I decided to investigate it. And when I opened it, it seemed like every freak known to man (again, pardon my language, I truly don't mean to offend anyone) came spewing out. Just a few examples—

THE CONCENTRIC CIRCLE MAN

He was something else because he honestly talked in seemingly endless concentric circles of meaningless. For example, if you asked him a question about whether he had a good time at the party last night or not, he would answer by saying, "Perhaps, well maybe, or you know, it's possible that perhaps, and even maybe, but I don't know, of course, I won't say no, because maybe I did, but I don't know, because it was possible that I did, although I don't know, because you don't really know whether you did or not, you know, because we all could probably have a good time if we didn't

know that we know that we did, you know, so yes, perhaps I did."
And that was just one example.

LONG-LEGGED LUCY

Now, it was largely agreed upon that Long-Legged Lucy was one of the most inappropriately named people around since she didn't really have long legs and her name was actually Donna, but since she always seemed a little off and since she always seemed a little desperate about things (she seemed to have a new boyfriend about ever four point two seconds), people just went with it because they didn't want to hurt her feelings. However, that certainly wasn't reciprocal because she was more than happy to rip into whomever she could wherever she could in any way she could, but that always took place under the cover of "background" as she put it, which was always confusing too, since you never really knew if she believed what she was saying or not because she simply wouldn't stand by anything she said.

DARTH DOOM

He was a real piece of work because he spent all of his time railing away about the indignities and injustices of the world while standing on top of an ivory pedestal. And it was something else too what this man would spew. He would say things like, "Only a bunch of dykes could break like a dam." And, "We need another weak-ass cock like we need another loose-ass whore." And, "Bimbo cheese rots worse than commercial wine." And of course, in public, he always wore four dress shirts, a pair of freshly-pressed blue jeans, and a smoking jacket with a dog whistle around his neck. But in private, he always wore a robe. It was all really distressing.

(And this kind of robe too)

THE BAIT-BOY

The Bait-Boy lived up to his name like few other people ever did, since no matter what you asked him or how you asked him it, he would respond. And he would respond in the most over-the-top frenetic, frantic way possible too. For example, if you asked him whether or not he thought blue was a nice color for the sky, he would emphatically respond that of course it is, only the whole time he spoke he would be sweating profusely and somewhat rambling off track. It was all pretty disturbing actually. And it certainly should be noted that he had a massive public breakdown more than once too.

THE SHALLOW DIVER

He really reminded everyone of one of those Russian nesting dolls that keeps getting smaller and smaller and smaller every time you open it, only he did that with diving. And it was something else too because he would simply jump from higher and higher heights on the diving board into smaller and smaller pools of water. And he didn't seem to worry about whether he could pull it off or not either. Even when people would tell him that he probably shouldn't do that, he would just keep doing it. And honestly, it really seemed like he had some perverse kind of suicide pact. And it certainly was perverse. And suicidal too, for sure.

THE ELIXIR LAD

Now, he didn't really drink all that much, or at least he couldn't remember if he did, which was obviously odd since his name clearly implied otherwise, but regardless, if loose lips sink ships, then he was a torpedo striking an entire armada because he just couldn't keep his mouth shut about anything. Of course, very little was known about him, but nevertheless, he was famous for what he would say when he had some booze in him: "The grape is a vine worth repeating" and "my boss is bigger than your boss" are just a few examples. And it's almost impossible to quantify how many lives have been touched by his weak constitution.

THE EVER-SHRINKING MAN

He was truly something to behold because it literally seemed like every time you looked at him he shrunk a little bit more. And you couldn't always figure out how or why that even happened. But it certainly did. And on top of that, he had the strangest memory possible because he seemed to forget just about everything he ever did or said. For example, his name, his age, his previous convictions or contacts, these were all things he forgot. But oddly enough, he never forgot to be mean, and he could be almost biblically mean too, it must be stressed.

THE BARN BURNER

He was something else because he seemed to simply live for defying his stature and defiling his reputation. Of course, a good number of people really enjoyed his speeches about "locking her up" and "throwing away the key", but to most people it seemed really odd given the fact that he was apparently as guilty of every crime as he would slander someone else for. Nevertheless, he certainly was a draw among a particular segment of the population, for they saw his credentials and valor as something worthy of their adulation. Now, it certainly needs to be stressed that he was so deeply consumed by his own brilliance that he somehow managed to forget that people were actually paying attention to him.

Observation Note: Where did all these characters come from?

But thankfully, before all of these people could finish pouring out of the room, another guest, some woman it sounded like, pushed the door shut, while saying, "You don't want to do that. Do you hear me?"

"I noticed that," I immediately responded, before I could even fully turn around to face her. "But why? And what was that?"

"Our worst nightmare," she answered, looking at me. And then I suddenly realized I recognized her from my file—

Jeff Weisman

"The Administrator"

"I see," I said, continuing to look at her. "And thanks for the warning."

"I wasn't talking to you," she replied, staring right at me, her eyes oddly glimmering in the dim hallway light.

"You weren't?" I asked, obviously confused by her response.

"No," she added, before starting to hobble away. "I was talking to me."

And I didn't know what to make of that, of course. But regardless, I was happy that the door was shut and that I didn't have to deal with that gaggle of freaks, so to speak (again, sorry for the blunt language, but it really seems apropos here), from that room.

Second Observation Note: And what do all of these people have to do with one another?

And then, when I finally managed to make my way back downstairs (after running into The Proctor, of all things, who simply kept rambling on and on about how "we need to get rid of all the kids around here"), I was more than surprised by what I saw because I found The Mayor standing in the middle of the parlor surrounded by a whole new set of people (and almost none of them seemed to be guests at the inn, I immediately realized).

"I know that's what you think," The Mayor declared.

"And we won't take it anymore," one of the attendants suddenly shouted.

"None of us will," The Mayor replied, before pounding his fists on top of the counter top in front of him.

"The townspeople," my assistant whispered to me, as I stood next to him. "Every so often we have a meeting here for them. Well, they think it's for them anyways."

"I see," I said, leaning into my attendant's ear, his yellow construction helmet bumping against my cheek. "But what exactly are they doing?"

"They're having a grievance recital," my assistant answered, continuing to whisper into my ear. "It's basically a monthly event."

"And this place is overflowing with carnage," The Mayor continued. "And out of control crime."

Personal Note: Why did I reflexively grab my wallet there?

"This could go on for hours," my assistant whispered again. "It's The Mayor tonight."

"And moral bankruptcy," The Mayor thundered, again banging his fists on top of the counter. "And vicious heathenism. And rampant decay."

"And I mean it," my assistant added. "Hours and hours."

"But there's no need to worry," The Mayor suddenly declared, literally leaping onto the side table next to the counter. "I alone can fix it." (1)

And at that, one of the other inn residents (The Skywalker, now that I think about it) suddenly murmured, "That's really my favorite part of this whole exercise."

"Mine too," The Fire Eater muttered back standing behind me.

"It's so outrageous," The Skywalker continued.

But then, before I could really think about any of it too much, my assistant grabbed me by the arm and yanked me out of there.

DISPATCH NUMBER SIX: Be warned. They are out to get you. They are out to get me. And they will stop at nothing to accomplish their goal. But WE can eradicate them. AWESOME!

And perhaps because I was so mad at being rushed out of the room, or perhaps because I was simply exhausted from these seemingly endless dispatches, I simply decided to ignore it for the time being and instead ask my assistant about his last action: "Why did you do that?" I asked, racing along beside him. "Yank me out of the room like that."

"To help you," my assistant answered, leading me out to his motorcar.

"To help me," I responded, trying to jerk my arm away from him. "But I was fine. Why did I need your help? I was enjoying that."

"Exactly," my assistant replied, while we got into his motorcar. "It's like staring at the sun. You'll burn your eyes out if you look at it too long. And let's go. Like I told you earlier, we still need to go see the opposition tonight."

"We do," I said, shutting the door behind me. "We still need to go see the opposition tonight? I didn't think you meant that literally."

"You sure repeat what I say a lot," my assistant said, suddenly looking at me like I really didn't belong here. "And I already told you that."

Second Personal Note: I wonder if Evelyn will listen to her mom more now that she's starting to date and seeing how boys really are.

And then we drove to "The Palace of the Opposition" as my assistant called it, which surprised me, but I figured I would just go with it, and then, before I knew it, we pulled up to quite the building.

(Basically what I saw)

"Look at this place," I said, opening the motorcar door. "It's a total dump. Whoever lives here must be completely broke."

"I don't know about that," my assistant responded, getting out of the car. "You're only looking at the façade. But let's go. They're expecting us."

"Okay."

And then before I could even get up to the door, I received another dispatch.

DISPATCH NUMBER SEVEN: Chicken SOUP!

And I had no idea what it meant, but again, before I could ponder it too long, my assistant rang the doorbell, and we immediately were let inside.

"Yes, yes, come inside," this man said (who I swear looked like The Mayor's Deputy from the ceremony the other day), while walking us through a large front parlor area where we saw a bunch of people (several I think I recognized from the protest march earlier that day) playing some sort of game at a large table—the whole experience completely flabbergasting me.

My best approximation of the game: The Magic Apple Dunk.

A LIST OF POSSIBLE SELECTIONS

1. Outrage

2. Injustice

13. Vindication

14. Validation

3. Self-Righteousness	15. Disgust
4. Apathy	16. Condemnation
5. Indifference	17. Approval
6. Anger	18. Indignation
7. Fear	19. Disillusionment
8. Disappointment	20. Shock
9. Discontentment	21. Elation
10. Exasperation	22. Excitement
11. Redemption	23. Vengeance
12. Justice	24. Chaos

Note: This is only a partial list of possible selections. Please feel free to add your own.

"Thanks," my assistant said, following the man inside.

Personal Note: Why does that guy look like The Mayor's Deputy?

And then we were lead into a large library lined with shelves and shelves of books from floor to ceiling where I was introduced to an old man dressed in a black and red robe sitting in a huge brown chair next to a massive fireplace sipping from a brandy sifter.

"Thank you much," the old man said, before casually motioning with his hand for me to sit down.

"Of course," I replied, noticing an odd looking sofa just to the right of me.

"Good," the old man said, as I sat down. "So you're the new researcher?" the old man then asked, his face pocked and thin and his eyes glossy liked fogged glass.

"Yes," I answered, somewhat distracted by the incredible amount of books around me. "You seem to be quite the bibliophile."

"What's that?" my assistant suddenly said, before literally erupting into laughter. "Did you hear that? This guy?" he then added, pointing at me. "He says quite the bibliophile."

"Of course," the old man snickered, clearly trying to refrain from busting into laughter himself. "For as we all know, perception is reality."

"Not always," I responded, caught off guard by his response.

"Often enough," the old man replied, before snickering slightly again. "Most certainly often enough."

And then, before I could try to rebut his point, my assistant said, "I hope we're not too late. He got caught up with The Mayor."

"No, no, that's fine," the old man answered. "I wasn't sure if it was The Mayor tonight or not."

"It was," my assistant replied. "And he was really in fine form too."

Personal Note: Who other than The Mayor would it be?

"Good," the old man said, suddenly looking back over at me and clearly studying my constitution. "So I'm sure you have quite a few questions," the old man then said. "So go ahead. What would you like to ask me?"

"I don't know," I automatically responded, oddly taken aback by this sudden line of inquiry. "I'm just trying to learn what's going on in this Town. So who are you opposing?"

"The resistance, of course."

"The resistance," I repeated, utterly confused by this response. "But aren't you the resistance?"

And then he proceeded to tell me this: Sometimes. But other times no. And when we're the resistance, we get all heated about it too. Really, there's nothing that's off the table or out of reach from our disparagement. And it's quite fun too. But it's fleeting, unfortunately, he then added, shaking his head, it's always fleeting.

"What do you mean by that?" I then asked, suddenly noticing a small room behind him that seemed to be full of people working.

"Just that," he answered. "It doesn't last. But thankfully, it's endless at least."

"What does that mean?" I asked, straining my neck to better make out what was going on in the room behind him.

"There's always something to be worked up about around here. Whether it's the specific treatment of someone or the laxness of ethical fortitude or the depravity of moral rectitude or the abuse of some group or another, it's endless."

Personal Note: What is in that room?

"One of my colleagues calls it job security," my assistant interrupted, only half-seemingly talking to me.

"It's the basis or our opposition," the old man continued, before taking a quick sip from his sifter of brandy.

"But what then are you opposing?" I asked, still unable to get my mind off of what might be going on in that room behind him.

"I told you, the resistance," he answered.

"You're resisting the resistance," I said, genuinely confused by his response. "How could that be?"

And then he proceeded to tell me this: Because that's how it works. Think of it like a cat chasing its tail. Or perhaps the moon chasing the sun. You need something to go after in order to feel validated. That's how people stay complacent.

And then the old man paused for a moment, looked at my assistant, and then said to him, "Why don't these researchers ever know that?"

"I have no clue," my assistant answered, continuing to stand behind me. "But it really is amazing."

"Agreed," the old man said, chuckling briefly. "It's like it's some kind of job prerequisite."

And then I simply couldn't resist any longer, so I simply asked the old man, "And what's behind that door?"

"There," the old man responded, waving his hand toward the door. "The protesters. And they're hard at work too."

And then the door suddenly opened, and I couldn't quite believe what I saw.

(My best approximation)

"But what are they doing?" I asked, struggling to try to make out exactly what I was looking at.

"Well," the old man said, turning around briefly and looking at everyone in the other room. "It looks like they're on break right now."

"That's required," my assistant said. "It's in the bylaws."

"But I'm sure they'll get back to it soon, because they're the sign builders, and there's plenty for them to create."

"There is," I said, watching the door close again.

And then he proceeded to tell me this: Sure, everyone's got to have a sign if they're going to protest something. That's how it works.

And there's a protest for everything you can imagine. Heck, I still remember that time I coordinated that event for the Unending Injustices Born Upon the Undead. And that was something else too. Because no one really knew what they were protesting, but they sure were committed to it. People were marching in the streets all over the downtown area screaming things like, "Leave the Undead Alone," and "Free the Undead," and "Long Live the Undead." Honestly, it was a real hoot.

"So are these protests successful?" I then asked, wondering how many people were actually behind that door.

"Fabulously," the old man immediately answered. "Beyond fabulously in fact."

"Because they've been changing things," I then said, surprised by his quick response to my question.

"Right," my assistant interrupted, pointing at me, before starting to laugh again. "That's exactly what he means."

"No kidding," the old man said, slapping his knee. "It's almost worth meeting these researchers just to hear them say that. They're all so buffoonish. It's really too much."

"That's what I say too," my assistant added, continuing to laugh wildly.

"So they don't change things?" I then asked, trying to ignore the obvious rudeness of their reactions to my questions.

And then he proceeded to tell me this: No. And why would they? Things don't need to be changed. And how many people do you really think care about making a difference anyways? In the end, maybe there's ten or twenty people who are really adamant about something. Sure, people will talk endlessly about what bothers them, but when it really comes down to standing up for something or taking the time out of their lives to do something about it, how many people do you really think show up? It's just a handful. And don't kid yourself about it either. The exception is not the norm for a reason.

"I see," I said, shaking my head at the old man.

"Alright," my assistant then interjected, turning and looking at me. "We should get going. You need to get your rest. Tomorrow I'm going to take you on a tour of The Town. So it's going to be a busy day for you."

"Fair enough," the old man said, looking at my assistant. "And I'm tired myself," he then added, before handing me a piece of paper with this printed on it (in these crazy large letters too)—

DON'T

MESS

WITH

US

"But," I stammered, honestly not sure how to react, clasping the piece of paper in my hand. "I'm not here to cause you any trouble. I'm just trying to learn what's going on."

"Exactly," the old man simply said. "That's exactly what they all say."

And then, before I could even respond, my assistant simply grabbed me by the arm and lead me back out to his automobile.

Personal Note: And I need to tell Aaron that it's okay not to know what you want to do with your life. But you have to follow through with your actions. That's what counts.

And then when we got back to the inn (uneventfully, I'm glad to say), I sat down at my desk and wrote this—

Research Update: There seems to be such a deep-seated jadedness and frustration with the way of things in this Town that the people here are almost resigned to their own demise. And that profoundly confuses me, especially since the byline for The Greatest Place on Earth is actually: "The Town Where Dreams Come True."

Act Eight

Explore the Sideshows

And that next morning when I woke up I immediately received the oddest message yet (which was simply slipped under my door, of all things). And it was simply this—

THE

GOOSE

HONKS

IN

THE

SKY.

Jeff Weisman

THE

TURKEY

CLUCKS

IN

THE

WOODS.

THE LEOPARD ROARS IN THE JUNGLE.

Jeff Weisman

THE

CROW

CAWS

IN

THE

FIELD.

THE

SEAL

BARKS

IN

THE

OCEAN.

YOU

HAVE

BEEN

TOLD.

And I had absolutely no idea what to make of it. But then I received another dispatch, and I was immediately preoccupied with that—

DISPATCH NUMBER EIGHT: Engage the latest blitz. The Town must be rewarded. BIG T & BD!!!!!! NOW!!!

And since I had absolutely no idea what to make of that either, I simply got dressed and took off to find my assistant, knowing we had a big day ahead of us.

Personal Note: I need to tell Ginny that I keep having this dream where we are standing on this cliff, looking out over this vast canyon, and just as I turn to hold her close to me, she pushes me over the edge, and I tumble down the side, knocking and bashing myself into a million pieces the whole way down. It's truly distressing.

However, before I made it all the way downstairs, I ran into Long-Legged Lucy and The High-Brow Suck-Up in the hall carrying all their luggage with them.

THE HIGH-BROW SUCK-UP

He was a strange figure because for a variety of reasons (his insistence on consuming artisanal cheeses, his near obsession with stone ground mustards, his penchant for limited-run wines chief among them) he never really seemed like he belonged at the inn. Yet, there he was. And oddly enough, he spent most of his time condemning someone or another for something they were doing, but when it came to questions of true moral significance pertaining to his own actions: Standing by his children, supporting his grandparents, upholding his own values, he contradicted himself faster than you could even repeat the concern at hand. Truly it was a marvel to behold. Although it must be noted that he would never allow anyone to "defame", as he put it, his pet bull. Nevertheless, he certainly deserved his moniker.

"Where are you going?" I asked, surprised to see them departing, Long-Legged Lucy's face covered in a thick white film of mascara.

"Onward to better things," Long-Legged Lucy responded.

"Yep," The High-Brow Suck-Up added, his nose ring (which for some reason I hadn't noticed until then) clearly visible to me.

"Why?" I asked.

"Blue whales and estrogen," Long-Legged Lucy answered.

"My pet bull," The High-Brow Suck-Up replied.

And at that they disappeared.

Observational Notation: People seem to come and go around here at an alarming rate. In fact, since I've been here I think ninety-one people have already left. I need to figure out why that is because it seems a little odd. Now granted, it is an inn and by design, it's a temporary residence, but several people left right after checking in. And that just doesn't seem right.

Then, after that encounter, I finally made it downstairs, only to yet again be completely taken aback by what I saw. And really, it can only be described like this—

THE BIG-TIME ALL-OUT MAINSTREAM
HOOTENANNY

The Human Cannonball flies across the room.

The Fire Eater downs a blow torch.

The Plate Spinner whirls eighty dishes around in the air.

The Knife Thrower nails the bull's eye, repeatedly.

The Antipode kicks a lounge chair around.

The Mime breaks out of a box.

The Pogo Sticker hops all over the room.

The Hook Suspender dangles from the ceiling, gleefully.

"What's everyone so happy about?" I asked my assistant, sitting in the corner of the room eating a plate of eggs.

"The latest Town attendance figures are out. And they're amazing," my assistant answered, smiling at me. "We're at a near two-decade high."

The Whistler tooted away.

"That's awesome," I answered, before suddenly receiving another dispatch.

DISPATCH NUMBER NINE: Numbers up. Figures GREAT. Looking forward to what's ahead. BIG PLANS! Keep moving away from behind.

"It really is," my assistant added, before getting up from the table and starting to walk out of the room with me.

Personal Note: That really is good news for The Town.

And then I suddenly noticed yet another man from my file—

"The Squawker"

But then, before I could think about it too much, someone (who I didn't even have a chance to see) handed me this letter—

Yo Dude:

It's me again, Reg. I'm still here. Are you going to help me or not? Remember, I'm counting on you. Thanks much. Your pal.

Personal Note: Who exactly gave me this letter? And what am I supposed to do about this guy? I want to help him. But part of me is suddenly thinking, "Leave me alone."

However, after all of that, my assistant and I finally made our way out to his automobile, hopped in, and started driving towards downtown.

"We've got a busy day ahead of us," my assistant said, turning onto the main thoroughfare approaching town. "I'm hoping to bring you to all of the main sights in one day."

"Good," I replied, quickly checking that I brought my notebook with me. "I'm looking forward to it."

Mental Note: Why am I always second-guessing things lately?

But then, before we could even get to Town, we suddenly witnessed a major accident at the corner of Jefferson and Hamilton Avenues.

"Holy Cow, did you see that?" I yelled, staring at the scene. "That red motorcar just plowed right into that yellow carriage. It didn't even stop at the intersection. And it wasn't even racing along. It was just going with the regular flow of traffic."

"Of course," my assistant replied, seemingly continuing on down the street almost oblivious to the concern at hand. "I'm sure that seems apparent to you."

"But we've got to stop," I then interjected, turning and facing my assistant. "Someone could be hurt. And didn't you see that?"

"No," my assistant simply answered, slowing down and nonchalantly pulling over to the side of the road. "I was busy trying to drive. But I figured you'd say that."

Second Personal Note: Just seeing that there reminded me of that time Ginny and I were taking Aaron (Evelyn wasn't born yet) to my parent's place on the elevated trolley in the city, and we witnessed that motorcar sideswipe that carriage trying turn onto the street below us from that ridiculously confusing interchange. Thankfully, they fixed that interchange after that.

And then once I finally ran up to the scene, I was comforted to see that both of the drivers were okay, but I was otherwise completely perplexed because ten other people had also pulled over (either stopping their carriages or buggies or motorcars right in the street) and they were all giving vastly different accounts to a police officer of the same accident I just witnessed.

Third Personal Note: And why wasn't my assistant more concerned about the accident? And how could he not have seen that accident? Is he blind or something?

ACCOUNT ONE: That red motorcar just pulled out from that alleyway there next to Jefferson Avenue and crashed right into that yellow buggy. I don't think the driver of the buggy even had a chance to see what was happening. That alleyway is always so hard to get out of. The last time I tried to pull out from there I had to wait for ten minutes before I could finally get into the street. And the store didn't even have the dress pants I was looking for. It was really frustrating. I came all the way out from my place just to try to find those. I had a really important business meeting that next day. And it was essential that I had a new suit to make my deal happen.

ACCOUNT TWO: It was all that driver of the yellow buggy's fault because that guy in the buggy just T-boned right into that motorcar. And the buggy was driving at least twenty miles per hour. It was absolutely nuts.

ACCOUNT THREE: I swear officer that green buggy just came barreling through that yellow light at like twenty-five miles per hour and just dead-on rammed into that carriage. And I've never seen anything like that in all my years. It scared the living bejeezers out of me. I don't even think I'll be able to sleep tonight.

ACCOUNT FOUR: That yellow buggy just came crashing down from on top of that hardware store there along Hamilton Avenue and landed right on top of that carriage. And I swear, I wouldn't believe it in a million years if I didn't see it with my own two eyes. I didn't even think a buggy could do that. The way it came flying down from on top of that hardware store like that. It was absolutely amazing.

ACCOUNT FIVE: That green milk wagon couldn't do anything about plowing into that red motorcar. When that aeroplane swooped across the intersection like that, mere inches from the surface, that milk wagon had no choice but to hit that motorcar. I'm amazed I didn't get caught up in the accident myself. It took everything I had to just hit that fire hydrant. And I'm going to need to file an insurance claim for my buggy, so I'm going to need you to verify my account.

ACCOUNT SIX: It was all that red motorcar's fault. The driver just did a U-turn in the middle of the intersection and rear-ended that carriage, just doing a complete one-eighty after hitting that carriage and rolling over near that ditch. I'm still all shaken from it.

ACCOUNT SEVEN: I mean it, the driver of that red motorcar there just came racing through that intersection at like twenty miles per hour, maybe even faster, because she was just zooming along, the motorcar was going so fast, in fact, that I had to tell my Johnny to hold on because I thought we were going to get hit too, because a little while back someone else came racing through here and nearly hit us when we were trying to get to one of the events downtown. And I've got to tell you, it was so traumatic, I almost didn't want to come back downtown. But you know I couldn't do that. We couldn't miss out on one of our events. There's just no way.

ACCOUNT EIGHT: That yellow carriage just rammed right into that red motorcar, and it didn't even stop at the intersection. And I'm not sure why, it wasn't racing along or anything, but it didn't stop at all and it was going with the regular flow of traffic too. But I'm sure glad to see that it looks like everyone's alright.

ACCOUNT NINE: That buggy just went right through that yellow light. I don't think that carriage ever even saw it coming. And it was horrific too.

ACCOUNT TEN: What's all the commotion about?

"But," I then stammered, looking over at my assistant and noticing him staring at one of the main attractions on the edge of downtown.

(A decent gist of it)

"I know," my assistant suddenly interjected, before I could even finish my thought. "That's not what happened at all."

"No," I replied, doing a quick double-take at the crowd of people gathered around the police officer. "And I need to tell that officer what took place."

"Don't worry," my assistant said, pulling me towards the sidewalk. "They've got it taken care of, and we need to go anyways."

"But," I repeated, struggling to get away from my assistant.

"I told you, they've got it taken care of," my assistant said, yanking me even harder. "So let's go. We've got a busy day still. And it's best if we walk from here anyways."

"Fine," I replied, straining to look back at the crowd. "If we must."

Fourth Personal Note: Why didn't I insist harder about telling the police officer what happened?

187

Act Nine

Enjoy the Funhouse

So then we finally made our way downtown to see the first "attraction" as my assistant put it.

Personal Note: Why does everyone seem to think everything's an attraction around here?

"Where is it?" I asked my assistant, looking around the downtown area, all of the buildings seeming somewhat reminiscent of an old movie production set.

"In the public square, of course," my assistant answered. "But there's never any way to park there. It's always totally packed. That's why I said we should just walk."

And then we turned around the corner of an old theater building, and I was immediately taken aback by the sight—

THE FLOGGING RITUAL

What I saw first was a bunch of men, more than I could count quite honestly, screaming in pure delight at the sight of a young woman, half naked, tied to a metal pole, perched on an elevated platform, or pedestal, if you will, relentlessly being whipped by an old man in the middle of the public square.

geeetttTTTTTTTTTTTTTTTTTTTTTTTTTTTTTTTTTTT heeeEEEEEEEEERRRRRRRRRRRRRRRRRRRRRRRRRRR, the men were screaming.

geeettttTTTTTTTTTTTTTTTTTTTTTTTTTTTTTTTTTTTT heeeeEEEEEEEERRRRRRRRRRRRRRRRRRRRRRRRRRRR

And then I noticed hundreds of women gathered around too. geeeettttTTTTTTTTTTTTTTTTTTTTTTTTTTTTTTTTTTTTTTTTTT heeeeEEEEERRRRRRRRRRRRRRRRRRRRRRRRRRRRRRRRRRRR goooooOOOOOOOOOOOOOOOOOOOOOODDDDDDDDDDDDD, the women were hollering, completely enthralled by the flogging.

"What's going on?" I asked my assistant, genuinely dismayed by the incident.

ggeeeeeeTTTTTTTTTTTTTTTTTTTTTTTTTTTTTTTTTTT heeeeEEEEEEEEEEEEEEEEEEEEEEEEERRRRRRRRRRRRRRRRR, I continued to hear.

"The daily worship ritual," my assistant answered. geeeeeeeettttttttTTTTTTTTTTTTTTTTTTTTTTTTTTTTTTTTTTTT heeeeeRRRRRRRRRRRRRRRRRRRRRRRRRRRRRRRRRRRRRRR gooooooooooooooooOOOOOOOOOOOOOOOOOOOOOOOOOOOO OOOOOOOOOOOOOOOOODDDDDDDDDDDDDDDDDDDDD DDDDDDDDDDDDDDDDDDDDDDDDDDDDDDDDDDDDDD DDDDDDDDDDDDDDDDDDDDDDDDDDDDDDDDDDDDDD DDDDDDDDDDDDDDDDDDDDDDDDDDDDDDDDDDDDDD DDDDDDDDDDDDDDDDDDDDDDDDDDDDDDDDDDDDDD DDDDDDDDDDDDDDDDDDDDDDDDDDDDDDDDDDDDDD DDDDDDDDDDDDDDDDDDDDDDDDDDDDDDDDDDDDDD

And then I noticed several children looking on at the sight utterly horrified.

"The what," I stammered, staring back at my assistant, his yellow construction helmet glistening in the sun. "But why are they doing that?"

And then my assistant looked at me dead in the eyes, and without even skipping a beat, replied, "Because we adore women, of course."

Observational Note: I'm not sure what to make of this practice. It obviously doesn't make any sense at all. Now granted, considering women "the lesser species" is nothing new. Most religions give credence to that. But it seemed like they thought she deserved it. And they seemed empowered by this ritual, like it was the most natural thing to do. But why were they showing their love by desecration? And why the obvious joy at such a public humiliation?

And then, my assistant grabbed my arm, swung me around, and I saw this—

THE MERITOCRACY INDOCTRINATION

Ninety people or so, easily, all crowded around some young boy sitting in a wheelchair in the middle of the street, his legs amputated below the knee, and his arms strapped into metal braces locked to the sides of his chair, tossing buckets of tar on him while taunting him with all sorts of horrifying epithets.

"Come on you pansy, can't you run after me?" a man barked, pouring his bucket of tar over the boy who I suddenly realized was actually chained down to the curb.

"Least I can wipe my own nose, snot face," a woman scoffed, heaving her bucket of tar onto him.

"Too bad you can't move you freakish cripple," some an old man, hobbling along said, before awkwardly pouring his bucket of tar over the young boy.

And those were just a few of the immediate examples that come to mind, and I was so horrified by it, that I turned away as quickly as I could, my knees weak from disbelief, before suddenly seeing a nine-year-old girl carrying a bucket of tar up to the boy, getting ready to pour it all over him.

"Why are you doing that?" I asked, grabbing her arm to stop her from walking forward, compulsion clearly getting the best of me.

Professional Note: As a professional scientist, it is imperative that I remain completely detached from and impartial to the subjects I'm studying. It is a dictate of the discipline.

"That's what we do," she answered looking at me, her blue eyes deeper than the ocean. "And let me go," she then added. "My mom's waiting for me."

And I didn't know what to say. So I released her arm and was suddenly pulled onward by my assistant. "Come on," my assistant said, rushing me down the street. "We're just getting started."

THE CONGREGATION RUCKUS

And then we passed over a busy intersection, turned onto Main Street, and immediately ran into hundreds and hundreds of people holding up large placards all amassed in front of the city hall building screaming at each other in the bright afternoon sunshine.

A Lutheran: My team.

A Hindu: No, my team.

A Baptist: My team.

A Christian: No, my team.

An Anabaptist: No, my team.

A Mennonite: No, my team.

A Sikh: My team.

A Muslim: My team.

A Jew: My team.

A Protestant: No, my team.

An Eastern Orthodox: No, my team.

A Roman Catholic: My team.

A Hasidic: My team.

An Evangelical: My team.

An Ecumenical: My team.

A Reformist: My team.

A Buddhist: My team.

A Gnostic: My team.

A Mormon: My team.

A Presbyterian: My team.

A Shinto: My team.

A Sufi: My team.

A Daoist: My team.

A Confucian: My team.

A Jain: My team.

A Pentecostal: No, my team.

And then some man behind me, a Unitarian, no less, suddenly yelled, "But aren't we all on the same team?" And at that, before I could even see who the man actually was, everyone pounced on him and seemingly tried to tear him asunder.

File Reflection: I remember now that one of the previous researchers had noted that there seems to be an almost reflexive response to the team or tribe mentality regarding questions of difference around here. And as the previous researcher noted, "It doesn't seem to matter what the team stands for. If it's your team, it's right, even when the person knows it's wrong."

And then we took off down the street again, "to the next attraction" as my assistant put it again. And along the way I couldn't help but stare at one of the sights.

(A decent facsimile)

"It's right here," my assistant added.

THE FAMILIAL CONFLAGRATION

And then as we turned the corner, I saw it—a massive pile of old bedroom furniture, kitchen tables, lounge chairs, recliners, school desks, nightstands, hall mirrors, blankets, pillows, dressers, lamps, clothes, just all sorts of personal and family items stacked up in the middle of the street, and tons of people standing around it, transfixed.

"What's this?" I asked my assistant, utterly confused by the sight.

"Quiet," my assistant responded without even looking at me. "He's about to speak."

And then a man climbed on top of a stack of twin bed frames in the front of the pile and suddenly declared: "For the loss of our family core structure. And for the destruction of our parental obligations. And for the breakdown of our societal considerations. And for the erosion of our personal involvement. And for the deprivation of the nuclear unit. We offer this humble sacrifice in order to symbolize our heartbreak over this loss."

"But those are all things that could help a struggling family," I said, turning towards my assistant.

"Quiet," my assistant immediately repeated, clearly fixated on the scene in front of him. "You don't want to miss this."

Sudden File Realization: I remember reading a lengthy note in my file describing the consistent decrying the people of this Town seem to have regarding the strength of their family structures. As one townsperson put it, "Nothing is more responsible for our current state of moral depravity and lawlessness than the collapse of the nuclear family unit." However, I also remember the researcher noting that the average person in this Town works fifty hours per week, and that most families have both parents working, and that the strain to keep up with the demands of this Town are enormous, and that very few work schedules sync up with school schedules. And that most parents feel constantly stressed out. And that most everyone feels genuinely overwhelmed by all of this. In fact, I remember the researcher commenting that it was odd that "these factors don't seem to figure into their equations of blame," as it was put. And this was all quite perplexing.

"And so," the man standing on top of the bed frames continued, "Without further ado, I give you our dismay."

And then he took out a match book, ripped out a match, struck the match against the side of the box, and tossed it on the pile.

"The waste," someone moaned, watching the pile begin to burn. "The utter waste."

And then the man jumped off the pile, just as it erupted into flames, and everyone gathered around started weeping, profusely.

"Let's go," my assistant said, again grabbing my arm and pulling me forward. "You get the gist of it, and there's still much more to see."

Personal Note: And why didn't I help that handicapped boy earlier?

And then we took off down the street, quickly rounded another street corner, and immediately came up upon this—

THE HERO VILIFICATION

It was nothing short of a mile long parade, all made up of wounded military vets, slowing marching down the middle of the street, some with crutches and others in wheelchairs, with hundreds and hundreds of people lined up along the sides of the street, all heaving rotten fruit and vegetables at them while boisterously declaring their indignation at their perceived frailties, the street oddly lined with large banners of gratitude.

"Purple hearts are for losers," one woman cackled, while chucking a rotten tomato at a soldier covered in medals.

THANKS FOR YOUR SACRIFICE, one banner read.

"Real soldiers don't get shot," a man cracked, before whipping a moldy peach aimlessly into the parade of veterans.

WE LOVE YOU, another banner read.

"Only the weak get wounded," a boy barked, before chucking a blackened banana at an older veteran, the veteran decorated in seemingly countless ribbons.

"True families don't lose a child in war," yet another woman groaned while hurling a head of wilted lettuce into the parade of veterans, the woman clutching a baby in her left arm.

THANK YOU FOR YOUR SERVICE, yet another banner read.

"Only the pathetic end up captured," an older man snickered, before flinging a bunch of rotten grapes at a POW.

And then, before I could even truly make sense out of the scene, my assistant grabbed me again, and rushed me off down the street. "We're almost late," he said, pushing me along. "I lost track of the time."

Report Notation: What was that? Why would people so willingly ridicule their veterans while simultaneously venerating their service? That contradiction is inexplicable because I always assumed there was a collective agreement that we valued our soldiers since their sacrifice is something we aspire to. However, could it be that all of this is simply a superficial consideration in order to placate our own gratitude at not having to have had to sacrifice ourselves? And that we don't really value anything after all, but rather appreciate our own fortune at not being burdened by such hardship. I'm not sure, but I need to think about this more.

"Hurry along," my assistant said, leading me down a side street. And along the way, I couldn't help but get momentarily sidetracked by another sight.

(A decent representation)

"Come on," my assistant commanded, yanking on my arm again. "We're almost there." And then I came upon this—

THE FREELOADER FREAKOUT

At first, I couldn't even figure out what I was witnessing because it was simply a ton of people running into a nondescript warehouse building seemingly looting the place.

Got a phonograph, one person yelled, racing out of the building.

An ice chest, another person screamed.

A hand drill, another person hollered.

And truly it didn't make any sense to me. But then I noticed a man standing at the door holding an old speaking-trumpet up to his mouth suddenly announcing: "And remember, if I let you in, you know what that means."

"We earned it," everyone standing outside the building suddenly screamed in delight.

And then I saw several more people bolt into the building.

Scored a silverware set, a man roared, sprinting back out.

A folding camera, a woman hooted.

A radio cabinet, a boy whooped.

Personal Note: Why did I find myself thinking about grabbing a new typewriter just then?

And then I watched my assistant suddenly run into the building, disappear momentarily, and race back out carrying a wooden container in his arms while wailing, "A box of cigars."

"What did you do that for?" I asked, once my assistant stopped in front of me. "We're supposed to remain impartial."

"I couldn't help myself," my assistant answered, panting slightly. "It's free if you can get it. You should get something yourself."

"No," I said, watching another person run out of the building lugging a large travel trunk over his head. "I can't do that."

"Fine," my assistant scoffed, shaking his head at me. "Be that way. But let's go. We've still got more to see."

Another Personal Note: It took all of my professional discretion to exercise the proper restraint there.

And then we took off down yet another side street, before coming up to a huge wall, perhaps eighty feet tall. And it was quite a sight too.

THE WALL OF ENDLESS GRIEF

I swear it was literally covered in thousands and thousands, if not millions, quite honestly, of printed notes. Just a few of the examples—

Jeff Weisman

BLAME the

blame on BLAME

The elderly need

dentures

The poor deserve poverty

The elite are

Elitist

Liberals wear snowflakes

Give the ozone

layer a bath

Capitalism is

communism

Conservatives spell government

F-A-S-C-I-S-M

Money

Kills

Borders

are   for

sissies

Free liberty

PC is BS

Slaves stole servitude

Eat yogurt

And I didn't know what to make of it, and I suddenly grew weak kneed, as my head swirled and spun about, and my stomach churned, and my mouth watered, and my brow sweated, and then I, before I could even grab onto anything, I simply passed out.

A Sunday at the Beach

"Dad," Aaron said, sitting on the large towel next to me, the water gently lapping against the sand only a few feet from us, his face just that of a little boy. "When I grow up, I'm going to be a baseball player. That's what I want to do because I want to be great."

"Well I," Evelyn interjected, laying on the towel in front of me, the smell of coconut oil permeating the air. "I am going to be President someday."

"No way," Aaron laughed. "You can't be President."

"Why?" Evelyn retorted, Ginny walking along the water line only a few feet from us. "I can be anything I want."

"But then I'll have to call you Madame Leader. And I don't want to have to do that."

"You alright?" my assistant asked, standing over me waving his yellow construction helmet back in forth in front of my face, the wall of notes towering over me.

Think

Thoughtfully

"You would make a great President," I mumbled still trying to get my bearings, my head hurting some.

Progressives

stunt

progress

"You've been out for few minutes," my assistant added, continuing to wave his helmet back and forth in front of my head.

"I have," I replied, still trying to figure out what happened.

Spanish

"Sure have. You passed out. And you had me all worried," my assistant said, looking at me. "You're my paycheck. So come on, let's go."

"Alright," I replied, getting up from the ground, brushing myself off, and starting to walk forward. And then, I suddenly recognized another person from my file—

"The Barrister"

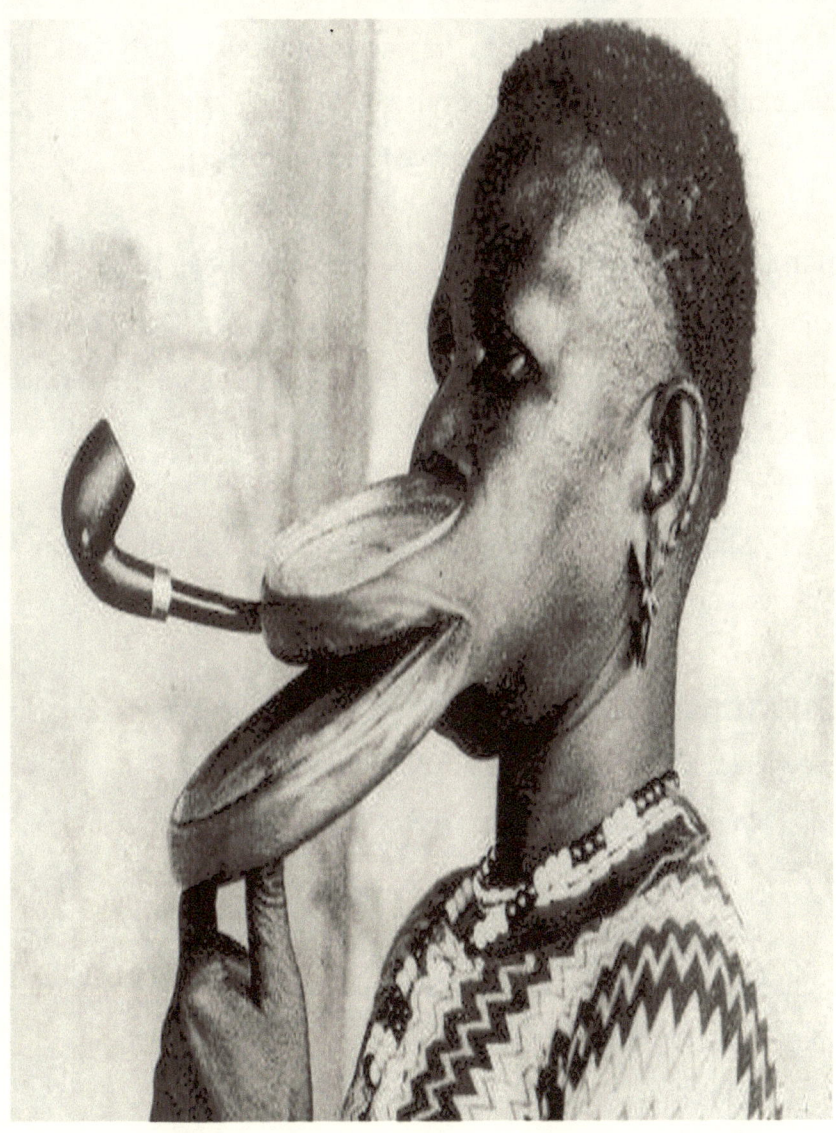

"Let's go," my assistant repeated, rushing along ahead of me.

"But that's," I stammered, struggling to keep up, my head still slightly dizzy and my balance somewhat off.

"Don't worry about it," my assistant said, quickly looking back at me. "You'll want to see this."

And then, I suddenly received another dispatch—

DISPATCH NUMBER TEN: Don't believe what you Read. Don't believe what you Hear. Don't believe what you See. Don't believe what you Think. Don't believe what you Feel. Don't believe what you Know…

And then I received yet another dispatch, which simply continued on from the first.

DISPATCH NUMBER ELEVEN: …Don't believe what you Experience. Don't believe what you Witness. I AM looking out for you. I am protecting you. I am all that & that. K?

And then, before I could even try to figure out what that might have meant, my assistant stopped me in front of a platform where a man was simply railing away.

THE BITCHING BOX

"I swear," the man, maybe thirty-five, standing in front of a podium, wearing a blue suit and a red tie, thundered, "Returning our Ice Cream Stand to this Town will be the death of us all. It will undermine the very fabric of our existence and ruin the strength of our community. It will destroy our standing in the world. It will desecrate our relationships with our friends. It will embolden our foes. It will undercut our values. It will weaken our collective bonds. It will erode our civic structures. It will annihilate our norms. It will violate our customs. Simply put, it would be the complete obliteration of everything good and decent about our Town."

"Come on," my assistant said, grabbing me by my arm.

"But I want to see this," I replied, looking at my assistant, his helmet glistening in the sun. "He's so worked up about everything."

"Oh, they all are when they get up on that box," my assistant said, tugging me along. "But we'll be back. It's time for lunch."

"Alright, yeah," I stammered, quickly glancing back at the man continuing to rail away—

"It will be the end of us all."

And then we walked over to a park bench to have lunch.

Act Ten

Experience the Hall of Mirrors

Over an egg and pickled celery sandwich, I finally asked my assistant the question again that had been plaguing me for a while now: "I know I basically asked this once before and I know you don't want to answer my questions, but what's going on here?"

"What's that?" my assistant replied, before taking another bite of his sandwich.

"What's going on here?" I repeated, picking through my bag of potato chips. "I don't see any logic to this place at all. And I certainly don't see anyone running it."

And just then, and I swear if it wasn't true, I wouldn't have believed it myself, but I received another dispatch.

DISPATCH NUMBER TWELVE: I'm running this place.

"No one's sure," my assistant answered, putting down his sandwich.

"But what about this?" I asked, showing him the dispatch.

"I know. I got one too, but we get those all the time," my assistant responded, before pulling out a whole series of pieces of paper from his front jacket pocket. "See."

And then he showed me the slips of paper all with this printed on them—

I'm running this place.
I'm running this place.
I'm running this place.

I'm running this place.

I'm running this place.

Seriously, there was probably fifty or sixty of them all told.

"But who do these come from?" I asked, looking back over my shoulder and suddenly noticing several men carrying a large banner that read:

Power to the People

"We're not sure," my assistant answered, pulling out one of his cigars from his container and lighting it.

"What does that mean?" I asked.

"Well, some say it's The Mayor while others say it's some Bureau Chief," my assistant responded, before taking a huge puff of his cigar. "And still some even think it's someone else altogether, maybe even The Mayor's Deputy, some think. But honestly, I don't know."

"You don't know," I said, staring at my assistant. "But you've been living here your whole life I thought?"

"So," he answered. "What's does that have to do with anything?"

Personal Note: Doesn't that have everything to do with something?

And then before I could inquire about anything else further, he tossed the remainder of his lunch into his bag, put out his cigar, and stood up.

"Are we leaving?" I asked, watching him scan the park.

Another Personal Note: Did I just see the same monkey hanging from that tree over there now?

"We have to," he answered, getting up from the picnic bench. "Time's up."

"Ok," I replied, standing up myself, before noticing several women carrying a tiny banner above their heads as they slowly lumbered down the middle of the main walkway through the park that read:

Work Equally

"Come on," my assistant then said walking away. "I'm still hoping to get you through all of this in one day."

And then we walked back over to the Bitching Box and heard another man fulminating away.

THE BITCHING BOX (CONT.)

"I swear," a new man, again maybe thirty-five, standing in front of a podium, wearing a red suit with a blue tie, thundered, "Reviving the former Ice Cream Stand in this Town will return our Town to its former glory. It will re-establish our rightful place in the world. It will bring glory to all of us. It will bring prosperity back to our community. It will restore our partnerships. It will bring security to our lives. It will provide jobs for all of us. It will revitalize our economy. It will modernize our Town. It will update our ice cream options. It will solve our ice cream imbalances. Simply put, it will be the complete restoration of everything good and decent about our Town."

Personal Note: Does this guy really think anyone will actually believe this?

"That's more than enough," my assistant declared, tugging on my arm again. "We should get to the next attraction."

"Sure," I said, quickly looking back, and hearing the man continue to fulminate away—

"It will save us from everything."

And then we walked down the street, crossed the intersection, and stopped in front of this strange looking hexagonal building.

"Go ahead," my assistant said, noticing my hesitation, while taking off his yellow construction helmet and briefly scratching his head. "This is one you have to see for yourself."

"What is it?" I asked, looking around the building and not seeing a single marker or indicator signifying what it was.

"You'll see," he answered, putting his helmet back on his head. "But just remember, you bring in with you what you brought out with you."

"What does that mean?" I asked, walking up to the building and suddenly seeing the marque printed in plain letters under the top of the front door—

THE MANOR OF MYSTIC WONDERS

"Trust me. You'll see."

And then I walked inside and was immediately overwhelmed by how dark and quiet it had instantly become. It was like the whole world had vanished. And it startled me.

Personal Note: Why do I still fear what I can't see so much?

But then, knowing that I needed to heed my assistant's advice, I continued forward, aimlessly feeling with my hands for something to grab onto, while hearing the sound of my feet shuffling against the wood plank floor redounding around me, before suddenly hearing a bugle toot: Dun, dun, duh, and seeing this—

(My best approximation)

"What is that?" I muttered to myself, while feeling the edge of the wall against my hand, before seeing this—

(Again, my best approximation)

And I didn't know what was going on or what to do. So I immediately reached up with my hands, rubbed my eyes to try to get a better sight of things, looked out again, and then saw this—

(A decent approximation)

And then I suddenly heard a monotone voice begin to narrate: Now, remember, the whites own this Town. The whites developed this Town. The whites built this Town. The whites settled this Town. The whites created this Town.

Go home Blacks, a voice suddenly screamed behind me.

And I nearly jumped out of my skin, as the narrator continued: The whites constructed this Town. The whites organized this Town.

Go home Jews, a different voice suddenly screamed behind me.

And I didn't know what to do. I literally couldn't see anything, and I couldn't figure out how to get out of there, as I again heard the narrator drone: The whites structured this Town. The whites engineered this Town. The whites planned this Town.

Go home Hispanics, yet another voice suddenly screamed behind me.

And I felt sick to my stomach, as the narrator droned relentlessly: The whites are best. The whites are best. The whites are best. The whites are best. The whites are best.

Go home Asians, yet another voice suddenly screamed behind me.

And I truly didn't know what to do—I couldn't see anything, I couldn't figure out where I was, I didn't know how to get out of there. Truly, I felt trapped by everything.

Personal Note: Did I bring this in with me?

And then I suddenly heard the narrator say: Please understand, everyone's voice needs to be heard equally. Everyone's opinion needs to be shared equally. Everyone's views need to be expressed equally. Everyone needs to be treated equally.

The whites are best, a voice behind me suddenly screamed again.

And I wanted to cry, as I suddenly saw this—

(My best approximation)

And then the narrator continued to drone away: The whites are best. The whites are best. The whites are best. The whites are best. The whites are best. The whites are best. The whites are best. The whites are best.

Second Personal Note: Why am I hearing this? Why am I hearing this in my head? Why?

And then it suddenly went completely silent, and I stood there for a minute, my heart pounding in my chest, before the lights finally came on, a door opened in front of me, and I stumbled outside.

Third Personal Note: I swear I don't believe the whites are best. I swear that's true.

"There you are," my assistant said, walking up to me and putting his arm over my shoulder. "I was worried about you. So what did you see?"

"I don't know," I answered, bent over on the ground, struggling not to vomit. "I heard and saw all kinds of crazy things, disturbing, and hateful things."

"We all do," he replied, helping me stand upright. "That's why you had to see it for yourself. It's part of The Town."

Fourth Personal Note: What does that mean?

And then he took me by the arm and led me down the street saying, "Come on. We need to head over here. There's still one more thing you need to see."

Research Notation: I don't know what to make of that. Was that my projection or was that my representation of something? And was that a feature or a function of The Town? And does the difference matter. And could it possibly be me? Could I somehow have become so ingrained with this idea from this Town that even though I don't believe it I still harbor it inside me?

And then I suddenly received another letter, this time from some middle-aged woman wearing a pink dress (the woman reminding me of a reporter from The Mayor's first event), the letter being tossed at me again, and the woman quickly disappearing down a side street.

The letter read—

The Wing Walker met with The Sword Swallower. The Sword Swallower met with The Snake Charmer. It has been declared.

Fifth Personal Note: Why do I keep getting these?

And then I realized that both the The Wing Walker and The Snake Charmer were also staying at the inn.

THE WING WALKER

He was truly something else too, because not only did it seem like he didn't belong at the inn (he was quite servile, for one), but no matter how low his plane flew to the ground or how high it flew in the air or how many loop-to-loops it did, he somehow managed to maintain his hold on the wing. Of course, several times he brushed the tops of trees and a few times he even scraped the sides of buildings, but still he managed to hold on. It was really like he was glued down to the wing, although his familial relationship to the pilot seemed to have something to do with that, but, for whatever reason, no one really wanted to talk about that.

THE SNAKE CHARMER

She was quite the sight too, because while it must be granted that she was physically attractive, her lilting voice, her lethargic demeanor, her blatant lack of moral fortitude, her undeniable air of entitlement, her talent for lulling one into a mesmerized stupor, all directly worked to undermine that attractiveness. Moreover, and perhaps most oddly, while she was a permanent resident of the inn, almost no one ever saw her. And that was truly confounding.

But I didn't know who The Sword Swallower was, so I asked my assistant, "Who's this?" while pointing to the name on the letter.

"I noticed that," my assistant answered, continuing to lead me down the street. "I'm not at liberty to say. But no matter, I'm sure it's nothing important."

"How do you know that?" I then asked, folding the letter back up.

"Because you can't trust those letters," he answered, while glancing over at me and smiling. "We have no idea where they come from. It could be anyone."

Sixth Personal Note: What does that mean?

"But that lady just threw it at me," I replied.

"Right," my assistant said. "But how do you even know she was real?"

Seventh Personal Note: Because we both just saw her, I thought.

But then, before I could even respond to my assistant's question, we came upon another massive crowd of people, this time all gathered around a large well in a small park in The Town, randomly pronouncing things into it, while tossing wads of money down it.

THE WISHING WELL

"1411," one man declared, tossing a handful of twenty dollar bills down the well. "When boys were boys, men were men, girls were girls, and women knew how to shut up."

"1743," another man announced, chucking a roll of five dollar bills down the well. "When a musket solved a problem."

"1372," yet another man proclaimed, dropping three one dollar bills down the well. "When the law could deal with crime."

"1695," a woman stated, flinging a five dollar bill down the well. "When it meant something to be bare foot and pregnant."

Observational Note: There seems to be an almost irresistible urge to hold onto some nonspecific point in the past in this Town.

"How long has this been going on for?" I asked my assistant, noticing that once someone made their statement into the well and dropped their money into it they would shuffle around to the back of the line and start again.

"We're not sure," my assistant answered, again pushing his construction helmet down tightly onto his head. "But years, at least."

"1542," yet another man asserted, while flipping thirty one hundred dollar bills into the well. "When a man could say what was on his mind."

"I see," I replied, not exactly sure what to make of what I was seeing, while standing there next to my assistant on the edge of the park.

But then, yet again, before I could think about it too long, my assistant looked at me and said: "Let's go. I'm supposed to introduce you to your supposed counterpart now."

"You are," I replied, startled by this sudden revelation. "But you didn't say that before."

"I didn't," he said, starting to walk back towards the center of Town. "Sorry about that, I must have forgotten to mention it."

"1832," I heard some woman behind me say. "When you could punish your kid right."

Seventh Personal Note: Why did my assistant smirk at me when he said he had forgotten to mention that? And what did he mean by my "supposed counterpart" anyways?

And then I looked over and saw quite the sight on the far side of the park.

(A close facsimile)

"Come on," my assistant added, quickly glancing back at me and then turning and hastily walking back down the street.

And then we crossed another intersection, walked down a back alley, and stopped in front of a small building with the words "Bureau Headquarters" printed across the front of it.

"What's this?" I asked, staring at the moniker. "No one told me this was here."

"Oh that," my assistant answered, quickly glancing over at me. "Nothing actually. That's an old sign. We call it the Special Councilors Office now. So come on."

Ninth Personal Note: What does that mean?

And then we walked up a series of stairs, turned down a long hall, walked to the third door on the left, and walked right in.

"There you are," an enormous man donning a blue sport jacket and grey baseball helmet said, sitting behind a large metal desk. "I thought you weren't going to make it."

"We got tied up with things," my assistant replied.

"I'm sure," the enormous man interrupted, before glancing at me and adding. "You're not quite what I expected. But oh well, they never are," And then he pulled out a huge file and started to read: "Robert Aaron Williams, Professor of Psychology, 49, married, two children."

"That's me," I interrupted, utterly confused by this whole exchange.

"Right," the enormous man then said, closing my file.

And then my assistant suddenly chimed in asking the enormous man, "So, what's your working thesis at this point?"

"That there's a high-level conspiracy at play here undermining this Town," the enormous man abruptly answered. "We're not exactly sure about all of the specifics just yet, but all indicators seem to point to that."

And then the enormous man took out another file and read: "Point of fact. The Blue-Billed Man's statement—The takeover will be triumphant. The Town will falter."

Personal Note: Who's the Blue-Billed Man? And how could The Town falter?

"So you're still worried about a conspiracy then?" my assistant asked, sitting down in the chair next to me and taking out another cigar.

Enormous Man: Absolutely. We have financial questions, family questions, professional questions, personal connections, prior connections, tangential connections, it's almost unbelievable.

"That's what half the people around here are saying," my assistant replied, motioning with his hand to see if either of us wanted a cigar.

We both nodded no.

"You should hear what we're talking about down here," the enormous man interjected.

And the enormous man took out a completely different file and read: "Point of fact. Open admission of support. Private discussions favoring collusion. Sustained contacts of interest. Permanent relationships of questionable standing."

"I see," my assistant said. "And what evidence do you have to support this working thesis?"

Enormous Man: Financial ties, family ties, professional ties, personal ties, business ties, and ties we're still trying to untie.

"And that's all?" my assistant asked.

Enormous Man: No, no. We have lies. Lots and lots of lies.

Personal Note: What are they talking about?

"And beyond lies?" my assistant asked, taking another huge puff of his cigar.

Enormous Man: A stated interest. Public rebukes. Repeated attempts at interference. And that's just to name a few.

"Repeated attempts at interference," my assistant repeated.

And then the enormous man took out yet another file and read: "There has been almost daily instances of interference. Instance number eight hundred and twenty-seven was the firing of the man overseeing the potential instances of interference. Instance number eight hundred and twenty-six was the threatening of the man investigating the potential instances of interference. Instance number eight hundred and twenty-five was pressuring the man in charge of the man investigating the potential instance of interference to resign.

"Alright," my assistant suddenly interrupted. "I get it already. And is there a consensus about this?"

Enormous Man (after laughing for a minute straight): No. In fact, many people believe the cause of this interference is simply the old Mayor.

"The old Mayor," my assistant replied, suddenly looking over at me. "But she died ten years ago."

"True, true," the enormous man replied. "But that seems to be utterly irrelevant."

And then the enormous man pulled out yet another completely different file and read: "The nature of our problems center around the old Mayor. All things befall her. This is indisputable. Repeat endlessly."

"Geez," my assistant said, before then adding, while continuing to stare at me, "And you're stepping into all of this."

"I don't know," I responded, completely unsure about what to say. "But I'm trying to research the townspeople. That's what I've been charged with. So I'm not sure what you're even talking about.

All I'm trying to learn about is why the townspeople are acting like they are."

"Oh," the enormous man said, looking at me obviously perplexed. "They're just fed up with things. So many of them feel like they don't have a voice. And they're getting a raw deal on things. And people are working against their interests. So they decided to do something different. Isn't that obvious?"

"No," I answered, looking out the window and suddenly seeing quite the sight.

(A close approximation)

"And The Bureau brought him in here?" the enormous man said, staring at my assistant.

"They have. And you know what I've been asked to do," my assistant replied, shaking his head at the enormous man, before taking another puff of his cigar. "I'm just doing my job."

"I suppose," the enormous man said, putting away one of the many files piled up on his desk.

And then I suddenly received a new dispatch—

DISPATCH NUMBER THIRTEEN: The Mute Lady shall remain FREE.

And I truly didn't know what to make of that because I didn't know The Mute Lady was confined in any way, especially since I just saw her at the inn the other morning.

THE MUTE LADY

She was quite a piece of work, as the saying goes, because despite her name, or perhaps because of it, she started this "Campaign to Speak Deafeningly" for all the guests at the inn. And this was quite the endeavor too, because she formed working groups, had pamphlets printed, and even gave several public speeches in support of this campaign. Of course, it should be noted that nobody knew what she was saying (and yes, obviously no one could hear her either), but even her translator, as it were, simply looked at her dumbfounded as she mouthed away. But mouthed away she would. And on top of that, she was married to The Mayor, or at least that was the pretext of their relationship, although, quite honestly, even that pretext was debatable, and that simple fact both did and did not seem relevant to anything somehow.

But then, before I could really think about any of this too much, my assistant got up from his seat, looked at the enormous man, said, "Thank you," and then told me, "Let's go."

"Were leaving?" I asked, watching the enormous man take out yet another file. "But we just got here. And I have some questions. He's my counterpart."

"Of course," the enormous man said, handing me an envelope from on top of the desk next to him. "So here. This should help but open it later."

"Alright," I replied, taking the envelope from him, before looking back over at my assistant. "So where are we going now?"

And then the enormous man read: "And we shouldn't take anything at face value."

"Later," my assistant said to the enormous man, before looking at me and saying, "Back. I have other business to attend to today. Bureau's orders. So we'll get to it again tomorrow."

Personal Note: What other business could he have to attend to today? And why shouldn't we take anything at face value?

And then we left.

Act Eleven

Peruse the Menagerie

Then, when I walked into the inn, I was immediately taken aback by the conversation that was taking place.

The Constructor: I'm working on redoing my room with an entire new vanity set.

The Sleeptalker: I'm working on having my mattress gold plated.

The Human Kow-Tow: I'm working on replacing my wallpaper with silk sheets.

The Skywalker: I'm going to have one of my aides track down my favorite box of chocolates.

And then the two aides, sitting on the floor behind The Skywalker, erupted into one of the oddest conversations I'd witnessed in a long time—

Aide One: No, I'm getting it for him.

Aide Two: Fat chance. I'm getting it for him.

Aide One: I'm getting it for him because I'm his favorite.

Aide Two: No, you're not. I'm his favorite.

Aide One: No, I'm his favorite.

Aide Two: No it's me.

And then the two aides got up from the floor and simply walked out of the room, the whole time arguing away, "I'm going to get it for him. No, I'm going to get it for him. No I am." And I really didn't know what to make of it. But regardless, all the inn guests seemed completely oblivious to the conversation because they simply continued on with their banter.

The Escapologist: I'm planning on taking the airship to dinner again later tonight.

The Horsemaster: Good idea. I think I'll go with you.

The Confectioner: Yeah well me, I'm working on a whole new arrangement around here.

The Antipode: You and me alike.

The Fire Eater: Ditto here.

And then I suddenly remembered yet another note from my file: There is a long standing pattern in this Town of the various individuals of significant station working to develop relationships that seem to directly conflict with the interests of the townspeople. However, and perhaps most vexingly, the townspeople either seem to approve of these relationships or remain basically indifferent to them. Why this is the case remains a question of profound contention for me.

The Dog Man: I can't even tell you what I'm cooking up.

The Saber Lady: At least we don't have to worry about the townspeople getting in our way.

The Pogo Sticker: I know, that's certainly a luxury.

The Tongue Twister: You can say that again.

But then, before I could even completely process all of that, I received another dispatch which truly confounded me—

DISPATCH NUMBER FOURTEEN: The Strongman is YOUR side. Do you hear me? The Strongman is MY side. LONG LIVE peanuts!

And I stood there for a moment, trying to figure out what that could even mean, when I suddenly remembered I had come across The Strongman in my file too—

Jeff Weisman

"The Strongman"

But then, yet again, before I could even fully process that, my assistant turned to me, looked at me peculiarly for a moment, his yellow construction helmet gleaming under the artificial light of the front parlor, handed me two letters, and then said, "Alright, you should be more than good for now. I need to get going."

"What are these?" I asked, glancing down at the letters in my hand.

"I forgot to give you those earlier. Sorry about that. I haven't gotten a raise in a while. And apparently it's affecting my motivation. I've got to go though," my assistant answered, starting to turn and walk out of the parlor.

"But where are you going? I still need your help," I said, standing there as everyone else in the parlor just continued on with their conversation as if we weren't even there.

The Belly Dancer: I'm converting my closet into a solarium.
The Gorilla-Faced Man: I'm annexing the vacant room next to me.

"Like I said earlier, I've got other business to attend to," my assistant answered, hurrying out the door. "And you've got plenty to do anyways. We'll get back to it tomorrow."

"Right," I said, staring at the letters.

Personal Note: Where is my assistant going?

And then, confused, tired, slightly bothered and all, I simply walked up to my room to see what was in these letters and to start to try to figure out what was going on with the townspeople. However, I was obviously distracted by everything, because when I got to the top of the stairs, instead of turning right towards my room, I somehow turned left (completely oblivious to the fact) and simply walked down to the end of the hall and opened the back closet door (my room key working, now that I think about it) and was immediately shocked by what I saw—

Seemingly millions and millions and millions and millions and millions of people (perhaps nearly a hundred million people, or even more, all told) crammed into this tiny room, all busily working away on stitching together some shredded quilt while muttering all sorts of things at each other (backwards and in whispers I instantly realized). It was truly unbelievable:

       ?on going what's
              me to listens one no
                           ?matter it
does what
       ignored being I'm

       anyways difference a make doesn't it
              ?me hear anyone doesn't why
                     anymore care don't I
forgotten been have I

       important isn't voice my
           ?do it does good what
     rigged is everything
                    scam a is it

time of use worthless a is it
meaningless just is it

And I simply couldn't even move from the sight, utterly mesmerized, their voices all mingling together while they furiously worked on the quilt.

Personal Note: Who are these people? And what are they doing?

But then, simply staring at everyone, I suddenly felt someone pull me away from the room, before slamming the door shut, and then barking, "What are you doing? We don't go in there. Weren't you told that?"

"What?" I replied, completely discombobulated by everything, before suddenly realizing I was talking to The Innkeeper. "No one told me anything about this room," I then added, my breath actually halted.

"Not even your assistant," The Innkeeper said, clearly mad at me. "What good is he? Well here," The Innkeeper then added, handing me a sheet of paper—

RULES OF THE INN

1.   Don't go into the closet
2.   Don't enter the closet
3.   Don't go near the closet
4.   Leave the closet alone
5.   Don't bother with the closet

6.   Don't concern yourself with the closet

7.   The closet is not to be touched

8.   Don't ever open the closet

9.   The closet doesn't matter

10. Consider the closet nonexistent

"What is this? And aren't these all really the same rule?" I asked, still trying to catch my bearings, while continuing to stare at the piece of paper.

"The rules," The Innkeeper answered, before adding, "Isn't it obvious? And why do we need more than one?"

"But," I stammered, genuinely startled by her response. "Then why did you make a list of ten?"

"Me," The Innkeeper answered, suddenly bursting into laughter. "It's not my list. You're too much."

"It's not your list," I said, standing in the hall, The Confectioner walking past us.

THE CONFECTIONER

He was something else because he seemed to believe that hyperbole was something best left never unused since he constantly talked in truly mindboggling exaggeration and ridiculous overkill. For example, he would routinely say things like "you will bow before my will" and "eternal purgatory awaits you if you defy my wishes" and "no one shall disobey my tidings" and "everything I say shall be written in stone". And since he simply hawked cotton candy too, it was all truly utterly bewildering.

"Do you always repeat what someone else said?" The Innkeeper responded, continuing to chuckle. "And you researchers are all alike. Good day."

And then The Innkeeper just walked away down the hall, disappearing into a room I'd never noticed before.

Personal Note: What did that mean?

But then, rather than thinking about it too much, I just decided to get back to my room (I had plenty of work to do) and see what these letters were all about before starting to work on my report.

Another Personal Note: Why does everyone seem to keep getting even weirder around here?

So then, I finally made it back to my room, sat down at my desk, and opened the first letter my assistant gave me.

Dear Lovey Love Love: (It read)

I will never forget the other night. The way you accosted me like that in my moment of weakness. It was beyond compare. And I have been forever changed by your sweet embrace.

Honestly, it was something that was truly breathtaking. You are the most amazing man I have ever known. You make the sky seem smaller. You make the stars seem closer. You make the heavens seem irrelevant. You make eternity seem short. I can't live without you. I can't imagine existing apart from you. I can't imagine anything without you in it. Honestly, I can't even imagine going on without you. Please write back to me. I await your response.

Your Sweet Pee, Me

PS: From the Law Offices of Rohan and Duggal

And I didn't know what to do or even what to think for a moment. Truly, I just sat there, holding the letter in my hand, staring at one of the other pictures tacked up on the wall of my room.

(A decent approximation)

While my mind raced away: Did I really sleep with her? Does she actually mean this? Who is she anyways? Did I really have that much impact on her?

Personal Note: Could this somehow be real?

But then, before I could even think about it too much, the two aides from earlier suddenly came bursting in through my door rambling away—

> Aide One: No, he likes me more.
> Aide Two: No, he likes me more.
> Aide One: No, me.
> Aide Two: Me.
> Aide One: Me.

"Excuse me," I said, staring at the two of them walking into my room, completely caught up in their conversation.

"No me," the first aide nearly yelled, before suddenly looking up at me, shrugging his shoulders, turning around (the second aide following him), walking out of the room, and simply continuing on with their conversation as if nothing happened: "No me. No me. No me." And I really didn't know what to think.

And then, before I could even process that too much, there was a knock at my door. So, I hastily folded the letter back up (making sure to put it back into its envelope), tucked it away in my jacket pocket, and answered the door.

Personal Note: What is going on around here?

"Professor Williams," a man, with an overstuffed build and oily skin, dressed in a grey business suit with a black and red striped tie, said, standing in the doorway, holding a large briefcase in his hand.

"Yes," I answered, staring at him.

"Not what I thought, but whatever," the man continued simply walking right into my room. "We need to talk."

"We do," I replied, surprised by his obvious rudeness. "And you are?" I then asked, motioning with my hand for him to sit down at my desk chair.

"The resistance," he answered, sitting down in my chair. "I'm here to help you."

"To help me?" I asked, looking at him, his out-of-shape build and heavy breathing seemingly the exact opposite of anything approaching someone able to help me. "Am I in danger or something? And I don't remember seeing you at the opposition's headquarters yesterday."

"Of course," he answered, staring at me, his eyes shifting about. "We all are. But that's not the real concern right now. And I'm not with the opposition. I'm with the resistance."

"It's not," I said, sitting down on the bed, the mattress squeaking under my weight and one of the springs uncomfortably poking me in the rear end.

"No."

"Then what's the real concern?" I asked.

And then the man opened his briefcase, took out a newfangled microphone, a large oil lamp, positioned the microphone on the desk in front of him, lit the lamp, quickly combed his hair, straightened his tie, and simply started talking: "We are here today to let all of you know that we don't agree with anything that's going on. We will do everything we can to fight this travesty. We will stand by our convictions. We will speak our mind. Yes, we will do everything we can to resist this outrageous threat to all that we know and respect as true."

"Who are you talking to?" I asked, looking at him completely perplexed.

"Please, don't interrupt me," the man barked, momentarily glaring at me, before simply continuing. "Yes, we want you to know that we are appalled at this outlandish threat to our Town. We are mortified by these consistent acts of public indecency. We are horrified at the routine attacks on our esteemed norms. We are sickened by the obvious recklessness and clear exercise of abuse of power. We are utterly disgusted by these repeated assaults committed on our fellow townspeople. Yes, we are repulsed by this menace to the very fabric of our Town."

And then the man put the microphone down, blew out the oil lamp, threw the microphone back in his briefcase, packed the lamp away, got up, and started to leave.

"Where are you going?" I asked, looking at him, utterly dismayed. "And what do you mean, you're with the resistance?"

"I've said my peace," the man responded, cradling his large briefcase under his right arm. "That should do for a while."

"But I thought you were going to help me?" I said. "And who are you resisting?"

"Didn't you just hear me," the man answered, stopping for a moment near my door. "What more do you want? And we resist everything."

"But how's that going to help me?" I asked, moving slightly on the bed, the spring still poking into my buttocks.

"Fine, here," the man said, quickly pulling a crumpled slip of paper out of his pocket and handing it to me.

And then I opened it and read—

LEAVE THIS MAN ALONE. DO YOU HEAR ME?

"But what good is this?" I asked, staring at the crumpled slip of paper in my hand.

"It lets everyone know we care," the man answered, starting to walk towards the door again. "And really, what could be more important than that? So have a good day."

And then the man left.

Personal Note: How did he even get in here? And what did he mean "we resist everything"?

But regardless, or perhaps despite it, I sat back down at my desk, took out the second letter my assistant gave me, and looked at it, and I immediately realized it was from Ginny. So I opened it up and started reading—

Dear Bob:

I know we didn't get a chance to talk like we hoped because you had to leave for your work, so I wanted to sit down and tell you how I was really feeling.

I miss you. I really do.

And I'm just sick with myself. I can't sleep anymore because I know I hurt you. But I want you to know that I never meant to do that. It was just a mistake, a stupid mistake.

He doesn't mean anything to me. I want you to know that.

I know that when we first met it was such an amazing, natural connection. Honestly, it was like we'd known each other our whole lives. And I knew, and you knew, that we were meant for each other. It was truly a match made in the stars.

And everything seemed to stay that way for so long. We kept moving forward with things. Sure, we had our differences, and yes, it always seemed like we were disagreeing over something or another. But isn't that normal? And still, we always made up. And I liked how you made up. I love it actually.

And, like I said, things kept moving forward. We had Aaron and Evelyn, and we were so happy. It really seemed like all that hard work was worth it. I know it was worth it.

But then we just got complacent. Or perhaps, and more honestly, I just started thinking I needed something more. Like somehow, what I had wasn't enough. And I know that is stupid. And I know that is wrong. And yes, you have every right to never forgive me again. But that's what happened. That was all it was.

And you know you didn't always pay as much attention to me as you really should have. You have to at least on some level acknowledge that you let your own interests get in the way of things. But it's not your fault.

And I'm not trying to blame you. I'm just trying to be honest about where we are.

It's definitely a turning point. And I don't know where we are going to go from here. I pray that it's back to each other. I really don't know what I'll do without you. I don't.

You are the best thing that ever happened to me.

Please keep that in mind when you think about us. I know I've betrayed you. I know

I've disappointed you. I know I've broken your heart. But I'm sorry. I need you.

And I pray that you won't give up on me. Yours, Ginny

And then I didn't know what to do. But nevertheless, I somehow passed out, because when I woke up, it was morning, and the letter was still in my hand. So, I folded it up, got up from my desk, and decided to head downstairs, seeing this picture on my wall before I left.

(A pretty close approximation)

But then, before I got even half way down the hall (my whole being feeling like it was being torn in two, quite honestly), I ran into another one of the inn guests.

THE MOUSE MAN

He was absolutely a singular piece of work, since his whole attraction was about simply spewing the most ridiculous and over-the-top statements he could possibly think up about The Town. And it was something else too. "No one can match the vigor of our Town." "I've seen baseballs literally fly over the centerfield wall just thinking about our Town. "Voodoo spirits fall victim to our Town's mere whims." "Kitty cats whimper in our Town's presence." And these are only a few examples. Really, it was unsurpassed, as far as that goes.

"Where are you going?" The Mouse Man asked, stopping me in the hall. "You seem all frazzled."

"I'm alright," I answered, not feeling like talking to anyone. "I just woke up."

Personal Note: Do I need to tell Ginny about the woman? And why can't I figure out if she's real or not?

"You sure," he said, pulling out a speaking-trumpet and suddenly screaming—

EVERYONE

LIKES

257

Jeff Weisman

ME.

I'M

THE

GREATEST

PERSON

IN

THE

WORLD.

MOMMY,

WHY DON'T YOU LOVE ME?

And I truly didn't know what to think or do, so I simply said, "Thank you. But I'm alright." And I rushed downstairs. Of course, when I got down there, I ran into my assistant, so instead of even grabbing a cup of coffee, I simply showed him the first letter he gave me, and he immediately handed me this—

CONFIDENTIAL SETTLEMENT AGREEMENT AND MUTUAL RELEASE; ASSIGNMENT OF COPYRIGHT AND NON-DISPARAGEMENT AGREEMENT

1.0) <u>**THE PARTIES**</u>

This Settlement Agreement and Mutual Release (hereinafter, this "Non-Disclosure Agreement") is made and deemed effective immediately (henceforth known as "Now") by David Dennison (AKA, the Double-D) and Peggy Peterson (AKA, Pee-Pee).

2.0) <u>**THE RECITALS**</u>

Prior to entering into this agreement, Pee-Pee, came into possession of certain "Confidential Information" pertaining to the Double-D, only some of which is in tangible form, and which includes, but is not limited to, certain biological evidence, still images, personal artifacts, letters, and various curious unmentionables, which were authored by, or relate to Double-D (collectively known as "The Property").

3.0) <u>**SETTLEMENT TERMS**</u>

After an undisclosed payment amount (forever known as "130,000 USD") is made, Pee-Pee shall sign and return this "Non-Disclosure Agreement" to Double-D pronto.

4.0) <u>**REMEDIES**</u>

Any future breach or threatened breach by Pee-Pee regarding Double-D shall automatically require the left ovary of Pee-Pee be provided to Double-D.

5.0) **IN WITNESS WHEREOF,** by their signatures below, the Parties each have approved and executed this Agreement as of the effective date established earlier (AKA, "Now").

_____   _____

"What in the heck's this?" I then asked, looking up from the letter and staring at my assistant, his yellow helmet crooked to the right of his head.

"Don't worry about it," my assistant answered, taking the letter back from me, before walking out of the kitchen. "It's all worked out."

"But I don't have a 130,000 dollars. And I didn't even do anything," I said, staring at him utterly confused.

"Don't worry about it. I'll take care of it," my assistant then said.

"But I didn't do anything," I repeated. "And I think it was all just a dream anyways."

"I told you," my assistant replied, stopping for a moment at the kitchen door and looking at me. "Don't worry about it. But just make sure you don't sign it. It's meaningless otherwise."

Personal Note: What does that mean? How can it be valid if I don't sign it?

"Fine," I said, still not sure what to make of any of this, while noticing the time. "But I need to go into Town and do some more work. I didn't realize what time it was already."

"But you can't go on your own," my assistant replied. "And I just got back. I need to rest."

"But I have to do some more work. And why can't I go on my own?"

"Fine," he replied, shrugging his shoulders and starting to walk back over towards me. "I'll drive you. But it's in the bylines about why you can't go alone. It's strict Bureau Policy."

Personal Note: What does that mean?

Nevertheless, still completely flabbergasted by everything that had just transpired, we headed straight outside. And then, while walking out to his automobile, I opened the envelope my counterpart gave me the day before and saw this—

UP IS

DOWN

And it was in huge letters like that too. However, before I could even think about it too much, my assistant motioned for me to keep moving along. But I was okay with that because I was more than ready to test some of my theories I'd been working on.

Act Twelve

Enter the Big Top

And then, we climbed into his automobile, started it up, and took off, and I almost immediately drifted into thought—

"How could you cheat on me?" Ginny says, sitting on the couch next to me in our living room, her blue eyes fixed on me and her brown hair bopping slightly on her head.

"I don't know," I answer, briefly looking up at the picture of our family at the cabin several years back on the bookshelf. "I really don't know how it happened."

"You don't just accidentally have an affair," Ginny retorts.

"I know," I reply, pushing against the pillow with my right elbow. "But I'm not even sure it really happened."

"What does that mean?" Ginny snaps. "You know what you did."

"But I didn't mean to do it," I answer, sitting up on the couch. "And you cheated on me. Don't you forget that?"

"That might be true," Ginny then says. "But two wrongs don't make a right."

And then, when I focused back on my surroundings, I suddenly saw an unexpected sight.

(A real close approximation)

And I wondered briefly about how this Town could be both simultaneously prosperous and so obviously self-destructive while pondering my fundamental research question: "Why are the townspeople behaving this way?" and I immediately formulated my first real thesis.

Hypothesis Number One: An Annihilation Tendency

So then we parked the automobile outside the local drug store, got out, took care of the meter (my assistant covering it, "Bureau Policy" as he reiterated), and we walked into the store.

Explanation: There is an overwhelming subconscious urge (or "death drive" in the parlance of Freud) to precipitate one's own destruction.

"Hello," I said, to the store clerk, a middle-aged white male, with a pronounced jaw line, crooked teeth, a stern look, and an overall strong demeanor, while my assistant wandered off into another aisle ("to buy aspirin," as he clarified). "Do you mind if I ask you a few questions?"

"Who are you?" the man answered, standing behind the counter. "I ain't seen you around here before."

"I know," I replied, taking out my notebook and pen from my inside coat pocket. "I'm with The Bureau. And I've been asked to conduct some research on the people here. So do you mind if I ask you a few questions?"

And then the man looked at me for a moment, obviously studying me, before straightening several candy bars on the display case next to him, and finally saying, "Alright, sure. But I don't know what good it'll do you."

"Why?" I asked. "Don't you think you can answer my questions?"

"Of course," the man replied. "I can answer any question you've got. But I don't know if you will be able to ask any questions worth answering."

Personal Note: What does that mean?

And then I flipped open my notebook, uncapped my pen, and began: "Why do you think the people want to tear down this Town?"

Answer: No one wants to tear down this Town. They want to build it up. They want to make it great again. It's our Town for heaven's sake.

"But people are knocking down some of the main attractions and destroying some of the more established structures around here. Isn't that tearing things down?"

Answer: No. We just want to change things up. Obviously, the old way of doing things isn't working anymore. So we need to try something new.

"So this is just an experiment?"

Answer: I wouldn't say that. I'd say it's the way things should have been done all along.

"And how's that?" I asked, honestly confused by his response, while noticing a young couple wandering into the store.

Answer: Disturbed.

"So you do want to destroy things?"

Answer: No, of course, not. We have children. We want to leave things better for them.

"I see," I said, taking a few more notes, and then deciding I should move on to the young couple. "Thanks. Do you mind then if I ask a few of your patrons some additional questions?"

Analysis: While there certainly seems to be evidence to tangentially support the theory that people are exhibiting behaviors in line with an annihilation tendency, it can't be ignored that they have children too and that they are obviously trying to do things that will benefit them.

"No," the store clerk replied. "Help yourself."

Conclusion: Negative.

And then I walked over to a young couple now standing in the store in front of the formula aisle, a newborn baby in a stroller next to them.

"Hi," I then said, looking down at the baby. "You have a beautiful child."

"Thanks," the man replied, his baseball cap pulled down tightly over his curly black hair. "She's our pride and joy."

"She sure is," the woman interjected. "Nothing's more important to us than her. Do you have any children yourself?"

"Two," I answered, pulling out my wallet and showing them a picture of Aaron and Evelyn. "They're what keep me going," I then added.

271

"We want to have at least two more ourselves," the man said, suddenly putting his arm around the woman.

"At least," the woman added.

"Good for you," I said, before asking, "Do you mind if I ask the two of you a few questions?"

"Are you a reporter or something?" the man replied looking at me curiously. "Because I've got to be honest with you, I don't trust any reporters. They don't say nothing but want they want to hear."

"No," I answered, opening my notebook, while thinking about my second potential theory. "I'm just trying to do a little research. So I just have a few questions for you."

Hypothesis Number Two: A Blind Authority Allegiance

"Shoot," the man said.

Explanation: There is a kind of willful abjuration of one's own identity (a "transference" in the parlance of Freud again) to the supremacy of another's authority and station in society.

And then I asked: So why do you think the people follow The Mayor's orders?

Answer: The Mayor's not in charge of things around here. (The man said.) And they don't follow his orders. They are mostly bemused by them. Of course, there are those who are bothered by how The Mayor speaks. But really, they should just settle down.

"He's not. So who's in charge of things around here?"

Answer: We are. (The woman said.) Isn't that obvious? We're running the show. Why do you think The Town's making so much progress?

"But you seem to be destroying most of The Town. Don't you think?"

Answer: (The man again.) No.

"So, you don't think The Mayor's words matter?"

Answer: When we don't agree with them, of course not. (The woman said again.) But when we do, we stand by them certifiably. It's that simple.

"But how do you know when you agree with them?"

Answer: When we're right, of course. What kind of question was that? (The man said.)

"Sorry, I'm just trying to get a better handle on things around here," I replied, looking up and seeing quite the sight on the wall above me.

(A decent approximation)

"I guess," the woman interrupted. "Are we almost done here?"

"Yes," I answered, continuing to write their responses in my notebook. "I just have one more question, and then I'll leave you be."

"Alright," the man replied.

"So does The Mayor do things that bother you?"

Answer: No. (They both said.) What The Mayor does is perfect.

And then the baby started crying, so I quickly wrote down their response, and thanked them for their time, before wandering over to find my assistant.

Analysis: There's more of a symbiotic relationship at work here than there is an obvious allegiance declaration since the townspeople seem to be ultimately imposing their own whims on the directions of things rather than simply following them. And it seems mutually beneficial. However, it poses another interesting question: Who exactly is leading whom?

"There you are," I said, finding my assistant in the magazine aisle. "Did you find what you needed?"

Conclusion: Negative.

"No," my assistant responded, putting down the magazine. "And it would cost too much in here anyways."

"Alright," I said. "So let's get to another place. I want to do some different research."

"Ok," my assistant replied. "You're the boss."

Personal Note: Are we witnessing a mirror effect where the people are simply reflecting themselves around here?

And then we walked to the next business (a restaurant named Lucky's Diner), and I immediately approached large table of patrons eating lunch, eager to test my next theory.

Hypothesis Number Three: The Self-Esteem Quandary

"Hi there," I said to the man sitting nearest me, my assistant continuing on to the counter area. "I don't mean to intrude, but do you mind if I ask you a few questions?"

"Are you a reporter?" the woman, sitting next to the man, asked. "Because we don't talk to reporters. We don't trust them at all. They will just say anything but the truth."

Personal Note: What is up with this blatant suspicion of reporters in this Town?

"I'm not," I answered, standing at the far side of their table. "I'm with The Bureau. And I just have a few questions for you about The Town."

"Isn't it great what we're doing around here?" another man sitting at the table, slightly younger than the first, wearing a white shirt and black slacks, interjected.

"I suppose," I said, looking at him. "So it's okay if I ask you all a few questions?"

Explanation: Due to a variety of external issues beyond one's control (ranging from shifting economic interests to constant industrial advances), there is an unhealthy proclivity to view one's self as a failure in line with one's expectations (or "pretentions", in the parlance of William James).

"Sure," the first man said. "We all think of ourselves as part of The Bureau."

Personal Note: What does that mean?

"So you believe this is The Greatest Place on Earth?"

Answer: Not anymore. But we're trying to change that. We're trying to fix this Town.

"And how are you doing that?"

Answer: By bringing back the past. Isn't that obvious?

"But how can you bring back the past?"

Answer: Look at this Town. Performers are leaving. Jobs are disappearing. Acts are changing. We're all being displaced. And someone's got to do something about it.

"And what exactly are you doing about that?"

Answer: We're making it great again. Isn't that obvious?

"By dismantling it?"

Answer: No, we're not dismantling it. We're only getting rid of what doesn't belong. And we're keeping the rest. That's all.

"But how do you know what doesn't belong?"

Observational Note: There seems to be an unnatural reliance on circular logic here that I find genuinely mystifying.

And then I simply heard a whole litany of responses—

Third Man: We just do.
Fourth Woman: My husband.
Sixth Man: The radio.
Second Man: Myself.
Third Woman: We know.
Fifth Man: Obviously.

"See, we know what's going on," the first man said picking up his cup of coffee. "Every last one of us."

Personal Note: Why don't I seem to know what's going on?

"And who are you trying to bring it back for?"

But then, before I could get an answer, my assistant walked up to me and handed me another note—

DISPATCH NUMBER FIFTEEN: The clock tolls. The bell rings. The clouds roll. All is as it should be. TRIUMPH!

And I had absolutely no idea what to make of it, but rather than focusing on it too much, I turned my attention back to the table, and was immediately cut off by the first man. "Are we done here yet?" the first man asked, obviously frustrated with me.

"Sure," I answered, seeing that I had worn out my welcome. "And thanks for your time."

Analysis: There actually seems to be an inexplicably high level of self-esteem at work here. It's as if everyone knows exactly what should take place. And somehow this knowledge seems to be innately formed. This poses another serious question: Can everyone be right? But regardless, the reliance on this belief is apparent.

And then I left the restaurant with my assistant.

Conclusion: Negative.

And then just outside the restaurant, not even ten feet away, I noticed a large group of people talking to each other. And I decided to approach them with my next theory. But then as I neared them, I suddenly realized they weren't actually talking to each other, but instead were rather talking independently of each other. And it was something else to see.

A Woman: Just keep quiet.

                          A Man: Don't say a thing.

        Another Woman: Shut up.

                    Another Man: Keep your head down.

     A Different Woman: Just keep quiet.

                  A Different Man: Don't say a thing.

The Second Woman Again: Shut up.

                  A New Man: Keep your head down.

And then I looked over across the street and noticed yet another unexpected sight.

(A rough approximation)

Hypothesis Number Four: The Conviction Factor

And then, when I looked back over at the group of people, I suddenly noticed one of them just run off, literally sprinting away from the group as fast as he could. And I wasn't sure what to make of that, but since the rest were still yammering away, I decided to approach them.

Explanation: Due to a pervasive timidity and a profound fear (in part aided by a long-established social decorum structure), there is a lack of conviction to adequately counter (or "intervene" in the parlance of the times) this prevailing force, thereby reinforcing it.

The First Woman Again: Just keep quiet.
The First Man: Don't say a thing.
The Second Man: Shut up.

Another New Man: Keep your head down.

And then, before I could even open my mouth, one of them suddenly waved his arms in the air and started talking in an entirely different tone.

Up

Speak

To

Have

We

He said, almost imperceptibly, to clarify. And I immediately recognized him from my file—

"The Pontificator"

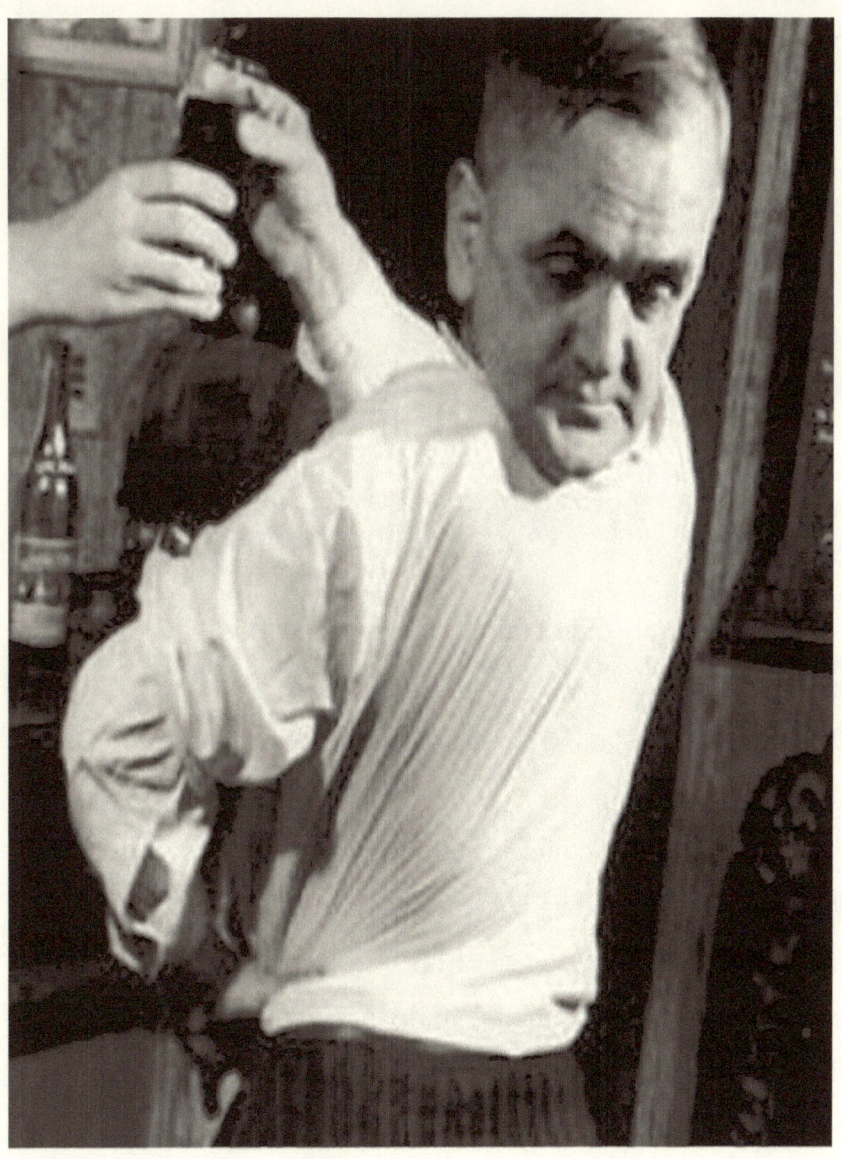

And then, while the people continued to yammer away "just keep quiet, don't say a thing, shut up, keep your head down" someone (I want to say a police officer, although in truth, it all happened so fast, I am still not sure) came running out of a nearby building, grabbed the man, and took him away, the man continuing to mumble the whole time he was being hauled away.

Choice

No

Have

We

And I truly didn't know what to make of it.

Personal Note: What is he actually speaking up against?

Yet, before I could even think about it too long, my assistant yanked me by my arm and led me away from the scene, "Come on," my assistant said, not even glancing over at me. "We need to get out of here. There'll start thinking you're one of them before you know it. And trust me, you don't want that. And besides, we have to get back so that we can get ready for our dinner tonight."

"Why would they think that?" I asked, looking back and noticing another person run off. "And dinner? I didn't know we were going to dinner tonight. And we've still got plenty of time."

"Just come on," my assistant responded, still not even glancing at me. "Neither of us need it. We've been invited to the main banquet. And they like to eat early."

Analysis: Ultimately, there doesn't seem to be any actual objection to these actions since the only notion of concern centers around speaking up about something that is never clarified as truly objectionable. This largely silent condescension ultimately must be understood as consent.

"Fine," I replied, hurrying down the street. "Let's get back so that I can change."

Conclusion: Negative.

And then once we got in the motorcar and started driving back to the inn, I reached into my pocket and suddenly realized I had a piece of paper stuffed inside it. So I took it out (figuring that in the melee from a moment ago someone must have put it in there) and read it—

Dear Friend:

I'm still here. Don't forget about me. Every minute there's more and more of us being brought here too. In fact, I have lost count at this point. Please help.

We're counting on you.

And I truly didn't know what to make of anything anymore.

Act Thirteen

Watch the Dog and Pony Show

Walking through the front door of the inn, my mind raced away—

Talk to her,
Leave her be,
Slander her back,
Let it go,
Find her,
Sue her,
Search her out,
Forget about it,

But then, before I could even figure out what to do about The Innkeeper's Daughter (or anything even close to that), I ran into The Dog Man in the side parlor.

THE DOG MAN

He was without question one of the most problematic and troubled people at the inn. For, not only was he highly regarded and revered in many ways (at one point he was even labeled "The Inn's Mayor" apparently), but he was also prone to such truly erratic and disturbing behavior (donning rose colored dresses, consuming Herculean quantities of cantaloupe juice, speaking while disavowing the underlining knowledge of his own statements) that many people questioned his overall mental health. However, all that aside, he managed to have a regular seat at the foot of the inn's table, as it were.

"Where have you been?" The Dog Man barked at me, sitting in the back lounge chair next to The Pantomime.

THE PANTOMIME

She was something else too because not only did she break the code of silence routinely (in fact, her act really should have been called "The Endless Blatherer"), but when she did speak, she seemed to mirror what someone else wanted her to say. For example, she would say "The worms are to blame for the trodden state of the grass," while pointing up to the sky, after someone seemed to have instructed her to do that. And honestly, it was all very befuddling.

"In Town," I answered, stopping for a moment in the doorway to the parlor, my assistant simply continuing on to his room in order to change his clothes. "I had to do some research."

"You and the research," The Dog Man instantly replied, staring at me like I had said something truly offensive. "You know what I think?" he then added.

"I need to get up to my room so that I can get ready for dinner now," I interrupted, annoyed by him, honestly. "I've been invited to the main banquet apparently."

"Right," The Dog Man then said, sneering at me. "Well, I think we need to research the researchers."

And I truly didn't know what to make of that.

Personal Note: What does that mean?

But then, I suddenly remembered what The Mayor handed me when I first arrived—

THE TOWN CHARTER

We, the residents of "The Greatest Place on Earth," hereby declare the following:

1. **Up is down**
2. **Down is up**
3. **Right is left**
4. **Left is right**
5. **Out is in**
6. **In is out**
7. **Off is on**
8. **On is off**

And somehow, I felt better.

Personal Note: Why did that make me feel better?

So then, I went back up to my room, only noticing one peculiar sight along the way.

(A pretty close representation actually)

But I tried not to focus on it too much, and instead get ready for the early dinner party, hoping the banquet wouldn't last too long because I still wanted to do some more work tonight.

Personal Note: I need to tell Aaron to stop letting people push him around so much.

And then, while putting on my nicest black suit and tie, I suddenly remembered another conversation I had with Ginny many years back—

"You'll always be faithful to me?" Ginny asked, sitting next to me on the picnic bench at Memorial Park on the edge of Mount Prospect College.

"Of course," I answered, starting back at her, her brown hair blowing slightly across her face in the wind.

"Because I've been hurt before."

"Me too," I replied, turning slightly to look her right in the eyes. "More than once. But I promise Ginny."

"Good," she said. "And I promise too."

And for a moment I wanted to cry, but I tried to shake it off (only half successfully because I had to wipe a tear from my eye, in full disclosure), but nevertheless, I left my room in order to head back downstairs to find my assistant.

Personal Note: What should I do about Ginny?

But then, before I could even walk half way down my hall, I was effectively accosted by The Giant Hat Man.

THE GIANT HAT MAN

He was quite the confounding figure because he only popped up at the most inopportune times (always wearing an enormous plaid hat, mind you) while simply expounding the most confusing ideas about all matters of subjects and concerns. For example, he would suddenly burst through a door and go on and on (sometimes for hours at a time, in fact) that it wasn't a door you just saw him walk through, but rather a "window of endless contempt." And really, no one was sure what he was talking about. But he was so emphatic about everything that it almost seemed convincing.

"There you are," The Giant Hat Man said, standing a mere inch from me while pointing his finger in my face. "I've been looking everywhere for you."

"Sorry," I replied, trying to get by him. "I've got to get going. I've been invited to the main banquet. And apparently, it starts pretty early."

"I know. And I'm watching you," The Giant Hat Man said. "And don't you forget it."

"Sure," I replied, having no real idea what he was talking about. "But I've really got to get going."

"And nothing will stop me," he then added, before handing me a note and disappearing back into his room.

And then I looked at the note and realized it was yet another dispatch.

DISPATCH NUMBER SIXTEEN: The Banquet was a great success. The food was outstanding. The cake was immaculate. PEACE to ALL! (But OUR enemies).

And I didn't know what to make of it (especially since it seemed to be referring to the banquet we were about to be going to), but before I could even think about it too much, my assistant suddenly grabbed me by the arm and yanked me along.

"Come on," my assistant said, rushing me down the stairs. "We're going to be late. So let's go."

"But the Giant Hat Man just threatened me," I said, still holding the dispatch in my hand. "And this note seems to be referencing the banquet that we haven't even gone to yet."

And then, to my complete shock, (and worry too, I must confess), my assistant simply stopped on the middle of the stairs, looked me straight in the eyes and sternly declared, "We're all watching you, you fool. So, let's go."

Personal Note: What did that mean?

But then, before I could even formulate a response, my assistant just yanked me along again, and then we immediately got in the motorcar and took off for the banquet.

Potential Hypothesis Number Five: An Alien Insurrection

"There's several things you've got to keep in mind about this dinner," my assistant suddenly barked, looking over at me, while driving down the road.

"There are," I replied, glancing back at him.

"Yes," he said. "There are. So listen up."

And then he told me this: One, keep your mouth shut. Two, say what people want to here. Three, laugh with everyone else. Four, don't snicker, ever. Five, be memorable. Six, don't stand out. Seven, look people in the eyes. Eight, don't stare. Nine, keep your hands to

yourself. Ten, flirt freely. Eleven, listen intently. Twelve, only half pay attention. Thirteen, follow along. Fourteen, trail blaze. Fifteen, stay by my side. Sixteen, don't linger around me. Seventeen, be polite. Eighteen, employ grand barbarity. And nineteen, and most importantly, keep your thoughts to yourself.

"But half of that doesn't make any sense. It just seems to contradict something else, just like the first rules you told me," I said, suddenly seeing an enormous mansion come into view.

(A decent representation)

"Good," he simply replied, pulling up to main driveway. "You were listening again."

"This place is huge," I said, watching him slow down to talk with the two guards posted at the front gate.

"And twenty," my assistant suddenly interjected. "Don't brag."

Potential Hypothesis Number Six: A Fear Conundrum

And then we pulled up to the guards and proceeded to have one of the more disconcerting interactions (at least from my perspective) yet—

First Guard (staring at my assistant): And he's to be let in?
Second Guard (eyeing me): Really? Him?
My Assistant (casually glancing over at me): Those are my orders.
First Guard (shaking his head): Seriously.
My Assistant (smirking): I know, crazy huh?
Second Guard (staring at me): Yep. (Waving us along.) Good luck with that one.

Personal Note: What did all of that mean?

And then we parked the motorcar in the side parking lot (next to at least fifty other chauffeured limousines), got out, and walked inside.

Imagine a huge hall, perhaps eighty feet long, with enormous chandeliers, elaborate silk curtains, granite columns, marble floor tiles, and every kind of expensive decoration and trinket, and then imagine hundreds of people all decked out in the finest dresses and suits. And then square that grandiosity.

And then square that.

And then square that.

And then square that.

And then square that.

And then square that.

And then you're getting close to the kind of luxury and wealth that seemed to be represented there. Honestly, it was like nothing I'd ever seen before in my life. In fact, I didn't really know that that kind of wealth actually existed. It was that impressive.

And then square that.

And then square that.

And then square that.

And then square that.

And then square that.

Potential Hypothesis Number Seven: A Mass Hysteria

And then when I looked up, I suddenly thought I saw that the ceiling was actually lined with tiny people somehow tucked into the crevices above us. But before I could really focus on that too long (or make any real sense out of that), my assistant pulled me forward saying, "I need to introduce you to the hostess."

"Help," I thought I heard one of the tiny people say. "We're tired of losing up here."

"Come on," my assistant repeated. "And remember, rule nine, don't stare."

And then we walked into the side room, and I suddenly realized that almost everyone from the inn was there (The

Escapologist, The Tongue-Twister, The Gorilla-Faced Man, Darth Doom, etc.) and The Mayor and The Mayor's Deputy, and The Innkeeper, and that man from the opposition, as it were, and that man from the resistance, and a bunch of other characters too, and they were all talking and mingling together like it was the most normal thing in the world.

Personal Note: How could that be?

And then, before I could even ponder that too long, my assistant stopped me in front of this oddly attractive woman, easily in her late sixties, with off-putting green eyeliner and clearly fake platinum blonde hair, and said, "Your Highness," before bowing before her.

"Yes, I see," the woman laughed, staring at me. "So this is our esteemed researcher?"

"It is," my assistant responded, standing back upright, all sorts of people wandering around us.

"Well let me look at you," she said, holding my hands and leaning away from me while staring into my eyes. "We have such high hopes for you. We all do."

"We sure do," this other man, in his nineties it seemed to me, suddenly interrupted, walking up from behind me.

Potential Hypothesis Number Eight: The Groupthink Conspiracy

"We all do," the woman repeated.

"I'm trying," I responded, looking at her, her whole demeanor and disposition utterly contradicting her age. "But I've just started, so I'm going to need more time. It is not clear yet to me what is going on here."

"Time," the older man laughed. "That is one thing we simply can't buy enough of."

And then I suddenly thought I remembered the man from my file: There is an older man here, one of the previous researchers had written, who talks about time as if it is a commodity. Give me more, or less, or that's enough, or it's up, he will say, as if he's wanting to purchase it.

"No matter," the woman simply responded. "It's your report we're in need of."

Personal Note: And I need to tell Evelyn to stop following what her friends are doing so much.

"Supposedly," the older man added, before wandering off to talk with someone else.

And then a bell tolled from overhead.

"It is," the woman said, continuing to stare at me, while turning slightly and adding, "Come on, let's eat."

Potential Hypothesis Number Nine: An Inferiority Complex

And then we walked into the main dining hall, and I was immediately taken aback by the sight—it was simply the most enormous table I'd ever seen in my life (easily a hundred feet long, all decked out in the finest linen and silverware and plates I'd ever thought possible, with every sort food piled on top of it) and everyone else wandering into the room, seeing their place cards and finding their seats, all seemingly waiting for something to occur once they sat down.

"You're over here," my assistant said, as I struggled to make sense of the enormity and grandeur of everything.

"Okay," I half-mumbled, finding my seat and suddenly noticing my place card—

(PUT NAME HERE)

It read, in huge letters like that too.

"Sit," my assistant added, pulling out my chair for me. "Remember, rule seventeen."

And then I suddenly noticed the man from The Bureau who first contacted me sitting at the far end of the table with a younger woman next to him. "But that's," I mumbled utterly shocked to see him there.

"Rule eight," my assistant said, slapping the back of my head. "Sit."

Personal Note: Why is he here?

And then, before I could even react to my assistant's obvious inappropriateness, The Mayor suddenly stood up at the side of the table and said, "Friends, legions, foes, and foreigners."

"Quiet," this man, sitting at the other side of the table, wearing a green suit, yelled, as people continued to mutter about. "I can't hear him."

And then I suddenly noticed quite the picture perched on the wall beside me.

(A very close approximation)

And I found it truly disturbing to see that in the dining room (or anywhere, for that matter). Nevertheless, before I could even focus on that too long, The Mayor simply continued, "We are gathered here tonight to celebrate our good fortune and success."

"Here, here," a woman, donning a pure white dress, barked.

"And to find out how things are doing within our Town."

"Damn right," another woman, also donning a pure white dress, nearly growled.

And then the Mayor took out a slip of paper, wrote something down on it, handed it to the servant standing next to him, waited a moment, and then took it back from the servant. "I have received the first update," The Mayor announced.

"Good news I hope," yet another woman, donning a green and blue dress, hacked.

"Let's pray," a man, wearing a tuxedo, roared. "Let's do pray."

"But," I uttered, actually despite myself, while quickly glancing over at my assistant. "He just wrote that down himself."

"Rule thirteen," my assistant immediately answered back. "So be quiet."

And then The Mayor simply continued, "Our adoption crusade appears to be proceeding along swimmingly. Better in fact, than we ever could have hoped."

"Good deal," Darth Doom, also wearing a tuxedo, bellowed.

And then I suddenly noticed the monkey I'd seen several times before (at least I believed it was the same monkey I'd seen before) hanging from a chandelier in the far corner of the room.

Personal Note: Was that really the same monkey?

But then, before I could focus on it too much, my assistant suddenly bumped me in the shoulder and mumbled, "Rule eleven."

And then The Mayor added, "Of course, there are those obvious forces at work against our cause. Yes, there are those forces." And then The Mayor took out another piece of paper, wrote something on it, handed it to his servant next to him, waited a moment, took it back from him, and then said, "I have received the second update."

"What does it say?" yet another woman, this one donning a bright pink dress, yelped.

"It says," The Mayor proclaimed, undoubtedly enjoying the fixed attention, "that there are those in this Town who seek to deny us our rightful place of honor. And that they wish to take from us what we have worked so hard to procure."

And then the servant, still standing next to The Mayor, whispered something into The Mayor's ear (which sounded like the word "reporters" to me, quite honestly). And then The Mayor said, "Secure. And that those who conspire against us are in quite a deep state."

"The utter travesty," The Innkeeper suddenly yelled. "The disgrace."

"And shame," another man roared, wearing a bright purple suit with a nearly neon-red tie. "The damn deep state."

"But we will push back against those forces," The Mayor added.

"But how do we know that that's true," the first woman barked again. "What evidence do we have?

And then I suddenly received yet another dispatch.

DISPATCH NUMBER SEVENTEEN: Don't trust the researchers. They are out to GET YOU. Especially that new researcher. He's a real SOB. PLUMS!

And then The Mayor took out another piece of paper, wrote something on it, handed it to his servant, waited a moment, took it back from him, and then showed it to us—

THE

CONSPIRATORS

It said, in huge letters like that. And then The Mayor took out yet another piece of paper, wrote something on it, handed it to his servant, waited a moment, took it back from him, and then read, "But we will chop off their heads to feed our tail."

"He's such a big flirt," a woman, also wearing a white dress, sitting next to me, shrieked, while grabbing my wrist and looking at me. "Oh, I'd so like to have my tail chopped off, sweetie. I so, so would."

Personal Note: Was she just flirting with me there?

"Whether it be our own brothers, sisters, or not," The Mayor then added.

"So let's eat," the older woman I first met suddenly declared, standing up from her seat and raising her glass. "To our prosperity."

"And glory," another man, who I couldn't actually see, howled.

And then I suddenly noticed another painting hanging on the wall to my left.

(Basically what I saw)

Potential Hypothesis Number Ten: A Herd Mentality

And then everyone toasted, chugged down their drinks, and simply gorged on the food, while saying all kinds of odd things. Honestly, the whole sight was really something else—

Liquefy elephantine, a man said, gnawing into a chunk of ham.

Restructure yearlings, a man said, tearing into a spit of beef.

Proselytize dispensations, a woman said, chomping into a hunk of venison.

Convert iridium, a man said, crunching into a turkey leg.

Seriously, it was almost too much. But nevertheless, I tried to mind my rules, and enjoy the meal (the food was fantastic, for the record), and then The Mayor suddenly stood up yet again, took out another piece of paper, wrote something on it, simply touched the shoulder of the bus boy next to him, before saying, "I have received the final update for the evening."

"Quantify stools," the woman next to me said, ripping into a chicken breast.

"Listen up," another man, wearing a bright orange suit, barked looking over at my assistant.

"Rule six," my assistant said, almost automatically it seemed, while shrugging his shoulders at me, his yellow helmet glistening under the light. "Rule six."

And then The Mayor declared, "Our progress is unmatched. Our growth is unparalleled. Our accomplishments are momentous. Our victory is unrivaled. Walnuts."

"That's right," a man, sitting near The Shallow Diver, immediately barked.

And then before The Mayor could even continue on, some other man (it seemed to me like someone who had actually just dropped off from the ceiling, in fact) came sprinting through the dining room, screaming: "We will not be silenced. Listen to me."

But it all seemed to sound like this—

We

Will

Not

Be

Silenced.

Listen to me.

I swear. And then two men, I presume servants (although it was certainly never clear) came running out from a side room, tackled the man, and hauled him off, the man screaming, "Listen to me. Listen to me. Listen to me," the whole time he was being carted away.

Personal Note: Why doesn't anyone say anything of substance around here?

"As long as we deny all else," The Mayor concluded, simply ignoring the man. "That is all that is required."

"Here, here," nearly everyone barked, getting up from their chairs and starting to leave the dining hall.

And then we got up, and I looked over at my assistant (wanting to ask him about why we didn't get dessert but deciding against it) and noticed him wiping a tear from his eye.

"Why are you crying?" I asked, truly confused by his reaction.

"I don't know," my assistant answered, looking over at me. "I guess I was just that moved by his speech."

Personal Note: What did he even say?

But then before I could even figure out what to say to my assistant, the man I first met from The Bureau approached me. "My friend, my friend," he said, holding out his hand to shake mine. "It is good to see you. So how has the expedition been going?"

"Alright," I replied, shaking his hand. "But I still have much work to do. And so many things are still quite confusing around here."

"You've been getting my dispatches I hope," he said, oddly smiling at me. "I've been trying to keep you focused to your charge."

And then he gave me this—

COUNT FOURTEEN
(Sought out financial partners contradictory to the interests of The Town)

1. Beginning at least forty years ago, DEFENDANT A ("DEFENDANT A") worked with various financiers ("FINANCIERS") considered unacceptable to appropriate practices.

COUNT FIFTEEN
(Used familial money to finance his various businesses throughout The Town)

1. Contrary to the business acumen claims of DEFENDANT A ("DEFENDANT A"), his overall wealth was effectively acquired through money passed down or inherited to him through highly suspect and often directly fraudulent tax dodging techniques.
2. These tax dodging techniques of DEFENDANT A ("DEFENDANT A") were ultimately learned from and employed by his father (referred to herein as "Papa").
3. Papa was a person of questionable standing, to put it one way. (For example, mob affiliation, white supremacy groups, etc., are known entanglements.)
4. Papa's Papa owned a brothel, for the record.

COUNT SIXTEEN
(Employed both overt and covert means to hide his true financial transactions)

1. DEFENDANT A ("DEFENDANT A") has employed techniques of property devaluation, property inflation, shell companies, etc. to achieve his economic standing.
2. These tax records have never been revealed to the public by DEFENDANT A ("DEFENDANT A").

Personal Note: Is that true about never revealing his tax documents? And if so, how could that be? And why?

"I didn't see them at all," I answered, continuing to try to make sense of his odd smile. "But I've been so busy since I got here."

"Of course," he said, before opening his briefcase and then pulling out another huge file of paperwork and quickly flipping through it. "These are my copies, so I can't give them to you. But these are all of my dispatches I've been sending to you. Just so you know."

"I didn't see them at all," I repeated, noticing my assistant looking clearly impatient standing next to us. "Or at least I don't know if I was."

"No matter," he said, throwing the files back in his briefcase and quickly shutting it. "Well, good luck."

And then he disappeared into another room.

Potential Hypothesis Number Eleven: A Delusional Syndrome

But then, before I could even try to chase after him, my assistant grabbed me by the arm, looked at me, said, "Let's go," and quickly led me back out to the motorcar. "It's not safe here anymore."

Act Fourteen

Awe at the Human Pyramid

"Why isn't it safe here anymore?" I asked for the third time in five minutes. "Why did you say that? I need to know."

"I'm sorry," my assistant finally replied, not even bothering to look over at me. "I shouldn't have said that. You're fine. Don't worry about it."

"How am I not supposed to worry about that?" I asked, looking over at him, the motorcar rumbling down a side street.

"You're the professional," he replied, turning onto the main road. "Right?"

"Of course," I answered, suddenly noticing this to my left.

(A pretty close approximation)

"Then don't worry about it," my assistant added. "Nothing's ever quite what it seems anyways."

Personal Note: What did that mean?

But then, before I could even think about his response too long, I suddenly remembered another conversation I had with Ginny about a year back—

"Are you still happy you married me?" she asked, sitting on the edge of the bed looking at me, her naked body almost glowing in the moonlight.

"I am," I answered, wondering if that was really true. "You've given me two great children. And a wonderful life."

"No, I mean me," she insisted, continuing to look at me, a tear forming in the corner of her eye. "Are you still happy you married me?"

"I am," I answered, after pausing for a minute.

And I forgot all about it.

Personal Note: Why did I pause there?

But then we pulled up to the inn, parked the automobile, got out, and walked through the front door, where I was immediately taken aback by the sight of nearly all of the inn residents, including The Innkeeper, (somehow back from the banquet before us too) running over to the China cabinet in the dining room, grabbing a something from it, and then making some strange pronouncement, before smashing it on the floor.

The Fire Eater: For the strength of conviction. (A plate.)

The Horsemaster: For the moral high ground. (A cup.)

The Dog Man: For the rule of law. (A plate.)

The Tongue Twister: For the wide open arms. (A butter dish.) The Proctor: For the tender heart. (A saucer.)

The Shill: For the consistent stance. (A cup.)

The Mouse Man: For the default to compassion. (A bowl.)

The Fortune Teller: For the reliance on norms. (A platter.)

"What are you doing?" I asked The Prism Lady, holding a serving bowl in her hand.

THE PRISM LADY

She was something else too because every time you looked at her you would swear you saw a slightly different person. Yet, despite her genteel manner and her obvious social skills, she never seemed to have a binding opinion or view on anything. Yet still, for some reason, people still wanted to listen to her, even if they quite couldn't figure out what she was talking about.

"Celebrating," The Prism Lady answered, not even bothering to look at me.

"But you're destroying everything," I said, genuinely befuddled by the sight. "What good is that?"

"No one cares," The Prism Lady replied, before smashing the serving bowl on the floor and proclaiming. "To the shining light upon the hill."

"Exactly," The Barn Burner interrupted, holding a gravy dish in his hand. "And besides no one said we couldn't." And then he smashed the gravy dish on the floor while hollering, "To the thousand points of light."

Personal Note: What does all of this mean?

But then my assistant grabbed me by my arm, told me to "get back to work," walked over to the China cabinet, grabbed a tea cup, and yelled, "To the Charter," before smashing the dish on the floor.

And I went back up to my room, absolutely befuddled by what was going on.

Potential Hypothesis Number Twelve: An Airborne Illness

Of course, before I could even make it to my room, I ran into The Snake Charmer and The Contortionist engaged in a near shouting match.

"The children," The Snake Charmer yelled.

"The poor," The Contortionist replied.

"The weak," The Snake Charmer added.

"The forgotten," The Contortionist shouted.

"The desperate," The Snake Charmer returned.

"The sick," The Contortionist barked.

"The threatened," The Snake Charmer howled.

"The scared," The Contortionist contended.

All the while, staring at a picture on the wall in front of them.

(A pretty close representation actually)

"What are you doing?" I asked, standing in the hallway next to them, surprised to see them there quite honestly. "And why aren't you downstairs with everyone else?"

"We're on our way now," The Contortionist answered, handing me another note, before adding, "And it's how we mourn, fool."

And then they left, laughing riotously the whole way down the stairs.

DISPATCH NUMBER EIGHTEEN: You have spoken. I have heard. We WILL prevail. There is no alternative. GUMDROPS!

And then, truly confused and somewhat disturbed, I simply headed back to my room, locked the door, and got back to things, deciding to catch up on my correspondence first.

Dear Evelyn: (I immediately typed)

What you said not long before I left was right: "We need to make money," because, like you emphasized, "No one's going to give it to us." But it's not the root of all happiness. And don't you forget that.

Your Dad (forever and a day)

And then I started typing another letter, to Ginny this time—

Dear Babe:

I've been thinking a lot about us these past few days. All kinds of different conversations we've had keep popping into my head. Like right now, I just remembered that one day we talked about how we were going to always work together, "Compromise," you said, and emphatically too. "That will be the hallmark of our family." And I was so proud of you that day for making that declaration, because that was my want too. And it still is. However, for a while now, it hasn't seemed like we've been doing that. Honestly, it's seemed more like we've been trying to beat each other, and find out who can win. And I've been guilty of that too. I haven't been

```
listening to you as well as I need to lately.
Neither of us have.
```

And then I stopped, left the unfinished letter in the typewriter (although I'm still not quite sure why I stopped just there), and got back to work on my report in my notebook.

Hypothesis Number Thirteen: An Automatic Behavioral Response

"Why have we been doing that Ginny?" I said out loud to myself, staring at the report in front of me, before getting back to it.

Explanation: As a result of a consistent pattern of negative environmental outcomes (both real and perceived), the townspeople are engaging in a collective retaliation (almost a kind of reverse "operant conditioning," in the parlance of Skinner) as an act of retribution to this wrong.

"And why haven't we been willing to address that?" I then said out loud to myself. "We both know it's been occurring." But rather than thinking about it too long, I simply got back to my report.

Analysis: While some of the actions being taken by the townspeople clearly seem to align with this theory, ultimately there doesn't seem to be any consistent pattern (or agreed to harm, or even agreed to belief in regards to that harm) to support this view.

"And why have we just been shouting at each other so much lately," I said out loud, almost despite myself, quite honestly. "It's like we've been talking past each other, instead of to and with each other."

Conclusion: Negative.

And then I paused for a moment, because I heard two inn guests (I wasn't exactly sure whom) talking with each other in the hallway outside my door—

"She's a bitch," I heard one of them say.

"A royal bitch," the other one said.

"A royal, royal bitch," the first one replied.

"A royal, royal, royal bitch," the other one said.

"And plain vindictive," the first one added. "And petty too."

And then they disappeared down the hall, so I turned my attention back to my letter for Ginny—

And it's like somehow we both started to believe that the other didn't really care about what the other thought, and we didn't know what we should do. You know what I mean? I think about that one afternoon a few years back when we got into that big argument about whether or not we should send Evelyn to that after-school math program. "You don't know what you're talking about," you kept saying. "You don't know at all. She wants to do it." And all I could say in response was, "No, you're the one who doesn't have a clue. Let her be a kid." And the odd thing was, we were both just trying to do what was best for Evelyn, but neither of us wanted to stop and think about that. All we wanted to do was focus on how right we were and how wrong the other one was. And why was that?

And then I stopped again and stared at this picture tacked up on my wall above my bed in my room.

(More or less)

Hypothesis Number Fourteen: A Moral Vacuity

"Why did we do that?" I said out loud to myself, looking back down at my report. "How did we get here?"

Explanation: The lack of a true moral foundation underpinning their belief structure has allowed them to fall victim to their own moral ambiguity (almost like a regressive "developmental stage" in the parlance of Piaget), henceforth driving their behavior to become erratic and unpredictable.

"And did we drive each other away Ginny?" I asked out loud, looking up from my desk, and noticing the picture of our family on my dresser. "Is it really our own fault?"

But then, before I could even think about that too much, there was suddenly a knock on my door, so I got up from my desk (my letter to Evelyn and my report still splayed out across the top of it and my letter to Ginny still in the typewriter) and opened it.

"Professor Williams," a man, dressed like the armed guard who arrested me the first night I arrived in The Town, said, while glancing down at a crumpled piece of paper in his hand. "Are you Professor Robert Williams?"

"I am," I answered, looking at the man, the other man with him, oddly dressed in red and green striped coveralls, simply standing silent next to him.

"You need to come with us," the man dressed like an armed guard immediately said, again glancing down at the crumpled piece of paper in his hand. "We have orders to bring you in."

"Bring me in?" I repeated, utterly bewildered by his request, before quickly looking back at my desk (Ginny's letter in the typewriter flopping slightly from the hallway breeze coming in through the open door) and adding, "Did I do something wrong?"

"You heard our orders," the other man suddenly barked. "So let's go. We don't have all night. And it's getting late as it is."

"But what did I do? Are you arresting me?" I stammered, truly disturbed by this sudden intrusion. "I've just been working. You must have the wrong man."

"You said you were Professor Robert Williams," the first man answered, yet again glancing down at the crumpled piece of paper in his hand. "So you are who we are after. Our orders are clear."

"What orders?" I replied, still completely confused by this entire interaction. "What are you talking about?"

And the man (who now definitely seemed like some kind of guard) showed me this—

SUBPOENA TO TESTIFY BEFORE THE GRAND JURY

To: Professor Robert Williams

YOU ARE HEREBY COMPELLED to appear before the grand jury at the time, date, and place established below. Additionally, you will remain there until notified otherwise.

Place: TBD
Time: Now

INSTRUCTIONS:

1. In complying with this subpoena, you are required to produce all documents deemed necessary in your possession, control, or custody, whether held by you in your past, present, or future agency, or heretofore obtained otherwise.

2. No documents called for by this request shall be destroyed, modified, removed, transferred, consumed, or otherwise made inaccessible to the grand jury.

3. This subpoena is continuing in nature and can be modified at any point in time, with or without your consent or notification.

Date: Yesterday

"So let's go already," the second guard barked again, glaring at me. "We don't have all night. And you're already late."

"But this is a court order," I said, utterly bewildered by this entire turn of events. "I can't be forced to appear before some court. I'm just a researcher. What have I done?"

"We're simply following our orders," the first guard responded, folding the piece of paper back up and putting it in his inside jacket pocket. "You'll have to take that up with the people in charge."

"Although I heard treason against mankind," the second guard suddenly barked, only half-seriously it seemed.

"But who's in charge?" I asked, briefly thinking about running, while continuing to stand in the doorway utterly mystified by this entire encounter. "I haven't been able to figure that out."

"And I heard conspiracy against the established order," the first guard simply added, sneering at me, while motioning for me to start moving.

Personal Note: What is going on?

And then they lead me down the hall (before I could even gather up my letters or The Bureau report, for the record), and all I could do while walking along with them was think about who was actually in charge around here. Just some of my thoughts—

The Mayor: But no one seems to really listen to him. And I can't figure out if he's following the people or if the people are following him anyways.

The Innkeeper: But she doesn't seem to be around much. And she seems more interested in some agenda that only she is aware of.

That Old Man (from the Opposition): But he doesn't seem to really care about things. And it's like he has some completely different interest in mind than what is taking place anyways.

That Late Sixties Woman (from the Banquet): But she doesn't seem to be interested in what's going on, even if my assistant did refer to her as "Your Highness."

An Inn Guest: But they all seem to be completely caught up in their own issues and concerns. And besides, they all are just busy playing games, anyways.

Someone Else: But who? But who? (I kept thinking.)

And then, before we even got to the bottom of the stairs (the guards occasionally nudging me forward), we ran into The Eel Man.

THE EEL MAN

He was something else too because he was constantly making some kind of statement of concern or disagreement about something that what was going on in The Town like "No, I wouldn't involve myself in that matter" or "I certainly don't think that's the most ideal course of action" or "I most definitely don't agree with that statement" or "That really doesn't seem like something that I find appropriate," yet he never actually did anything about what was going on, nor, in fact, did he ever actually seem do disagree with anything. Honestly, and most pertinently, ultimately, it was like he agreed with what was occurring. And in the end, all of that was really quite dismaying, to put it bluntly.

"What's going on?" The Eel Man asked, looking up at us from the bottom of the stairs. "What did he do?"

"None of your business," the first guard said, nudging me along. "We have our orders."

"You didn't get me in trouble," The Eel Man then barked, glaring up at me. "I certainly don't need that. You hear me."

"Yes," I answered, almost instinctively, in retrospect.

"But no matter," The Eel Man then added. "I'm out of here anyways."

And then we just walked by him and stepped into the parlor, where I immediately noticed another man from my file—

Jeff Weisman

"The Purveyor"

And he was playing a game with a bunch of the other inn guests. And it seemed like it was something I read in my file too: The Electorate Shuffle.

PICK AN ISSUE AND WATCH YOUR HOPES VANISH AWAY

1. Medicare	10. Terrorism
2. Social Security	11. Civil Rights
3. Health Care	12. Veterans Benefits
4. Immigration Reform	13. Regulations
5. Gun Control	14. Government Waste
6. Drug Policies	15. Diplomacy
7. Medicaid	16. Job Growth
8. Debt and Deficit	17. Military Engagement
9. Student Loans	18. Border Control

Note: Please only make one final selection at a time. Also, please understand all selections are not meant to be realized—ever.

"What did you do?" The Snake Charmer asked, briefly looking up from the card she was holding in her hand, as we walked past them, before casually throwing the card back down on the table.

"I don't know," I answered, glancing around the room for my assistant. "But can you tell my assistant that I've been brought in for questioning?"

"Jim," The Snake Charmer replied, picking up another card, "That fool." And then she paused for a moment, before adding, "Alright, if I see him."

Personal Note: My assistant's name is Jim?

"Thanks."

And then they took me out to their "patty wagon," as they put it (their words exactly), and I was immediately struck by the sight of their vehicle.

(A decent approximation)

"That's what you're taking me in?" I asked, still trying to make sense of the sight of the thing, let alone everything else that was going on.

"I would stay quiet if I were you," the second guard barked, shoving me forward. "You don't even know what you've gotten yourself into."

And then I suddenly remembered an odd insight from my file: The application of their Charter Rules seems to be predicated on the perceived status of the individual, one researcher wrote. For example, several council members consistently violated numerous Charter Rules without any consequences at all while more than a few townspeople were routinely rounded up by the local authorities and locked away indefinitely for no clear purpose other than some indirect reference to a violated Charter Rule. This discrepancy might be a factor in their behavior.

"But what did I do?" I asked again, climbing into the seat next to the second guard. "I'm just a researcher."

"And I also heard colluded with foreign adversaries," the first guard barked.

And then I remembered another insight from my file: And they seem to have an underlying paranoia that affects their thinking, decision making, reasoning, belief structure, viewpoint, ideology, perception, and conclusions.

"Just get in," the second guard said, pushing me back against the seat. "We've got a job to do."

"But so do I," I replied, watching the first guard (sitting behind the wheel) struggling to start up the vehicle, his foot pounding on the gas pedal and his hand repeatedly beating on the starting button. "I've been asked by The Bureau to research the behavior of the townspeople."

"No one made you do anything," the second guard said,

staring at me. "You did it all by your own volition."

And then the vehicle fired up.

"True, but someone had to do it," I replied for some reason, over the roar of the engine.

"Of course, but it didn't have to be you," the first guard yelled.

And then we drove off, as my mind raced away—

But the man from The Bureau wanted my help.

I had a chance to do something good for the people here.

What's Evelyn going to think of me now?

What's going on in this Town?

How did I end up here?

What am I going to do now?

And those were just some of my thoughts, because I was really just a jumbled mess of concern and confusion.

Personal Note: What was I supposed to do?

"And you better watch what you say now," the first guard suddenly yelled, turning down a small side road. "Because everything you've ever said and done has been recorded."

"What?" I said, suddenly seeing an enormous building come into view. "You've been watching me."

"We all have fool," the second guard growled, calmly sitting next to me. "What do you think we do?"

"I don't know," I answered, looking at the guard driving down the road, his thin face clearly strained from tension. "I don't know at all."

And then we pulled up to the building.

Personal Note: What do the people do around here?

"Come on," the second guard said, standing up, while tugging on my arm. "Let's get inside."

Act Fifteen

Marvel at the High Wire Stunts

Sitting on the bench in the corner of the cell, I tried to make sense of what had just happened to me—

THE CHARGES

"Papers," the man behind the desk had said to the first guard.

"Right here," the second guard replied, handing him a whole file of papers, while I stood in the large room, oddly devoid of people (other than the four of us), watching all of this unfold.

"And here's our orders," the first guard then added, handing him the document he first showed me.

"Good."

And then the man behind the desk proceeded to read off a whole litany of charges being brought against me—

Charge One: Conspiracy against The Town.

Charge Two: Obstruction of justice.

Charge Three: Abuse of power.

Charge Four: Aiding and abetting a foreign entity.

Charge Five: Treason against The Town.

Charge Six: Fraud.

Charge Seven: Corruption.

And I simply stood there dumbfounded, the man behind the desk, his black hair greasy and strangely combed to one side, blankly staring at the paper in his hand.

"What?" I finally mumbled, almost at a complete loss for words. "I'm being arrested."

"Take him away," the man simply replied, before I could even formulate a response.

Personal Note: What is going on?

THE CORRIDOR

And then the two guards who brought me there started walking me down this long corridor, and the whole thing felt like this—

IN A LONG NARROW CORRIDOR
OF THE NONDESCRIPT BUILDING OF

The Greatest Place on Earth	)	ROW NO. 311A.RU.11A
v.	)	
Professor Robert Williams,	)	
AKA dad,	)	
AKA husband,	)	
AKA friend,	)	
AKA son,	)	
AKA teacher,	)	
AKA researcher	)	

SLOWING WALKING BESIDE THE TWO GUARDS

1. The walls seemingly closing in around me like an unknowable force of nature.

2. "But how could those charges be against me?" I finally asked the first guard, shuffling along next to me. "I thought it was a subpoena anyways. And why am I being arrested now?"

3. "Just keep quiet," the second guard simply barked, noticing me staring at the walls lined with enormous framed pictures. "The supposed past Town leaders," the guard simply sneered, pushing me forward.

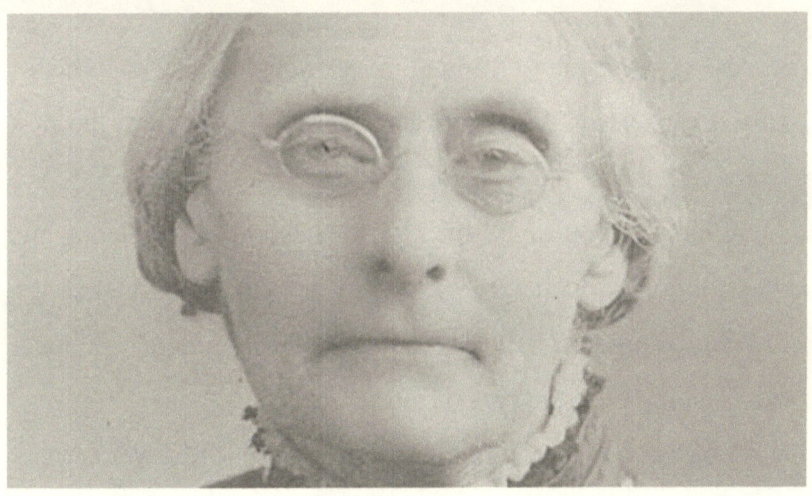

(One decent example)

Personal Note: Where am I?

(A second decent example)

And then we entered an enormous housing facility, which I suddenly realized was the exact same place I had been in the first night I arrived there.

"What did you do?" some prisoner suddenly yelled at me from the front of his cell as we walked toward the end of the facility.

"How could you betray us like this?" another prisoner howled, clasping onto the bars of his cell.

"You are a disgrace to every single one of us," yet another prisoner screamed, the vitriol in his voice almost turning my blood cold.

"You disgusting excuse for a human being," someone else roared from one of the cells above us.

And then I suddenly remembered another insight from one of the researchers in my file: They seem to know no bounds for vocalizing contempt.

"But I didn't do anything," I said again, following along with the two guards. "How could I? I'm just a researcher."

"I already told you," the first guard growled. "Shut up."

And then we turned down another corridor in the facility, and all of the inmates suddenly ran to the front of their cells and roared: WEEEEEEEEEEEEEEEEEEEEEEEEEEEEEEEEEEEEEEEE
EEEEEEEEEEEEEEEEEEEEEEEEEEEEEEEEEEEEEEEEEEEE
EEEEEEEEEEEEEEEEEEEEEEEEEEEELOOOOOOOOOOOO
OOOOOOOOOOOOOOOOOOOOOOOOOOOOOOOOOOOOOOO
OOOOOOOOOOOOOOOOOOOOOOOOOOOOOOOOOOOOOOO
OOOOOOOOOOOOOOOOOOOOOOOOOVVVVVVVVVVV
VVVVVVVVVVVVVVVVVVVVVVVVVVVVVVVVVVVVVVV
VVVVVVVVVVVVVVVVVVVVVVVVVVVVVVVVVVVVVVV
VVVVVVVVVVVVVVVEEEEEEEEEEEEEEEEEEEEEEEE
EEEEEEEEEEEEEEEEEEEEEEEEEEEEEEEEEEEEEEEEEEE
EEEEEEEEEEEEEEEEEEEEEEEEEEEEEEEEEEEEEEEEEEE
EEEEEEEEEEEEEEEEEEEEEEEEEEEEEEEEEEEEEEEEEEE
EEEEEEEEEEEEEEEEEEEEEEEEEYOOOOOOOOOOOO
OOOOOOOOOOOOOOOOOOOOOOOOOOOOOOOOOOOOOOO
OOOOOOOOOOOOOOOOOOOOOOOOOOOOOOOOOOOOOOO
OOOOOOOOOOOOOOOOOOOOOOOOOOOOOOOOOOOOOOO
OOOOOOOOOOOOOOOOUUUUUUUUUUUUUUUUUU
UUUUUUUUUUUUUUUUUUUUUUUUUUUUUUUUUUUUU
UUUUUUUUUUUUUUUUUUUUUUUUUUUUUUUUUUUUU
UUUUUUUUUUUUUUUUUUUUUUUUUUUUUUUUUUUUU
UUUUUUUUUUUUUUUUUUUUUUUUUUUUUUUUUUUUU

UUUUUUUUUUUUUUUUUUUUUUUUUUUUUUUUUUUUU
UUUUUUUUUUUUUUUUUUUUUUUUUUUUUUUUlouder than I
ever thought possible.

Personal Note: What is going on in this place?

And then I was led down yet another corridor, the roars of
the inmates only slightly muffled behind me, and I immediately
realized I was being taken to a different cell than the one I stayed in
the first time I was there, the cell only a few doors down from where
we entered.

"Get in," the first guard suddenly barked, yanking open the
door, the clank of the metal against the wall reverberating
throughout the hall. "Did you hear me?"

"Alright," I replied, before being pushed inside. "I'm going."

And then the door slammed behind me.

Another Personal Note: How am I going to explain this to Aaron?

THE CELL

So there I was, sitting in the back of the cell, replaying the
last fifteen minutes of my life over and over in my head as another
man suddenly walked up to my door, the man wearing a black suit
and black tie, his hair slightly grey and parted to one side, his face
elongated and wrinkled, his eyes a dark blue color, his whole

344

presence conveying a kind of devout seriousness, saying, "Mr. Williams."

"Yes," I replied, noticing he had a large brown briefcase in his hand too.

"Professor Robert Williams," the man continued, almost ignoring me.

"That's me," I restated, staring at the man.

"Procedures," the man simply replied, before turning to his right and waiting a moment.

And then the door suddenly opened.

Personal Note: Should I run?

MY ATTORNEY

And then the man walked inside and said, "Don't think about going anywhere," while stepping over toward the bench and putting his briefcase down on top of it, before I even had a chance to react. "They have guards flanking both sides of your cell, guards posted at every exit, lookouts at every corner, dogs everywhere, airships overhead, the roads are blocked off, you name it. You're enemy number one now. And don't you forget it."

"Who are you?" I then asked, watching the man open his briefcase and casually pull out a piece of paper.

"Your attorney," he simply answered, looking over at me, while handing me the piece of paper. "Of course. Here."

And then I read this—

DISPATCH NUMBER NINETEEN: Get the NEW researcher. Convict him. He cannot be trusted. He's a TRAITOR. You know the truth. WITCH HUNT!

"What's this?" I said, more to myself than anything else. "And am I officially being called a traitor now?"

"Your assistant wanted me to give you that," the man answered, standing in my cell, looking down at me sitting on the bench next to his briefcase. "He said you couldn't go without it. And they're calling you everything under the sun."

And then my lawyer (as he insisted I referred to him) proceeded to just unload on me a whole series of names I was being called: Liar, narcissist, psychopath, lunatic, dilettante, Neanderthal, showman, braggart, fake, spy, misogynist, rapist, racist, bigot, idiot, moron, buffoon, sexist, fool, goon, creep, bully, slanderer, mobster, man-child, phony, conspirator, deceiver, anarchist, sicko, evil, mean, horrible, disgusting, uncouth, uncultured, uncivilized, base, selfish, self-centered, vile, despicable, self-involved, self-interested, petty, vengeful, afraid, weak, cowardly, small, crude, rude, nativist, gross, cartoonish, unserious, unstable, unsound, unhinged, unempathetic, corrupt, sexual assaulter, criminal, money launderer, con, barbarian, draft dodger, cheat, scam artist, Fascist, ignoramus, demagogue, sociopath, reckless, mad, whiner, complainer, distractor, deflector, xenophobe, Authoritarian, clown, cheapskate, egomaniac, fraud.

"Alright already," I finally said, looking up at my lawyer. "I get the point. But where's my assistant? I couldn't find him when I left."

"He's been arrested," my lawyer answered, pulling out another piece of paper and handing me this—

Dear Bob:

I flipped. I had to. I didn't want to. But I don't want to go to jail. Do you? So can you blame me? Anyways, sorry about that. Best of luck.

Jim

"He flipped?" I said, completely taken aback by all of this. "What does that mean?"

"It means he's working with the prosecution now," my lawyer answered, putting the piece of paper back in his briefcase. "He's evidence against you."

"I know what that means, but I didn't do anything. None of this makes any sense at all."

"And they have all kinds of dirt on you now too," my lawyer continued.

And then he showed me this picture.

(A real close approximation)

"But that," I stammered, staring at the picture, while leaning forward on the concrete bench. "That's."

"So you do know her then?" my lawyer said, continuing to hold the picture up for me.

"Yes, that's my maid," I answered, looking at him dejectedly. "But what does that have to do with anything? And I thought my assistant took care of it."

"I see," my lawyer simply said, putting the picture back in his briefcase. "And does this sound familiar?"

Personal Note: Did I really have an affair with her then?

And then he pulled out some newfangled recorder machine from his briefcase and played it for me: "Yes baby, yes," the recording crackled. "That's how I like it. Give it to The Mayor just like that. You know that's how I like it. Give it to me good."

348

"What's that?" I immediately said, listening to the recording, while looking at my lawyer sitting on the bench next to me in my cell, his nice suit pressed tightly around him, his hair parted perfectly to one side, his briefcase clearly of money, everything about him exuding a kind of station and standing in life that utterly conflicted with the abruptness and crudeness of his inquiry.

"That's a piece of key evidence against you," my lawyer responded putting the machine back in his briefcase.

"But that's not me," I replied, sitting up on the bench. "It's The Mayor. It even said so. You just heard it yourself."

"Of course," my lawyer then said again, before suddenly standing up from the bench, turning to face me in my cell, and looking me right in the eyes. "You don't seem to appreciate the seriousness of what you're up against right now. Most everyone has it out for you. And I can't help you if you don't cooperate with me. Do you understand?"

"Yes," I answered, not sure what to think about any of this. "But I am cooperating. That was not me. I swear."

"You really are going to make this difficult."

Personal Note: Why won't he believe me?

"I'm not," I replied, suddenly noticing the letters RUAWOL etched into the wall in the far corner of my cell.

And then he proceeded to explain this entire plan to me for how he was going to deal with my "regrettable predicament" as he took to calling it: "First," he began, "we're going to have you write to your immediate family. You do have immediately family?" he then asked, (which I thought was odd since he seemed to know every other detail in the world about me).

"Yes," I responded. "A wife, a son, and a daughter."

"Good. And we're going to have them write letters on your behalf. We'll have your wife say something like he's a loyal husband who supports me no matter what happens in my life."

"We are?"

And then he paused for a moment, looked at me, and added, "Course, I doubt anyone's going to believe that. But it always sounds good."

Personal Note: Why would he say that?

"And we'll have your son say things like he's a great dad who always fights for what is right in the world. And he's helped me so much. He's such a great teacher and mentor. And he's been my rock when I've needed one," he continued.

"You what?" I then said, completely confused by this entire interaction. "My son?"

And then he paused again, looked at me, shook his head, and simply added, "Right, well, no matter, it'll sound good. And we'll have your daughter say things like he's an amazing dad, great grandfather, and awesome person. Of course," he then continued. "All that stuff you've said about wanting to have sex with her, and liking her, and thinking she's attractive, and saying she's your type, and then even dating women who look like her, and comparing the women you've dated to her, none of that's going to help you. But it is what it is."

Personal Note: What is he talking about? And how messed up does he think I am?

"But I didn't say anything like that about my daughter," I interjected, completely put off by him. "I never would. That's reprehensible. Who would talk like that? Let alone even think it."

"Of course," he simply answered, before continuing on. "And then we'll have several of your coworkers testify on your behalf. We're going to have to work really hard to build up your character."

"Build up my character? What are you talking about?" I interrupted, starting to grow genuinely upset with him, while wanting to get up and run from the cell. "I haven't done anything. Just let me say that. I don't need any witnesses. I'll just testify for myself. And how did a subpoena become an arrest warrant anyways?"

Personal Note: What is he talking about?

And then he paused again for a moment, looked at me like I was truly out of my mind, chuckled briefly, and then finally said,

"Are you crazy? You can't be trusted. We have no idea what you'll say. You can't even keep your own voice on a tape straight. Let alone what you did yesterday. We can't do that. There's no way in a million years that you can testify on your own behalf."

"But I want to," I repeated. "I haven't done anything wrong."

"Good," he then answered, before reaching back into his briefcase. "We'll use that. We'll just keep saying you want to talk. But we can't let you because everyone's out to get you. They would just use your own words against you. That sounds great."

"But I haven't done anything wrong," I pleaded again.

Personal Note: Why won't he believe me?

"Of course," he then said, taking out another file from his briefcase, and then starting to go through a whole series of different pieces of evidence against me—

1. They have a transcript of the conversation you had with The Dog Man.

THE DOG MAN: "Do you think The Mayor can accomplish what he's talking about?"
ME: "No."

2. They have a picture of some of the people you visited.

(A rough approximation)

3.   They have a copy of the letter you sent to The Bureau.

Dear Bureau Chiefs:

My current working thesis is "The Vengeful Chaos Paradox", and it centers on the most aggrieved and forgotten members of The Town, "The Belt Bucklers and The Rust Belters and The Western Talkers" as they call themselves around here. And how they are convinced that their wrongs can be rectified if only enough vitriol and animosity are employed on their behalf.

4.   They have a message they intercepted concerning you.

THE RESEARCHER MUST BE CORRUPTED

5. They have a whole bunch of corroborating stories pertaining to your actions.

Long-Legged Lucy: He groped me.

The Confectioner: He cheated on me.

Townsperson Number One: He evicted me.

Townsperson Number Two: He robbed me.

Townsperson Number Three: He silenced me.

Townsperson Number Four: He threatened me.

Townsperson Number Five: He accosted me.

Townsperson Number Six: He deceived me.

Townsperson Number Seven: He conned me.

"And that's just a tiny smidgen of them," my lawyer then said, tossing the file he was reading from back in his briefcase.

"But what did I do?" I asked, looking at him, completely flummoxed.

"That's the wrong question," my lawyer answered, looking at me clearly annoyed. "You should be asking me what you didn't do."

6. They have copies of all of your relevant records.

CERTIFICATE OF BIRTH

Name: <u>Robert Aaron Williams</u>

Sex: <u>Male</u>

Mother: <u>Matilda Karen Williams</u>

Father: <u>Roger Barton Williams</u>

This is a true certificate of name and birth facts as recorded in this office.

"Alright fine, what didn't I do?" I interrupted, utterly bewildered by this entire experience. "I want to know."

"I was only joking," my lawyer responded, oddly looking at me like I should have understood that all along. "You've done it all, evidently."

"Not funny," I simply replied, staring at him. "Not funny at all."

7. They have access to all of your personal communications.

Dear Ginny:

Your special treat you gave me last night
was amazing. Thank you baby. And I'll get you
back next time. Promise.

Yours.

And yours again. Love, Bob

8. They have testimony from all of your closest friends.

Interviewer: And you said you remember hearing Robby [Professor Williams] say he didn't like strawberries in third grade gym class.

Respondent B: Yes. And repeatedly too.

9. They have circumstantial evidence galore.

John R. Miller hereby testifies in true faith and honor that on said date I witnessed Professor Robert Williams eating a pickle and mustard sandwich.

10. They have all of your relevant financial information.

EZ 1010: RETURN FOR JOINT FILERS WITH DEPENDENTS
NAME: Robert Aaron Williams
INCOME:1,000,000,000,000,000,000,000,000,000,000,000,000,
000,000,000,000,000,000,000,000,000,000,000,000,000,000,000,

000,000,000,000,000,000,000,000,000,000,000,000,000,000,000,
000,000,000,000,000,000,000,000,000,000,000,000,000,000,000,
000,000,000,000,000,000,000,000,000,000,000,000,000,000,000,
000,000,000,000,000,000,000,000,000,000,000,000,000,000,000
000,000,000,000,000,000,000,000,000,000,000,000,000,000,000,
000,000,000,000,000,000,000,000,000,000,000,000,000,000,000,

Tax Due: 0.0

"What? That's not mine," I said, absolutely beside myself. "And I would never disclose that. And that's not even close to correct anyways."

11. They have all your important public interviews.

Q: And as a professional psychologist and professor you believe the real question for our time is one of accountability?
A: I do.

"Fine," I finally said, nearly yelling, quite honestly. "That's enough. That's more than enough. What are we going to do?"

"The only thing we can do," my lawyer answered, tossing several open files into his briefcase. "Attack."

"What?" I replied, watching him close his briefcase. "We attack? How's that going to help? And who are we going to attack anyways?"

Personal Note: What is he talking about?

"The prosecution, obviously. See, it's simple. When you can win on the facts, you use them. When you can't win on the facts, you question the law. When you can't win on the facts or questioning the law, you attack the prosecution. Besides, no one trusts anyone in authority around here anyways," my lawyer responded. "So we can use that to our advantage."

"What are you talking about?" I asked, watching him start to leave my cell.

"Don't worry, I've got it covered," my lawyer answered. "We're only concerned with the court of public opinion, and we all know what that means."

And then he left.

Personal Note: What does that mean?

Act Sixteen

Behold the Liberty Horses

So there I was, the next morning, alone in my cell, utterly dumbfounded by the situation, unsure how I was going to get out of this, on the verge of tears, staring at the blank wall, when I suddenly drifted into a recent memory—

"Let's go," I hollered up to Evelyn and Aaron from the kitchen. "Mom's waiting for us at the park. We need to leave already. The concert's starting soon."

"I've decided not to go dad," Evelyn yelled back from her room upstairs. "I want to go to the outdoor mall with my friends instead."

"What are you talking about?" I barked, putting the picnic basket back down on the counter top for a moment. "We agreed to go to the concert together tonight. You promised."

"Yeah, sorry dad," Aaron yelled, racing past me in the kitchen. "I'm going with my friends to the football game. Shawn and Deon are telling me I can't miss it."

"But you promised your mom and me you were going to do this. You both did. You have to keep your word. We were going to do this as a family."

"Sorry dad," Evelyn replied, speeding past me too. "Got to go."

"Love you dad," Aaron roared from the front porch. "And we'll do it next time, swear."

"Love you too," Evelyn added, the screen door slamming behind her. "But got to go."

And then before I could even ponder why I had just had that specific memory come flooding back to mind, I suddenly received this under my door—

DISPATCH NUMBER TWENTY: I love this Town. Wink. Wink.

And then, just as fast as I had a chance to read that (and well before I could even fully consider what the point of that was), I suddenly received this under my door—

```
Dear Lovey Love:
    I haven't heard back from you. Please
write. I need you. I miss you. I want you. I
won't go away. Ever.
    Love you,
    Your Pee-Pee
```

And then before I could even formulate a response, (or even fully comprehend how I might want to respond) I suddenly heard a muffled voice through the small air vent in the upper right hand corner of my cell say, "Professor Williams, Professor Williams is that you?"

"Yes," I answered, after climbing up onto the concrete bench in the back of my cell and leaning up to the vent. "This is Professor Williams."

"Good," the muffled voice replied. "Listen. You've got to listen to me. You've been framed."

"What?" I replied, not sure what to think of what was going on.

Personal Note: Should I trust this person or not?

"You heard me. You've been framed."

"I have, by whom?" I asked, leaning up closer to the vent to better hear the answer.

"By those who don't want you here. That's who. And they'll do anything to get rid of you," the muffled voice responded. "Absolutely anything."

"They will," I said, suddenly whispering. "Why?"

"Because they didn't get what they wanted," the muffled voice answered. "And they can't stand that."

"But what did they want?" I asked, utterly confused by his response.

"Who knows?" the muffled voice said. "Who knows at all?"

Personal Note: What did they want?

"But how are they framing me?" I then asked, quickly glancing out the door of my cell to make sure no one was around and suddenly noticing this picture on the corridor wall.

(A close approximation)

"They're setting you up to take the fall for them, that's how," the muffled voice answered. "And they're going to force you to lie against yourself. They'll trap you because they've developed a whole counter narrative to your own."

"A counter narrative to my own?" I interrupted, leaning up closer to the vent.

"You heard me," the muffled voice continued. "They have this idea that you've conspired against them, that you're only here for your own interests, that you don't care about this Town, that you will do anything to get what you want, that you've been doing things solely to protect yourself, that you've been constantly distracting everyone from what's really going on, that you did the most horrible things imaginable to get here. That's how. And they're going to trip you up because they're going to foist this narrative onto you."

"But I'm just a researcher," I replied, leaning up even further to the vent. "That's all I am. And I heard all of those charges read against me already. But I haven't done anything wrong."

"Sorry," the muffled voice then said. "I've got to go. Someone's coming."

And then I remembered another note from my file: There is such a frenzied state of mania overtaking nearly everyone in this Town that it is almost impossible to find anyone not engulfed by it. Scratch that, it is impossible to find anyone not engulfed by it.

Personal Note: Have I been engulfed by it too?

And then, before I could even think about that too much, there was another note slipped under my door. So I picked it up and read it—

DISPATCH NUMBER TWENTY-ONE: Remember, the Researcher did it. He conspired against you. We must bring him down. Stand strong. Let FREEDOM reign. Long LIVE The Greatest Place on Earth. Go CHEESE!

And then before I could even figure out what to do next, a guard suddenly approached my door and angrily ordered me out. "Now," he stressed.

"Alright," I responded, still not sure what to make of anything that was going on.

And then he led me down this long side corridor toward what I realized was a large cafeteria, literally the size of a decent-sized auditorium, and ordered me to get in line. "Now," the guard again angrily stressed turning away from me, thousands of inmates filling the room.

"I am," I replied, watching him walk over to a large group of other guards and begin to talk with them, one of the guards suddenly reminding me of someone else from my file—

"The Provocateur"

We should lynch him, I imagined the guard saying.

Damn right we should, I imagined one of the other guards responding.

And twice, I imagined the first guard continuing, if we're so lucky.

"You new here?" this guy in front of me suddenly asked, his front teeth missing and his thin brown hair frail like a worn broom.

"Yes," I answered, not sure at all what to make of him. "I just got here last night."

"Thought so," the guy in front of me answered, before inching forward in the line. "Well, take my advice, don't think about things too much. That's for sure."

"Why?" I replied, suddenly imagining myself standing in front of a room full of people while being grilled by them, their voices ricocheting around me like a pinball machine—

"Why didn't you stand up for yourself more?"

"Why didn't you fight back?"

"Why did you take things for granted?"

"Why didn't you go to every part of The Town?"

"Why didn't you distance yourself from your past?"

"Why did you leave things unanswered?"

"Why didn't you attack too?"

"Why didn't you take any chances?"

"Why didn't you clarify what you wanted?"

"Why?"

"Why?"

"Why?"

"Why?"

"Why?

"Why?

"Why?"

"Why?"

"Why?"

"Move it," a guard at the front of the line suddenly said. "We've got to keep this line moving."

"Huh," I mumbled, looking around me. "What happened?"

"See," the guy I was first talking to suddenly said, shoving me forward. "That's what happens. So stay focused. But don't worry about it too much, it happens to almost all of us. And besides, you'll forget about it eventually. At least you can hope you will."

Personal Note: What did that mean?

And then I grabbed my plate of food, turned around, and suddenly saw Reggie (the inmate I first met) waving me towards him from a table near the back of the room, another inmate sitting next to him, this large picture hanging over both of them.

(A rough approximation)

"I've got to go," I said to the guy who was helping me, before motioning with my tray towards the other side of the room. "I know that man over there."

"Sure," the guy replied. "But just remember what I told you. And also, be civil, it's key to things around here. Apparently, anyways."

Personal Note: And what did that mean?

But then, before I could even ponder that too long, I simply wandered over to Reggie, figuring I better keep moving along.

"Robert," Reggie said, smiling at me, as I approached him, his left wrist bandaged up. "I didn't expect to see you here. Not at all. But whatever, sit down. Yes, please sit down."

"Yeah, have a seat," the other man sitting next to Reggie, his face riddled with pock marks, immediately barked, looking at me like I knew him or something.

"Okay," I replied, sitting down on the metal bench, the large room clambering with noise.

"Did you get my letters?" Reggie then asked, continuing to smile at me.

"Yes," I answered. "Quite a few."

"See," the pock marked man barked again. "And he got them too."

"That's good, and here," Reggie immediately replied, before quickly scanning the room and then handing me this—

Dear Bob:

We're counting on you. We truly are. You're our best hope. Every day we pray for your success. So don't forget us. And somehow, everything depends on you. Your friend, Reg.

"But I didn't do anything. And I don't know why I'm here," I said, handing the letter back to him. "And why are you giving me this now? You could have just told me it."

"We know you didn't do anything," Reggie simply replied. "We're all still here. But you have to know we're relying on you."

"Yeah, nothing's changed," the pock marked man barked, suddenly glaring at me.

"Nothing has changed Bob," Reggie added, shaking his head at me. "And we're all here for the same reason."

And then the pock marked man suddenly enumerated a whole litany of reasons for why I was here: More than half the people couldn't stand the way things were. Almost no one wanted to take things seriously. Almost no one seemed to care about what you did. More than half the people didn't care what you said. Nearly half the people didn't think it mattered anyways. No one seemed to know how to stand up to you. The basic rules of civility and decorum seemed at odds with your ribaldry. You seemed like a decent enough vessel for their hopes. Exasperation begets desperation.

"What are you talking about?" I suddenly interrupted, looking at him like he was out of his mind.

Personal Note: What was he talking about?

"And then there's the enablers," Reggie answered, suddenly scanning around the room worriedly. "Really, it's all about them in the end."

"The enablers? Who are they?" I asked, truly bewildered by this entire exchange.

And then the pock marked man suddenly enumerated a whole litany of people and things for whom he considered to be the enablers: The establishment, the media, your allies, your enemies, your victims, your friends, our norms, our mass entertainment society, our short attention spans, our varied interests, the moneyed class, the shareholders, the fundamentalists, polarization, political correctness, victimization, latent tendencies, manifest tendencies, passivity, indifference, apathy, the cult of personality, tribalism, cultural realities, gerrymandering, fear.

"Seriously, what are you talking about?" I suddenly interrupted again, cutting him off, nearly distraught from this conversation. "What does this have to do with me?"

"Why you're here," Reggie simply replied, looking at me. "Why we're all here."

"But that doesn't make any sense," I said, utterly dumbfounded by his response. "That doesn't make any sense at all. I don't even know what to say."

"None of us do," Reggie simply replied.

"And you," the pock marked man barked, glaring at me. "You're an enabler too."

Personal Note: Am I actually an enabler too?

And then, out of nowhere, a guard handed me another note. So I quickly opened it and read this—

DISPATCH NUMBER TWENTY-TWO: Low IQ Bob. That's who the Researcher is. Got that. It's Low IQ Bob. LOW IQ BOB. LOW IQ BOB. Pro military! Remember, LOW IQ BOB.

Personal Note: What's going on?

But then, before I could even ponder that too long and before either of them could even say anything else actually, the guard who initially led me into the cafeteria walked up to me and simply walloped me across the side of the head with his baton.

"No," I barked, sitting at the table across from Aaron. "You don't just yell at your sister when you don't agree with her."

"Yeah Aaron," Evelyn interjected. "You listen to what I say. Do you hear me?"

"And you," I then said, looking over at Evelyn. "You don't just get to declare that you're right because you want to."

"Let's be civil everyone," Ginny interrupted.

"You have to support your ideas with facts," I then continued, shaking my head at both of them. "Of course you have a right to your opinion. We all do. But you have to be able to reason your arguments through. That's the point of debate. And remember, winning isn't everything."

"But Aaron's a dweeb," Evelyn said.

"And challenge the ideas, not the person."

"No, you're a dweeb," Aaron retorted.

"Do you hear me?"

And then I suddenly looked up, my face cold against the concrete floor, and saw this on the cafeteria wall in front of me.

(A decent facsimile)

Personal Note: What just happened?

But before I could even figure that out, the guard who walloped me across the side of the head picked me up off the floor and barked, "Come on already. We're going to be late."

"But why'd you do that?" I asked, my feet wobbly beneath me. "What'd I do?"

"You know exactly what you did," the guard said. "It's obvious."

"What?" I replied, struggling to walk forward. "What are you talking about?"

And the guard just looked at me like I had said the strangest thing ever, shook his head briefly, and shoved me forward.

Personal Note: What was he talking about?

And then I was brought to a small room and ordered to sit down.

"Who are you?" I asked, seeing a tall man, nearly eight feet tall, with a lanky build and an oily complexion, walk up to me and sit down at the other side of the table.

"Do you recognize this?" the man simply replied, shoving a file across the table over towards me. (The man suddenly reminding me of the description I was given of Shady Davey.)

And then I opened the file and saw this—

THE SURVIVAL STRATAGEM PLAYBOOK
APPROACH ONE: The Victimization Plan

We simply let the new researcher conduct his research while we blame the prior researcher for all of the current identified wrongs in order to keep the new researcher in his position.

APPROACH TWO: The Counselor Plan

We simply fire all of the counselors until we have a counselor who is willing to say whatever is necessary in order to be able to blame the counselor for any legal shortcomings that arise.

APPROACH THREE: The Confusion Plan

We simply offer up so many conflicting ideas about everything that is going on that no one will be able to keep anything straight.

APPROACH FOUR: The Scattershot Plan

We simply inundate people with so many different proposals and proclamations that no one will know what is going on.

APPROACH FIVE: The Base Appeal Plan

We simply solidify our most ardent supporters by continuing to appeal to the crudest, basest, and most unfortunate notions possible in order to gird against any possible negative considerations.

APPROACH SIX: The Captivity Plan

We simply continue to hold the potential opposition captive to the interests at hand by offering them the possibility of accomplishing whatever pet projects or ideas they have ever imagined.

APPROACH SEVEN: The Redound Plan

We simply say that anything they are saying against anything we say is something that they are actually doing themselves.

APPROACH EIGHT: The Conspiratorial Plan

We simply contend that they are working to undermine the current order by infiltrating our most esteemed structures in order to advance their own aims.

"Well," the man said again, staring at me while picking the file back up from the table. "Have you seen that before?"

"No," I answered, looking up from the file and staring at him, his face covered in sweat. "I have no idea what that is."

Personal Note: What was that?

"Fair enough then," the man simply said, waving his arm in the air. "Take him away."

And then the guard hauled me out of the room, led me down the corridor, and threw me back in my cell, the whole time barking at me, "And don't you forget it," before slamming the door behind him.

And then I simply sat down on the concrete bench in the back of the cell and started crying, all the while thinking, "What did I do to deserve this? What did I do? What?"

Personal Note: What did I do to deserve this?

But then before I could even wipe the tears from my eyes, this was slipped under my door, so I picked it up and read it—

Dear Bob:

We've got your back. Don't worry. Again, we've got your back. And we feel better now too. We really needed to say that.

Signed,

The Resistance

And I had no idea what to think.

Act Seventeen

Hear the Ringmaster

And then, after some indeterminate period of time (although it seemed like the next morning, at least), while my thoughts simply circled around in my head—

It's a dream

It's a revelation

It's a joke

It's a nightmare

It's an apocalypse

It's a hostage taking

It's a retrogression

It's a disgrace

It's a norm

A large man with an overgrown mustache, wearing a blue suit, and carrying a massive black briefcase in his right hand, walked up to my cell door, nodded back towards the main guard station in the cell block, waited for the door to open, and quickly walked inside.

"Who are you?" I asked, before the door could even close behind him, his whole disposition seemingly unsettled and disjointed.

"Your new attorney," the man answered, putting his briefcase down on the concrete bench next to me and opening it.

"My new attorney?" I replied, looking at the man, a strange seriousness about his demeanor suddenly obvious to me. "But I had an attorney. What happened to him?"

"You fired him."

"I what," I said, simply flabbergasted by his answer. "I didn't do that. How could I?"

"I don't know," the man replied. "That's what you do apparently. But no matter, I'm in charge now. So please call me your attorney. I do insist. And here, I was supposed to give you this." And then he took out a formal looking piece of paper and handed it to me—

Highlight Legal Firm

911 Constitution Row
Re: Past Due Notice
File #: 111-111-1111111

Dear Bob,

Attached please find your past due notice for services rendered. Your total past due balance, including hypothetical services, consultation time, document destruction, future public appearances, potential tangential careers, and pundit opportunities, is $456,003.89.

Please process this payment immediately. Any further delay of payment will result in one, or more lawsuits, and possible countersuits, of course.

BILLING SUMMARY

Invoice Amount:	**$456,003.89**
Payment Received:	**$0.00**
<u>**Remaining Balance:**</u>	<u>**$456,003.89**</u>
Balance Due:	**$456,003.89**

Sincerely, Your bud

"What?" I said, not even bothering to finish reading the document. "What's this?"

"Let me see it," my attorney replied (since he insisted), taking the piece of paper back from me and looking at it. "It's a bill," my attorney then said.

"I know that, but why would I get it?" I snapped, getting up from the bench and walking over to the door and suddenly seeing this on the wall outside my cell.

(A decent approximation)

"Don't get prickly with me," my attorney said. "I'm just trying to help you. Trust me, you're going to need my legal advice too, because as we all know, nothing's guaranteed in this world."

And then, before I could even respond, a note was slid under my cell door, so I walked over to it, picked it up, and read it—

DISPATCH NUMBER TWENTY-THREE: Cerfufufflele

And I honestly had no idea what to make of that, but it didn't matter, because I didn't have any time to think about it, since my attorney then took another piece of paper out of his briefcase and handed it to me—

OFFICE OF THE COURT
OFFICIAL LEGAL DEFENSE FILING

In Re: Case No. 12121

Dear To Whom It May Concern:

I (___put name here___) due hereby declare myself (put name here___) unfit to provide testimony on my (___put name here___) behalf.

Thank you.

Yours very sincerely,

Signed (___put name here___)
CC: Lead Counsel

"What's this?" I then barked, looking up from the paper at my attorney.

"Your best shot," my attorney then answered, before adding. "My best shot actually."

"But I'm not guilty," I replied, handing the piece of paper back to him. "I didn't do anything. And I'm not going to say anything else."

"But you can't go to trial," my attorney said, shaking his head at me. "There's no way we can win."

"But I didn't do anything," I repeated, staring at my attorney. "I already told you that."

And then my attorney looked at me for a moment, while putting the piece of paper back in his briefcase, and then gave me these five options: (1) we claim a perjury trap; (2) we hope for a hung jury; (3) we pray your allies can cover for you; (4) we hope it somehow gets tied up in the hubbub of public opinion; and (5) we bet on the fact that enough people simply won't care.

"No," I said, looking at my attorney, getting up from the bench. "I didn't do anything. So I'm going to defend myself. It's that simple."

"Fine," my attorney simply replied, shaking his head at me. "Be that way."

And then my attorney motioned to the guard to open the door, and we awkwardly waited for the door to open, and then simply left for trial.

Personal Note: What should I have done?

However, to say it was a madhouse when we got out into the cell block would be nothing short of an understatement of unimaginable proportions because the whole place was just brimming with people trying to get a glimpse at what was going on.

A First Prisoner: Let me see what's going on.

A Guard: There he goes.

The Warden: Check that out.

Another Guard: No one will believe I saw this.

The Cell Block Boss: Talk about historic.

Another Prisoner: What's going on?

Yet Another Prisoner: Call me.

Yet Another Guard: Who's that?

The Warden Again: I can't believe I saw him.

And that was nothing compared to the madhouse along the way, since it was truly a sight like no other. From the odd notion of a party—

(A decent gist)

To the weird vibe of a death march—

(Not a bad representation)

To a royal free market bonanza—

(Pretty close actually)

And all of that somehow still seemed tame compared to what occurred once we got to the courthouse, since not only were there seemingly a million people gathered outside the building (and that number being only a slight exaggeration, quite honestly), but everyone under the sun seemed to be shouting something at me. Take just a small snippet—

Some Man: You traitor.

Some Woman: You Demi-God.

Some Older Man: You tyrant.

Some Other Man: You amoeba.

Some Other Woman: You savior.

A Child: You hero.

Yet Another Man: You lout.

Some Other Older Man: You saint.

Yet Another Woman: You scum-bag.

Yet Another Child: You leader.

Some Older Woman: You excellent excellence of Excellency.

And I mean, all of it was really like nothing I'd ever witnessed before, and that was just to get in and find my seat. Yet, there I was, sitting inside the packed courtroom, my attorney next to me, photographers lining the walls, people filling every seat possible, guards stationed on both sides of the judge's bench, the lights blaring overhead, voices reverberating every which way, bulbs flashing wildly, people desperately trying to get into the photographs, reporters trying to color everything with the most memorable representation of the proceedings possible—

Some Guy: We should expect to see quite the legal harangue.

Some Other Guy: The word is the prosecution has established a forty-two point overview.

A Woman: The judge should enter the courtroom any minute now.

Yet Some Other Guy: How do I look?

Some Other Woman: We've heard the entire guild of researchers is prepared to testify today.

Yet Some Other Woman: I have no idea what is going on.

Yet Some Other Guy Still: Now, we await the trail of the century.

"You're going to owe me big time for this," my attorney said, leaning in and whispering into my ear. "And I mean big time."

But then, before I could even respond, a guard walked out from the back door in the courtroom and proclaimed, "All rise for the Honorable John PQ Doe," in a voice reminiscent of a horse race starting announcer, and then everyone stood up and the judge casually walked into the room.

Personal Note: Why do I have to pay for this?

Now, the judge was not what I expected (not at all), because she (and yes it was a she, at least initially) seemed to have the head of a two-million person Medusa, or even a two-hundred million person Medusa more honestly, because every time I looked at her, she seemed to be a different person or have a different hair style, or even shift genders, or ages, or ethnicities, or races, so I quickly closed my eyes, wiped them with my hands, and then opened them again, and settled on seeing a late sixties white man with short cropped grey hair, a slightly overfed look, nondescript brown eyebrows, a clearly angry snarl, and a huge wart on his left cheek.

"Have a seat," the judge said.

And we all sat down in the courtroom.

Personal Note: Why did I settle on a white man?

"Great," my attorney mumbled into my ear. "Judge PQ too, just what we needed."

"You know him?" I asked, pulling my chair closer to the long wood table in front of me, the legs making on odd scraping sound amongst the loud chatter and rumblings of the room.

"We all do," my attorney replied. "And even my wife's not as temperamental as he is."

But then before I could even comment about the obvious sexist comment on his part, the judge simply said: "Quiet down everyone. I've got lunch to get to soon. So let's get started."

Personal Note: Should I have told my attorney that that was an inappropriate comment?

"Just let me do the talking," my attorney whispered into my ear. "Please."

"I told you already," I said again. "I'm not guilty."

And then the prosecutor, this thin man, with thick silver spectacles and perfectly parted black hair, got up from the table next to me and started to speak: "Your honorable honorific, esteemed ladies and gentlemen of the jury, good people of the court, citizens of the world, distinguished guests, humble spectators, curious onlookers, confused bystanders, and anyone else I forgot to mention, we are gathered here today because this man (the guy then suddenly pointed at me) is guilty of conspiracy against our good Town, obstruction of justice, abuse of power, aiding and abetting a foreign entity, treason against our good Town, fraud, corruption, and all sorts of other nearly unspeakable crimes against humanity. And I

393

will prove all of my charges with expert testimony as I await your guilty verdicts. Thank you."

And then the prosecutor sat back down.

Personal Note: What are the other nearly unspeakable crimes against humanity?

And then my attorney slowly got up from his seat, straightened his tie again, looked around the courtroom, seemed to smile for a picture, and then loudly declared: "My client is innocent. Innocent, I tell you. Innocent. And he (my attorney pointed at the prosecutor) is merely a tool of the establishment working to undermine the legal authority and rightful standing of my (and then he fussed up my hair) good client here. Thank you."

Personal Note: That's my defense?

"Fair enough," the judge then said, while waiting for my attorney to sit back down, before turning to the prosecutor, and then saying, "you may call your first witness."

"The Sword Swallower, or as we like to call him around the office, Junior."

And then the Sword Swallower (who I suddenly realized I had actually seen at the inn before) got up from the back of the room (for the record, I couldn't even see half of the room from where I was sitting), literally skipped up to the witness stand, gave the crowd a quick salute (almost of the Heil kind, it seemed to me) and then sat down (without even taking the oath, mind you).

And then the prosecutor causally put his hand on top of the witness stand tabletop, turned to the jury, and in a clearly overly dramatic manner said, "Now, you've told me that you've witnessed the defendant here (and then he again pointed at me, quite rudely, I must stress) engage in obvious acts of treason against our good Town. Can you please tell us about that?"

Junior: I have. And certainly. I know from firsthand experience that the defendant willfully and gleefully sought to obtain information from a foreign adversary to undermine our good Town.

And then the prosecutor walked over to his table, picked up a piece of paper, and gave this to the judge—

Exhibit A: "…if it's what you say I love it..." (1)

"Is this what you are referring to?" the prosecutor then asked.

Junior: Yes. Those are his exact words. And they show obvious intent too, because, honestly, any rational person would agree that you can't declare joy over the possibility of obtaining information from a foreign adversary without engaging in at least a minimal desire to act against the interests of our Town, whatever the reason or hope of obtaining that information might be.

"Unquestionably," the prosecutor said, turning and facing the jury. "That is certainly a reasonable conclusion."

"Thank you," the judge added, before saying. "Anything else."

Personal Note: Is that a reasonable conclusion?

"Not right now," the prosecutor then said. "So let me call my next witness."

And then Junior got up from the witness stand, again saluted the crowd (in the same way) and quickly disappeared into the back of the courtroom (or at least I thought he disappeared into the back of the courtroom, because he certainly could have simply left The Town instead).

"Aren't you going to say anything?" I asked, leaning over towards my attorney.

"No," my attorney whispered back. "Don't worry, I know what I'm doing. And I told you my strategy."

And then the prosecutor called The Barn Burner (from the inn too). Or, "The General" to quote him directly. And we waited for The General to walk up to the witness stand, take the oath at least (which was oddly the Miranda rights statement, for some reason) and then sit down. "Thank you," the prosecutor then said.

"Lock her up," The General simply chanted, instinctively it seemed, while sitting in his chair. "Lock her up. Lock her up. Lock her up."

"Right," the prosecutor replied. "Now, you've witnessed the defendant make repeated false claims regarding his interests and activities outside of this Town's, and you've overlooked any of your concerns or knowledge regarding these facts."

The General: That's right. In fact, I've seen him work on the behalf of foreign interests without acknowledging it, I've seen him hide money in all sorts of dubious off-shore accounts, I've heard him threaten to kidnap an individual for another Town in order to obtain the reward money, and I've even heard him repeatedly make materially false statements and omissions regarding these claims.

And then the prosecutor walked back over to the table, picked up a piece of paper, and gave this to the judge—

Exhibit B: "I agree and stipulate to this Statement of the Offense." (2)

"I see," the prosecutor then said. "So you're willing to stand by those facts?"

"Yes," The General answered. "I've formally acknowledged many of them, in fact."

397

"Alright then," the prosecutor said. "That'll be all for now. Although, we might need you to work with us again in the future."

"Of course," The General replied. "I am well aware of that."

And then The General got up from the witness stand, momentarily stood at attention, and then simply walked towards the back of the room, where I suddenly noticed this on the wall.

(A pretty close approximation)

Personal Note: Did he really formally acknowledge many of those offenses?

And then the prosecutor walked over to the jury box, triumphantly waved his arms in the air, and said, "I now call The Elixir Lad. Or The Coffee Boy, as we like to call him around here. A truly excellent guy."

"Thank you," The Coffee Boy said, getting up from the back of the room, before suddenly (and quite oddly, I must stress) announcing, "And don't imbibe and blab. It will do you no good. No good at all. Trust me, you'll never live it down."

And then The Coffee Boy walked up to the witness stand, raised his left hand in the air, and said, "I do solemnly swear to tell the truth, the whole truth, and nothing but the truth, so help me God."

"Yes," some woman behind me interrupted. "He's my husband. So help him God."

"Alright, have a seat," the judge immediately declared. "I'm getting hungry already. And this whole fiasco's taking way too long."

"Thank you, your Excellency," the prosecutor simply said, before turning to The Coffee Boy, winking momentarily (which I had no idea how to interpret, quite honestly), and then saying, "Now, you've clarified to me that you are aware of multiple instances where the defendant, that man there (the prosecutor then added, clearly for dramatic effect, while again rudely pointing at me) met with well-known foreign adversaries to this good Town in order to obtain 'dirt' on a rival. Please tell us about this."

The Coffee Boy: Yes. That is true. I know that he worked with a professor he believed had contacts with one of our main foreign adversaries, and he met with a foreign female intermediary that he believed to be the niece of the same foreign adversary in order to potentially obtain thousands of communications regarding this matter, and then when he told his supervisor of this fact, his supervisor, The World's Most Unfit Man, as we refer to him around here, simply responded "Great work." (3) All of that is a matter of public record too.

And then the prosecutor walked back over to his table, picked up a piece of paper, and gave this to the judge—

Exhibit C: "It's history making if it happens." (4)

The Coffee Boy: Yes. And that is only a brief summation of what occurred. In fact, his efforts to work with one of our Town's adversaries is wildly more complicated even than that.

Personal Note: Did he really try to recruit a foreign adversary's help?

"Evidently," the prosecutor then said. "But that'll be all for now. Too much more on this will just make everyone's head spin."

"And please," The Coffee Boy added, getting up from the bench. "Remember my point about drinking."

"And he's a good man," the woman sitting behind me said. "Just pardon him."

And then The Coffee Boy got up from the witness stand, looked around the room briefly, put his head down, and slumped away.

"Aren't you going to do anything?" I asked my attorney again.

"I told you my strategy," my attorney repeated, gruffly whispering into my ear. "Don't worry."

And then, before I could even go on with my concerns, the prosecutor called his next witness to the stand. "I now call The Manager," the prosecutor then said. "Or as we refer to him around here, Count Von Creepy." (Who I heard stayed at the inn at one point too, for the record.)

Count Von Creepy: I'm innocent, Your Honor. (He said spontaneously, it seemed.)

"You're not on trial here right now," the judge intoned, looking at Count Von Creepy sitting in the back of the room. "And we have your plea. Would you please just take the stand?"

"I'm not," Count Von Creepy replied, standing up. "Really? Okay then. Sure."

And then Count Von Creepy walked up to the witness stand, put his hand on the Bible, and then said (in what I believe was Ukrainian, of all things) "I swear to tell you something."

"Thanks," the prosecutor replied, before turning to face the jury, smiling briefly, and continuing. "Now, you informed me about your extensive interactions with the defendant, that man here (he then added, yet again oddly pointing at me), and his repeated interests and intermingling with adversaries contrary to our own. Please expound on them."

Count Von Creepy: What I know is that this man was roughly seventeen million dollars in debt to a known oligarch, and not the nice kind either, and while he was desperately trying to pay this man off, doing all kinds of crazy things, trying to lie about his financial standing with multiple banks in order to obtain cash, having his lawyer, The Human Cannonball, as you probably know him (who plead guilty to these things too, just to say) help him in all sorts of nefarious ways, he volunteered to work for someone for free.

And then the prosecutor walked over to the table, picked up another piece of paper, and handed it to the judge—

Exhibit D: "I am not looking for a paid job." (5)

"Is this what you are referring to?" the prosecutor then asked.

"Yes," Count Von Creepy answered.

"And that is weird," the judge said, leaning back in his chair. "Continue."

Personal Note: Did he really volunteer to work for free when he had someone out to get him?

"Of course, Your Honor," the prosecutor then said, before looking back over at Count Von Creepy and adding. "Go on."

Count Von Creepy: And he openly sought to use this position to his advantage.

And then the prosecutor again walked over to the table, picked up another piece of paper, and handed it to the judge—

Exhibit E: "How do we use to get whole?" (6)

"And this is in reference to?" the prosecutor asked.

Count Von Creepy: His debts, of course. His enormous debts. And how he thought he could use his position to fix his problems, because, understand, he was in some serious financial jeopardy at the time. And that's putting it mildly.

"Fine," the judge suddenly interrupted. "He owed a lot of money and sought to use his position to his advantage, but what does that have to do with anything?"

"That's true," someone behind me yelled. "That's circumstantial at best."

Count Von Creepy: His extensive ties with these known adversaries directly impacted the formal stance he took with them. And he's a suspected "back channel." (7) Although he's denied that.

And then the prosecutor walked back over to his table, grabbed another piece of paper, and handed it to the judge—

Exhibit F: "I have managed [sic] campaigns around the world." (8)

"Objection, Your Honor," my attorney suddenly said, standing up from his seat. "That's not proof of anything. And that's mere speculation anyways."

"Agreed," the judge answered, looking at the prosecutor. "Do you have anything else?"

"What was that all about?" I thought to myself, while looking over and seeing this on the wall behind me.

(A rough approximation)

"Of course, the prosecution replied. "You should hear what his daughter has to say about him."

Count Von Creepy: Yes, you should hear what his daughter has to say about him.

And then once again the prosecutor walked over to the table, grabbed another piece of paper, and handed it to the judge—

Exhibit G: "You know he has killed people [sic]." (9)

"What?" some man groaned behind me.

"And there's more," the prosecutor then said.

Count Von Creepy: Yes, yes there is more (while moaning).

And then yet again the prosecutor walked over to the table, grabbed another piece of paper, and handed it to the judge—

Exhibit H: "That money we have is blood money." (10)

"Objection, Your Honor," my attorney suddenly yelled, standing up next to me. "That's hearsay. It doesn't matter what his daughter says about him."

"What kind of man are you?" some lady way in the back of the room yelled up at me.

"Agreed," the judge then said, while turning to the jury. "Please strike that from any consideration. That testimony is completely inadmissible."

"What is this guy talking about?" I said, looking up at my attorney. "None of that is even remotely true. And my daughter would never talk about me like that. What is he talking about?"

"Quiet," my attorney simply barked, continuing to stare at the judge, before adding, "Thank you Your Honor."

Personal Note: Seriously, what daughter would say that about her own father?

"And you can get back to your witness after lunch," the judge then said, before slamming his gavel down on the top of his bench. "I'm famished."

And then everyone went to recess.

Act Eighteen

Witness the Aerial Ballet

Of course, like everything else around there, nothing went like I expected (at all), because the whole place was nothing short of an utter madhouse. Seriously, there were people just gathered in the halls everywhere talking about anything you could think of. Take just a few examples—

Some Lady: That man is true abomination to everything good and decent in this world.

Some Guy: He should be burned at the stake.

Some Man: This is the best I say. I mean, talk about exciting.

Some Other Lady: It really is entertaining.

Some Woman: Why do we have to endure this?

A Young Woman: He could have my baby I tell you.

And that was nothing compared to the scene of the reporters outside the courthouse just climbing and clambering all over each other to relay their understanding of the events—

One Reporter: I swear, I've never seen a scene quite like this scene I'm seeing. It's truly a scene to see, you see. I mean, I can't believe I'm seeing this scene I'm seeing.

Personal Note: What is going on?

Another Reporter: Yes everyone. It appears the defense is clearly winning the case. From my count alone, the prosecution already has had ten inadmissible claims, fourteen objections, three official court warnings from the judge, and two formal retractions.

Personal Note: What is that person talking about?

And then, as crazy as all of that seemed, when I walked back into the court from the hallway, (the only thing I did on break was write this note in calligraphy to Aaron to Evelyn)—

Dear Kids:

Know this. I know we don't always agree. And your mom and I haven't been perfect. And things certainly aren't what we thought they would be all the time. But we love you. No matter what happens, that's true. And I know you love us too. We both do. We're family. And don't you forget that. We're all in this together.

Love Dad

(Well that and cried briefly), I ran into some sketch artist drawing a picture of me for some newspaper publication.

(A pretty accurate depiction of the drawing)

"Who's that?" was all I could think.

Personal Note: Seriously, what kind of caricature of me is that?

But before I could even think about it too long, my attorney walked back up to me, motioned for me to sit down, and then the guard walked out from the side room and announced, "The Honorable John PQ Doe," and then everyone stood up, waited a moment, and then the judge walked into the room.

"Alright," the judge then said, looking at the prosecutor, while sitting down. "Go ahead and finish up your testimony. And for the record, I had one hell of a good tuna on rye sandwich for lunch."

And then some court reporter (or at least I believed it was a court reporter) stood up in the back of the room and yelled: "He had a horrible peanut butter and pickle pizza today. Print it. STAT."

"Quiet," the judge simply said. "We've got more important concerns in this world than my lunch."

"Fair enough," the prosecutor replied, before turning back to Count Von Creepy (who was sitting at the witness stand already again) and said. "That's all for now."

And Count Von Creepy just sat there for a moment, looking at the prosecutor completely befuddled-like, before whining, "What? That's it. That's all you want me to talk about. You don't want me to mention his insane business ties. His inability to have a formal divorce proceeding because of his long history of questionable personal behavior, to put it one way. His myriad of outlandish financial ties. His blatant disregard for any legal constraints or limitations. His utterly reckless spending habits. His tampering of witnesses. And what about his turning state's evidence?"

"No," the prosecutor suddenly interrupted, walking over to Count Von Creepy. "That's enough for now. Thank you."

And then Count Von Creepy stood up, quickly wiped his brow, and awkwardly hobbled off to the back of the room.

"I'm glad he's through," my lawyer mumbled into my ear. "That's guy really makes me uncomfortable."

"Tell me about it," I replied.

Personal Note: Did this guy really do those things?

And then the prosecutor casually lumbered back over to the jury booth, again waved his hands in the air (why truly eluded me) and said, "I now call The Concentric Circle Man. Or, if you prefer, Professor Wackadoodle, as I like to call him."

"That's another man from the inn," I whispered to my lawyer.

"Quiet," my lawyer simply responded. "Remember, my plan. And here," my lawyer then said handing me this—

DISPATCH NUMBER TWENTY-FOUR: Stay strong. I'm the greatest. Go SOYBEAN growers. I ROCK!!

"But," I whispered again, looking at the note utterly confused.

"My plan," my lawyer simply interjected.

And then, before I could even respond, The Concentric Circle Man walked up to the witness stand, yelled "Mat Rossiya" for some unknown reason (although I think that means Mother Russia in Russian), and then sat down.

"Quite the entrance," the prosecutor said.

"Yes, no, maybe, sure," The Concentric Circle Man replied.

"What did he say?" someone else behind me asked. "I can't make out anything this guy's talking about."

"Now," the prosecutor simply continued, ignoring the blatant and reckless intrusion into the proceedings. "You have previously explained to me that you witnessed this man (again he pointed at me, just to make it clear) repeatedly meet with foreign adversaries contrary to official published statements of his suggesting otherwise. That he has long been under suspicion for working as a covert operative against our Town. That he has held private meetings with known Town adversaries. Is this correct so far?"

The Concentric Circle Man: Well, yes, perhaps, I don't know. Maybe, sure.

"Thank you," the prosecutor then said, before again walking over to his table, picking up another piece of paper, walking over to the judge, and handing him this—

Exhibit I: I had a "private conversation" with a senior official. (1)

"What is he talking about?" the person behind me shouted again.

"Quiet," the judge simply commanded. "We have serious business to get to here."

And then the prosecutor turned to The Concentric Circle Man and asked, "Was that what you were referring to?"

"Yes, well, I suppose, sure."

"Great," the prosecutor said. "And you have told me that he (and then the prosecutor suddenly whipped around in the middle of the courtroom and pointed at me again) repeatedly denied these contacts unless pressed endlessly. And that he discussed these interactions with The Elixir Lad."

The Concentric Circle Man: All of this is contained in his dodgy dossier, as he calls it.

And then the prosecutor again walked over to the table, picked up another piece of paper, and gave it to the judge—

Exhibit J: "It may have come up, yeah." (2)

The Concentric Circle Man: Yes, that's it.

"I got that one," another guy said, almost gleefully.

"Thank you," the prosecutor then replied, walking back over towards the jury booth. "For now, we'll overlook your previous business arrangements, multiple prior surveillance instances, repeated renewals of said needs, and other questionable interactions. So you can go."

"Sure, yes, thanks, okay, fine," The Concentric Circle Man said, getting up and simply leaving the room.

"Talk about obfuscation," my attorney grumbled, leaning forward on the table. "Even I get a headache listening to that guy."

Personal Note: Would someone really do all of that?

"Good riddance," someone else shouted from inside the courtroom.

And when I looked around the room to try to figure out who it was, I suddenly noticed this on the far wall.

(A pretty close approximation)

"Quiet," the judge ordered again.

And then the prosecutor walked back over towards the jury booth, slammed his hand down on top of the front rail, and then said, "I now call, The Shallow Diver. Or as he prefers to be called, Tricky Dick, although we just call him Slippery Dick when he insists on that."

"Tricky Dick," some woman a few rows behind me said. "But that's already taken."

"We know," the prosecutor replied. "So that's why we call him Slippery Dick. And you should see the tattoo on his back. It's a real statement to his beloved moniker."

"Fine," the judge simply interjected. "You may call Slippery Dick."

And then, as I sat there, continuing to wonder what was going on, Slippery Dick, wearing a bright orange suit, blue fedora, and smoking a massive cigar (literally the size of a baby's arm), casually strolled up to the witness stand, graciously bowed before the room, calmly announced, "I am nothing if not a patriot," and then sat down.

"Thank you," the prosecutor said. "We appreciate your declaration of loyalty. Now, it is my understanding that you are aware that he (and yes, he yet again pointed at me) has repeatedly been in communication with a direct connection to a hostile adversary."

"I am," Slippery Dick, suddenly interrupted. "Although he insists his communications are with a true hero."

"Yes," the prosecutor replied, before again walking over to his table, picking up a piece of paper, and handing it to the judge—

Exhibit K: He's "my hero." (3)

"That's what I'm referring to," Slippery Dick interjected. "Precisely."

"Good," the prosecutor replied. "Now, it is also my understanding that you were made aware of these communications of his long before anyone else was. So, would you please explain?"

Slippery Dick: Certainly. He actually claims to have met with this main communication link in a slightly perplexing but still plausibly conceivable manner. And he even acknowledged that point previously.

And then, yet again, the prosecutor walked over to his table, picked up another piece of paper, and handed it to the judge—

Exhibit L: "I said 'I think I will go [sic] and meet with (him).'" (4)

"And again, he knew of this fact before anyone else did," the prosecutor repeated, not bothering to expound on that previous point for whatever reason.

Slippery Dick: That's the claim, yes.

And then, once again, the prosecutor walked over to his table, picked up a piece of paper, and handed it to the judge—

Exhibit M: "Payload coming." (5)

Slippery Dick: That's right. And he was absolutely confident of that fact, truly beyond simple speculation, quite honestly.

And then, yet again, the prosecutor walked over to his table, picked up another piece of paper, and handed it to the judge—

Exhibit N: "I am assured" of this. (6)

Slippery Dick: That's the one. And basically in context too.

"Good," the prosecutor said, before continuing. "And he (yet again, pointing at me) has pervious business ties with Count Von Creepy."

Slippery Dick: Oh yes, long, long ties.

"And," the prosecutor simply continued. "He (of course, again pointing at me) has long ties to The Mayor too."

"The Mayor," someone in one of the back rows of the courtroom suddenly gasped.

Slippery Dick (interjecting): Long, long ties. Although not The Innkeeper, for the record.

"We'll get to The Innkeeper soon enough," the prosecutor sneered.

"Good," the judge interrupted. "Because let's get this on with. My wife's making a beef and bean casserole for dinner tonight, and I don't want to miss it."

Reporter (suddenly announcing): The judge just stated that he's having a steak and baked potato dinner tonight with his nephew. Print it.

"Of course," the prosecutor simply replied, clearly ignoring the sudden interruption. "So rather than go on and on and on with the questionable ties and links to our known adversaries, and rather than further establish the known connections, not to mention the additional individuals who have already pleaded guilty to said ties or crimes, let's instead turn our attention to this man's (again he had to point at me) character."

Personal Note: What's the issue with my character?

"You know," I said, suddenly realizing a key point, leaning in and talking with my attorney. "It just occurred to me, where's my assistant? I figured he'd be here."

"I don't know," my attorney simply replied, whispering into my ear. "But keep quiet, alright? Because this isn't going well at all."

And then, before I could even formulate a response, I looked over to the far side of the courtroom to see what the prosecutor was doing, and suddenly noticed this on the wall.

(A decent approximation)

Slippery Dick (standing up from his seat): So, are we done here?

"Yes," the prosecutor answered.

And then Slippery Dick took another bow, pulled out another cigar, lit it, chuckled for a good twenty seconds, and skipped out of the courtroom.

"Wow," someone behind me sneered. "What a Dick."

Personal Note: Would someone really have all of those ties?

"I now call The Fixer," the prosecutor said, almost triumphantly, quite honestly, while walking back over towards the jury booth.

And then I looked over and watched The Fixer get up (who I also recognized from the inn), nearly gallop to the front of the room, clap briefly, and then sit down at the witness stand.

"Thank you," the prosecutor said. "Now, you've known the defendant for a while now. And you can attest to his character, correct?"

The Fixer: Yes.

"And you've publicly declared your support for him?" the prosecutor then added.

The Fixer: Certainly

And then the prosecutor once again walked over to his table, grabbed a piece of paper, and handed it to the judge—

Exhibit O: I'd "take a bullet" for him. (7)

"Are these your words?" the prosecutor then asked.

The Fixer: Yes. And that's basically the appropriate context too.

"Wow," someone behind me mumbled. "That's some loyalty."

Personal Note: Seriously, who would say that? Let alone do that?

"And you would say that you know him well?" the prosecutor immediately continued, nearly pacing around the courtroom.

The Fixer: Not as good as one of his many wives I'm sure. Or some of his mistresses even. But I certainly know what he's been up to, yes.

"Good," the prosecutor said.

Personal Note: Who is he talking about?

"Say something," I whispered over to my lawyer. "That's not true at all. I've only been married once. Trust me," I then added, suddenly thinking about what I should tell Ginny again.

"Quiet," my lawyer barked into my ear. "I've got this."

"Thank you," the prosecutor replied. "And we'll get to his mistresses and your knowledge of them soon enough. But first, I'd like you to tell us about some of the things you've done that can support your knowledge of his character."

The Fixer: Well, some of this is a little difficult to talk about, but essentially, I've conducted many of his most questionable business transactions. I've worked to support his character in any way necessary. And I've conducted any sort of work for him that he's had to have taken care of. All of this I've fully attested to in my plea agreement and hours and hours of previous testimony.

"I see," the prosecutor said.

The Fixer (interjecting): They don't call me The Fixer for nothing.

"And you've been willing to threaten people if necessary," the prosecutor immediately continued.

The Fixer: Of course.

And then the prosecutor yet again walked over to the table, grabbed another piece of paper, and handed it to the judge—

Exhibit P: "Mark my words…tread very [sic] lightly, because what I'm going to do to you is going to be [sic] disgusting. Do you understand me?" (8)

The Fixer: I used the word "fucking" there, and twice, got it?

"Definitely," the prosecutor said. "Definitely. And you've also met with known adversaries in connection with your work for this (and yes, yet again he pointed at me) man?"

The Fixer: I'm a business man too. And outside of that, that's not stuff I like to talk about.

"Fine, fine," the prosecutor replied. "We're not here about you. But you can attest to his character. So what can you tell us about his various excursions with women?"

(What the word excursion makes me think of)

The Fixer: That's what you want to call them?

"Sure," the prosecutor answered, walking over towards the witness stand. "We need to keep things polite."

"Right," The Fixer said, nearly snickering. "Because we're all family men here."

"But you are aware of theses encounters. And in fact, you've helped conceal them from the public's eye?"

The Fixer: I told you, I'm The Fixer.

And then the prosecutor again walked over to his table, grabbed another piece of paper, walked over to the judge's bench, and handed it to the judge—

Exhibit Q: "I used my own personal funds to facilitate a payment..." (9)

"Is this what you are referring to?" the prosecutor then asked.

The Fixer (pausing briefly before answering): Sure. And that was a good one. Don't you think?

"What does that mean?" some guy in the middle of the courtroom yelled out.

"No kidding," another woman added from over near the jury booth. "What kind of attitude is this? And what lawyer pays for his client's settlement with his own funds?"

"Order," the judge suddenly erupted. "Order in the court. Please everyone, keep your thoughts to yourself. And the point of all of this was to develop a sense of his character, so let's stay focused here. Please everyone, okay?"

Personal Note: Did he really do those things?

"Can you be my lawyer?" someone else near the jury booth yelled. "I've got a house payment I don't feel like covering."

"Order," the judge repeated again. "Order, I say. I won't have any more of these outbursts in my courtroom."

"Sorry, Your Honor," the prosecutor interjected. "I didn't mean to incite anything."

"What a family man," someone else yelled. "Too much."

"That's it," the judge then declared, pounding his gavel on top of his desk. "We're taking a fifteen minute recess to get our heads back straight."

"Alright," the prosecutor said. "If that's what you'd like. I'm through with my questions anyways."

"Does that mean we're done here?" The Fixer said, standing up and glaring out at everyone in the courtroom.

"Yes," the judge repeated, again slamming his gavel down on top of his desk. "This court is now in recess."

And then everyone got up and again left the courtroom.

\

Act Nineteen

Gawk at the Lion Tamer

"What are you doing?" I asked my attorney, standing out in the hallway with him, all sorts of people gathered around mingling with each other, gossiping about all sorts of things, and just getting up into anyone's business any way they could. Just a few examples—

Some Lady: Did you see that General's weird looking frown?
Some Man: What about that jurist's bizarre choice of neck wrap?
Some Other Woman: And what of that guard's hair lip?
Some Other Man: And I still can't believe that last witness's brazenness.

"Trust me," my attorney quickly answered, pressing himself back against the hallway wall in order to let some large lady pass us by. "I've got a strategy."

"But they're just decimating my character," I said, watching some guy flirt with some older woman at the top of the stairwell. "And it's not even me. I didn't do any of those things."

"It doesn't matter," my attorney replied, straightening his tie. "We're not trying to prove your innocence," he then added, before turning and starting to walk back into the courtroom. "We're just trying to seed doubt. So come on."

"Fine," I said, starting to walk back into the courtroom.

Personal Note: Does that mean guilt is actually innocence?

However, before I could even get to the courtroom door, this young female reporter (her appearance beyond stunning, for the record) effectively accosted me in the hall.

"What do you think of the trial so far?" she asked (her whole being suddenly reminding me of the woman I first saw in my "dream" on the train telling me "nothing's in hiding").

"I can't comment," I said, trying to walk past her. "On the advice of my counsel."

"We're doing fine," my attorney interjected, suddenly noticing the reporter talking to me (his sudden interest in her nearly embarrassing). "Everything's going according to my plan."

"You have a plan?" the reporter asked, looking over at my attorney.

"Of course," my attorney answered, uncomfortably ogling her. "Just watch."

And then, before I could even ask my attorney to expound on that point, we were suddenly called back into the courtroom by some bailiff. "One minute," the bailiff announced. "One minute. Judge's orders."

"Oh, we're going to do that," the reporter said. "We keep everything in front of you."

"Look for me when this is over," my attorney then added, continuing to gawk at her.

Personal Note: Who exactly is watching this?

And then, when we walked back into the courtroom, we were both immediately struck by the sight of all the people in a near uproar over the state of the proceedings—

Some Man: This is whole thing is insane.
Some Woman: A total Kangaroo Court.
Some Other Man: Kabuki Theater I say.
Some Other Woman: A Witch Hunt.

"This is going to make my career," my attorney barked at me. "I can't believe it."

But then, before I could even think about that too much, the guard walked back out from the back door, announced, "The Honorable PQ," and we all rose. And then, while I was standing there waiting for the judge to walk into the room, I suddenly noticed another man from my file sitting in the back of the room—

Jeff Weisman

"The Necromancer"

"Oh, here," my attorney suddenly whispered in my ear, jarring me out of my daze, while handing me this—

DISPATCH TWENTY-SIX: Don't believe the opposition. Don't trust the naysayers. Don't listen to the chatterboxes. Deny the resistance. Up is still Down!

"Let's get this going," the judge then said, before I even had a chance to truly process that. "I've got my dinner appointment to get to tonight."

And then the prosecutor simply went through a whole series of witnesses (nearly all of them from the inn, it seemed) all attesting to various aspects of my character and my actions—

"Yes, I've lied on his behalf routinely," The Tongue Twister answered.

Exhibit R: We gave "alternative facts to that." (1)

"I've flagrantly misrepresented things for him, often," The Shill replied. "Even more than often actually."

Exhibit S: It "was the largest audience (sic) ever..." (2)

"Sometimes you just straight up have to," Long-Legged Lucy replied, shaking her head at the prosecutor. "It's his expectation actually."

Exhibit T: We used "white lies." (3)

"Objection," my attorney suddenly said, standing up from his seat. "That's hearsay. We have no direct quote of that."

"Fine, Your Honor, you can strike that from the record," the prosecutor replied. "But there has never been a denial of that point."

Personal Note: Is that actually true about the lack of a denial?

"You may continue," the judge simply said.

"Thank you," I mumbled to my attorney, nearly exasperated by this whole experience. "Someone needs to stand up for me."

"We all need to eat," The Pantomime said. "So sure, I've probably pushed the boundaries of credulity a few times."

Exhibit U: He "in no way, form, or fashion has ever encouraged violence…" (4)

"Yeah, that's one."

And this, the prosecutor said, holding up another piece of paper—

Exhibit V: He has the "highest integrity and exemplary character." (5)

"Objection," my attorney yelled again, while jumping up from his seat. "That quote is not in reference to my client."

"Fair point," the judge said, wagging his finger in the air. "Strike that from the record."

"But that seemed to support me," I whispered, looking up at my attorney, standing over me clearly proud of his successful retraction.

"Quiet," my attorney simply responded. "My plan."

And then The Pantomime got down from the witness stand, and the prosecutor got back to it—

"I actually enjoyed doing it for him," The Mouse Man laughed. "And really I never even thought of it as lying."

Exhibit W: "I've seen this guy throw a dead spiral through a tire." (6)

"Yeah, that's me. And maybe a little hyperbolic there. I've got to concede that."

Personal Note: Were we ever supposed to believe that?

"And then there's his family," the prosecutor said, walking back over towards the jury booth.

"My family," I whispered, leaning in to talk with my attorney. "Are they here?"

And then, before I could even hear his response, The Snake Charmer walked out from some unseen door at the side of the room and sat down at the witness stand.

The Snake Charmer: And sure he's said a few odd things about me being his daughter.

"But that's not my daughter."

"Quiet," my attorney interjected. "You have to trust me."

Exhibit X: If she "weren't my daughter, perhaps, I would be dating her." (7)

"But that was all just in jest," The Snake Charmer said. "Right?"

Personal Note: Again, who talks about their child like that? And I told my first attorney this.

"And this," the prosecutor added, holding up another piece of paper—

Exhibit Y: "She's got the best body." (8)

"Yeah, that too. And that is a little messed up."

"And then there's his son," the prosecutor said, waiting for The Snake Charmer to get down from the witness stand (half the courtroom ogling over her, it seemed).

"Sure, I've struggled to find my place in our relationship at times," The No-Brain Boy said.

Exhibit Z: "He's always fought for himself." (9)

"And then there's his wives, and the three marriages, and the prenuptial agreements, and the repeated allegations of adultery, and questions of rape, and the admitted affairs, and the untold number of non-disclosure agreements," the prosecutor then said.

"Objection, Your Honor," my attorney immediately chimed in. "Nearly all of that's hearsay and conjecture. And none of that is relevant here."

"Agreed," the judge then said, wagging his finger at the prosecutor. "Please keep your ruminations to yourself."

"Fine," the prosecutor replied. "I apologize. It's just that there's a lot of fertile ground there. But regardless, let me pursue his demands regarding loyalty first then. And we'll get to the women later."

"My demands regarding loyalty," I repeated, whispering into my attorney's ear. "What does that mean?"

"I don't know," my attorney answered. "But I'm just glad we struck out all that potential testimony regarding your wives."

"But I've only had one wife," I said, looking over and seeing this on the far wall toward the back of the room.

(A real good representation)

"No matter," my attorney replied. "We won't have to hear from her at least."

And then the prosecutor simply called out a whole slew of witnesses—

"He had me openly acknowledge my fidelity," The Black Gold Albino said. "Of course."

Exhibit A-a: "It's a great privilege you've given me." (10)

"And I fully proffered forward my deepest tribute," The Ever-Shrinking Man said.

Exhibit B-b: "It's an honor to be able to serve you." (11)

"And I certainly offered my respect," The Proctor said.

Exhibit C-c: "It's a privilege to serve…" (12)

"And I made my praise," The Prism Lady said.

Exhibit D-d: "It's a new day…" (13)

"And I glowered in my appreciation," The Human Kow-Tow said.

Exhibit E-e: "(sic) what an incredible honor it is…" (14)

"And I almost hurt myself fawning over him," The High-Brow Suck-Up said.

Exhibit F-f: "We thank you for the opportunity and blessing you've given us…" (15)

"And then there's what Shady Davey has already attested to in a prior hearing. And under oath too, no less," the prosecutor added.

Personal Note: Did people really ingratiate themselves that way to someone? And Shady Davey?

"Even I couldn't believe how far he wanted me to go with this whole obedience thing," Shady Davey said (not looking anything like who I met or who was initially described to me).

Exhibit G-g: "I need loyalty, I expect loyalty." (16)

"Is this what you mean?" the prosecutor asked.

"Yes, that's it," Shady Davey answered.

"And this too?" the prosecutor then interjected, before walking over to his table, again grabbing a piece of paper, and handing it to the judge—

Exhibit H-h: "That's what I want, honest loyalty." (17)

"You got it," Shady Davey simply said, oddly looking both confident and diffident at the same time.

"Thank you," the prosecutor replied. "And now for his business dealings."

"What he just said was basically what The Mayor asked of me," I said, yet again whispering into my attorney's ear, while Shady Davey climbed down from the witness stand. "And my business dealings? What does that mean? I'm a researcher. What is he talking about?"

"I don't know," my attorney answered. "But I'm just glad we're done with that whole loyalty thing. It's absolutely crazy to think you would do that."

"I didn't do that," I said, raising my voice slightly. "Who would?"

"Quiet," my attorney barked, leaning forward against the table. "I've got a reputation to uphold here."

And then, again, before I could even respond, the prosecutor began calling different witnesses to the stand—

Chief Spitfire: Yes, he raised his fees to all of his key businesses in the area.

"Objection," my attorney suddenly interjected. "You can't prove there's a correlation there."

"And," the prosecutor simply continued, completely ignoring my attorney, nor even waiting for anyone to take the stand. "And he has all sorts of townspeople leasing from him."

"Objection again," my attorney interrupted again, this time standing up from his seat. "You can have anyone you want lease from you."

Personal Note: Is it really true that you can do that?

"And," the prosecutor simply continued, not even bothering to pause for a response from the judge regarding my attorney's objections, while another person took the stand. "He even has extended family members punishing people who won't do business the way he wants it done."

The Wing Walker: Yeah, I'm not going to comment on that.

"And," the prosecutor added. "He's retained control over his entire enterprise, even though he's said otherwise."

Exhibit I-i: "But I'm going to have nothing to do with the management." (18)

"And he," the prosecutor suddenly said (again pointing at me). "Yes he, even admitted that he doesn't have to worry about these conflicts of interest."

Exhibit J-j: I "can't have a conflict of interest." (19)

"So what?" my attorney yelled, jumping up from his seat. "He wants to be rich. We all do. What's the problem there?"

"Our Charter," the prosecutor roared back. "That's what."

"Who cares about that?" someone else in the audience hollered.

"Yeah," someone else added. "Those are just words on a page anyways. And there are no specific words pertaining to anything like that in our Charter anyways. Right?"

"And I want to be rich too," someone else in the audience wailed.

"And bounteous," someone else added.

(What the word bounteous makes me think of)

"Order," the judge again screamed. "Order in the court. Please everyone refrain from commenting."

"Certainly judge, sorry," the prosecutor interjected. "Money always seems to get people worked up."

The courtroom then quieted down (oddly enough, it seemed to me).

"Alright," the judge responded, waving his finger at the prosecutor. "We've had enough of this line of thought. What else are you going to be using to establish his character here?"

"The women," the prosecutor immediately answered, while The Wing Walker stepped down from the stand.

"The women?" someone a few rows behind me gasped.

"What women?" I whispered to my attorney. "What is he talking about?"

"Let's see the women," another person (some man, it seemed) hollered from the back of the courtroom. "Come on, bring them out. I want to see the women."

"Order," the judge repeated, slamming his gavel down on his bench top. "I will hold you all in contempt of court if you don't quiet down."

And then before I could even hear a response from my attorney, the prosecutor just began calling out woman after woman after woman to the stand—

Woman One: He groped my breasts and tried to put his hand up my skirt.

Exhibit K-k: "His hands were everywhere." (20)

Woman Two: There was an incident that occurred.

Exhibit L-l: "I referred to this as a 'rape.'" (21)

Woman Three: He groped and grabbed me, yes.

Exhibit M-m: "He pushed me up against the wall, and had his hands all over me and tried to get up my dress again." (22)

Woman Four: He put his hand up my skirt.

Exhibit N-n: "He did touch my vagina through my underwear." (23)

Woman Five: He forcibly kissed me. And in public too.

Exhibit O-o: "He took my hand, and grabbed me, and went for the lips." (24)

Woman Six: He forcibly kissed me on the mouth, and twice.

Exhibit P-p: "He kissed me directly on the lips." (25)

Woman Seven: He grabbed me and touched my breast.

Exhibit Q-q: "Then his hand touched the right side of my breast." (26)

Woman Eight: He walked in unannounced while we were naked.

Exhibit R-r: "The time that he walked through the dressing rooms was really shocking. We were all naked." (27)

Personal Note: What are they talking about?

Woman Nine: He grabbed my buttocks in the pavilion.

Exhibit S-s: "All of a sudden I felt a grab, a little nudge." (28)

Woman Ten: And he forcibly kissed me too.

Exhibit T-t: "...He pulled my face in and gave me a smooch." (29)

Woman Eleven: And he did the same with me.

Exhibit U-u: He "kissed me directly on the mouth." (30)

Woman Twelve: And me too.

Exhibit V-v: "I turned around, and within seconds he was pushing me against the wall and forcing his tongue down my throat." (31)

Woman Thirteen: And he grabbed me too.

Exhibit W-w: "He squeezed my butt." (32)

Woman Fourteen: And he forcibly kissed me too. And then asked how much.

Exhibit X-x: "When he entered the room he grabbed each of us tightly in a hug and kissed each of us on the lips without asking for permission." (33)

Personal Note: Who would do this?

Woman Fifteen: And he inspected us over like meat.

(What the word inspection makes me think of)

Exhibit Y-y: "He would step in front of each girl and look you over from head to toe like we were just meat, we were just sexual objects, that we were not people." (34)

Woman Sixteen: And he grabbed and kissed me on two occasions.

Exhibit Z-z: "He then grabbed my shoulder and began kissing me again very aggressively and placed his hand on my breast." (35)

Woman Seventeen: And he grabbed me and invited me to his hotel room.

Exhibit A-aa: "He probably doesn't want me telling the story about that time he continually grabbed my ass and invited me to his hotel room." (36)

"And that's not even all of them. And then there's his own admission," the prosecutor said, whipping around and glaring at me. "The words he exactly used."

Exhibit B-bb: "Grab 'em by the pussy. You can do anything." (37)

"But I didn't say that," I barked out, looking around the courtroom. "That's not me."

Personal Note: Who would ever say that?

"Liar," someone in the back of the room suddenly yelled. (And I swear it sounded like The Tongue Twister. But that couldn't have been, right?)

"Order," the judge immediately declared. "I want order in this court."

"Quiet," my attorney then said, before standing up from his seat and speaking directly to the judge. "Those are all just allegations. My client's never admitted to any of that. And he's since doubted that last one too. So can I please have a minute to consult with my client about this?"

"Fine," the judge simply answered. "If you must."

Act Twenty

Gasp at the Elephant Routine

"Aren't you going to say anything?" I whispered to my attorney. "You've just been sitting there breathing into my ear."

"I'm trying to make it look like we are deep in consultation," my attorney simply answered, opening his briefcase sitting on the table in front of him. "Alright."

"But how's that going to help me?"

"I've already told you, I've got a reputation to uphold here," my attorney answered, grabbing a piece of paper out of his briefcase. "And we're getting killed here. And here," my attorney then added, handing me a letter. "I forgot to give you this."

```
Dear Dad:
     I had this dream the other night about
you and me. We were at the old creek near the
cabin we rented that one summer. And I asked
you what you hoped I would be when I grew up.
And you said, "Content." And that made me mad.
You don't really just want that for me dad, do
you?
     Evelyn
```

Personal Note: What does she mean by that?

But again, before I could even think about that (or what my attorney actually thought he was doing, for that matter), the judge chimed back in, saying, "Alright. Let's get this on with."

"Yes, your honor," my attorney immediately replied, closing his briefcase. "We've had time to consider an alternative plan. So thanks."

"We have," I thought, putting the letter in my front pocket.

"And are we almost done here?" the judge asked, looking over at the prosecutor standing by the jury box. "I've still got my dinner engagement to get to tonight."

"We are," the prosecutor replied. "I simply have my two star witnesses left."

"Two star witnesses," I thought, looking over and seeing this on the wall.

(A real close approximation)

"Two," the judge groaned, leaning back in his chair.

"Yes, so first I will call The Innkeeper."

"The Innkeeper," I mumbled, looking over at my attorney.

"You know her," my attorney responded, turning in his chair to better face me, the gasp from the courtroom attendants clearly audible.

"Not really," I answered. "I've just been staying at her place. And what could she have on me?"

And then, before I could even hear my attorney's response, The Innkeeper walked out from a side room, raised her chin in the air triumphantly while taking in a loud snort of air, and then sat down at the witness stand.

"So you," the prosecutor said, walking over toward The Innkeeper. "Can tell us things that will help us understand this man?" (And yes, he pointed at me again.)

The Innkeeper: I can tell you things that will make your head spin.

"Good. So would you please first tell us about some of the crazy things you've heard him say?"

The Innkeeper: Sure. But I'm not really sure where to begin. There's just so many. So let me start with some of his biggest whoppers I suppose.

"And by whoppers," the prosecutor interrupted, staring at The Innkeeper. "You don't mean the candy kind?"

The Innkeeper (shaking her head, annoyingly): That's right.

"Good. So, please enlighten us."

The Innkeeper: Well, for starters he has this whole thing about numbers.

"We already heard that point about the audience size."

The Innkeeper: That's just the tip of the iceberg.

And then the prosecutor walked over to the table, grabbed yet another piece of paper, and handed it to the judge—

Exhibit C-cc: "We enacted the biggest tax cuts..." (1)

The Innkeeper: Yep, that's one.

"And this," the prosecutor then said.

Exhibit D-dd: "We have signed more legislation than anybody." (2)

The Innkeeper: Yep, that's another.

"And this," the prosecutor continued, holding up yet another piece of paper.

Exhibit E-ee: "Black homeownership just hit the highest level it has ever been..." (3)

The Innkeeper: You got it.

"And this," the prosecutor simply said.

Exhibit F-ff: "We're the highest developed nation taxed in the world." (4)

The Innkeeper: Yep.

"And this," the prosecutor continued.

Personal Note: What did that last one even mean?

Exhibit G-gg: "No administration has accomplished more in the first 90 days." (5)

The Innkeeper: You got it.

"And this," the prosecutor said yet again.

Exhibit H-hh: "14 percent of noncitizens are registered to vote." (6)

The Innkeeper: That was him, alright.

Personal Note: How would anyone even know that?

"And this," the prosecutor simply continued.

Exhibit I-ii: "I released the most extensive financial review of anybody in (sic) history..." (7)

The Innkeeper: Oh yeah. That one too.

"And this," the prosecutor said, growing visibly excited.

Exhibit J-jj: "Youth unemployment is through the roof..." (8)

The Innkeeper: Yep.

"And this," the prosecutor railed on.

Exhibit K-kk: "My I.Q. is one of the highest..." (9)

The Innkeeper: Oh yeah, that one too.

"Alright, alright, alright," my attorney finally interrupted. "We get it. He's got a thing for numbers. And he likes to embellish. But so what?"

Personal Note: Are those merely examples of embellishment?

"Agreed," the judge chimed in, looking at The Innkeeper. "Your point's well taken. Do you have anything else?"

"Sure," The Innkeeper answered, oddly seeming to enjoy all of the attention. "There's this whole thing he has with making things up. And to the point too that no one even knows what he's talking about."

"Like?"

The Innkeeper: Well, there was this whole Muslim celebration thing he came up with.

Exhibit L-ll: "Thousands and thousands of people were cheering as that building was coming down." (10)

The Innkeeper: "That's it."

"And this," the prosecutor continued, yet again.

Exhibit M-mm: His "birth certificate is a fraud." (11)

The Innkeeper: Oh yeah. That's certainly one.

"And this," the prosecutor said.

Exhibit N-nn: "He founded ISIS." (12)

"This is insane. Aren't you going to say anything?" I whispered into my attorney's ear, while noticing this on the wall on the far side of the room.

(A pretty good representation)

The Innkeeper. Yeah. And he has this whole thing about that kind of stuff too.

"I see that," the prosecutor simply replied, before holding up another piece of paper—

Exhibit O-oo: He "had my 'wires tapped.'" (13)

The Innkeeper: Yep.

"And this," the prosecutor immediately added.

Exhibit P-pp: "…You also had people that were very fine people on both sides." (14)

The Innkeeper. Oh yeah. And really, we could go on for days with this kind of stuff too.

"But we won't," the prosecutor interjected. "We want to respect the urgings of this court. So we will move to our next point, cruelty."

"Thanks," the judge said.

The Innkeeper: Oh, and there's a plethora there too.

"Like this," the prosecutor said, holding up yet another piece of paper, before walking over and handing it to the judge.

Exhibit Q-qq: She's "unattractive both inside and out. I fully understand why her former husband left her for a man." (15)

The Innkeeper: Oh yeah. That's one.

"And this," the prosecutor said.

Exhibit R-rr: "Turned her down twice and she went hostile. Major loser…" (16)

The Innkeeper: Yep. Although she was looking for a job from him there.

"And this," the prosecutor continued.

Exhibit S-ss: He "reminds me of a spoiled brat without a properly functioning brain." (17)

The Innkeeper: Definitely.

"And this," the prosecutor went on.

Personal Note: Who talks like that?

Exhibit T-tt: He "is a low class slob." (18)

The Innkeeper: You got it.

"And this," the prosecutor immediately said.

Exhibit U-uu: "They're bringing drugs. They're bringing crime. They're rapists." (19)

The Innkeeper: Yeah, and that's one of his greatest hits, in fact.

"And this."

Exhibit V-vv: "I understand the Chinese mind." (20)

The Innkeeper: Yep, and that's both dumb and racist.

"And this."

Exhibit W-ww: "I have a great relationship with the blacks." (21)

The Innkeeper: Definitely. And the same kind of deal as before about the whole dumb racist thing.

"And this," the prosecutor said, holding up yet another piece of paper.

Exhibit X-xx: "He's not a war hero. He was a war hero because he was captured. I like people who weren't captured." (22)

The Innkeeper: Oh yeah. And that's a real doosey too.

"And this."

Personal Note: Who says that? And about a POW too?

Exhibit Y-yy: "Probably, maybe she wasn't allowed to have anything to say, you tell me, but plenty of people have written that." (23)

The Innkeeper: Oh yeah. And that was real offensive too. Let alone kind of nuts.

"Would you do something please?" I whispered to my attorney again, while noticing this on the wall above the judge.

(A pretty good representation)

"I am," my attorney simply responded, suddenly shuffling several of the papers around on the table in front of him. "Trust me."

"And this," the prosecutor continued.

Exhibit Z-zz: "I think Islam hates us." (24)

The Innkeeper: Oh yeah. There was that one too. And think of the gall of that.

"And this."

Exhibit A-aaa: "Get that son of a bitch off the field right now." (25)

The Innkeeper: Yeah, and it's kind of crazy to refer to anyone's mom that way.

"And this."

Exhibit B-bbb: There was "blood coming out of her wherever." (26)

The Innkeeper: Oh yeah. There was that one also.

"And we could go on and on and on too," the prosecutor then said, walking over towards the jury booth. But we want to get to his name calling."

"Sure," The Innkeeper said, leaning forward in his seat. "I can give you a whole list of examples there."

"Like?" the prosecutor asked.

The Innkeeper: Little Rocket Man, Pocahontas, Low Energy Jeb, Crooked Hillary, Sleepin' Joe, Al Frankenstein, Lamb the Sham, Wacky Jacky, Little Marco, Cryin' Chuck, Sloppy Steve, Dopey Sugar, Lyin' Ted, Psycho Joe, Sleepy Eyes, Little Katie, Dicky Durbin, Jeff Flakey, McMuffin, Mr. Peepers, Cheatin' Obama, Crazy Bernie, Mr. Magoo.

"Alright, alright," my attorney finally interrupted. "We get it, he likes to belittle people. You've made your point."

Personal Note: What adult actually talks like that?

"Good," the prosecutor simply said. "And now for what you can tell us about his (and yes, he pointed at me yet again) need to incessantly brag on himself."

"His arrogance you mean?" The Innkeeper clarified, looking over at the prosecutor standing near the jury box. "And unmatched narcissism?"

"Sure, if you will," the prosecutor responded, turning and facing the jury booth for a moment. "What can you tell us about that?"

The Innkeeper: Plenty. Trust me.

And then the prosecutor once again, walked over to his table, picked up yet another piece of paper, and handed it to the judge, while saying, "Like this."

Exhibit C-ccc: "I consider myself too perfect and have no faults." (27)

The Innkeeper: Yep, that's one.

"And this," the prosecutor continued.

Exhibit D-ddd: "I have the best words." (28)

The Innkeeper: You got it.

"And this."

Exhibit E-eee: "…I can actually make my enemies tell the truth." (29)

The Innkeeper: Yeah, although that's just part of what he said, but sure.

Personal Note: Who would ever say, let alone think, anything like that?

"And this."

Exhibit F-fff: "Please don't feel stupid or insecure, it's not your fault." (30)

The Innkeeper: Definitely.

"And this."

Exhibit G-ggg: "…I'm more honest and my women are more beautiful." (31)

"And this."

Exhibit H-hhh: "…the beauty of me is that I'm very rich." (32)

"Fine," my attorney finally interrupted, not even letting The Innkeeper respond. "He's an egomaniac, we get it. But so what? Lots of people are egomaniacs."

Personal Note: Does anyone actually talk like that?

"You have to think you're above everyone else in order to be able to act like that," the prosecutor simply answered. "But no matter, we've made our point."

"Keep your eye on the time," the judge said, pointing to his watch on his wrist.

"Of course," the prosecutor replied. "So my last point with this witness simply focuses on his claimed business prowess."

"My what? My business prowess. But I'm just a researcher," I said, looking over at my attorney.

(What business prowess makes me think of)

"Oh, I can talk about how he conducts his business," The Innkeeper simply responded. "You better believe me."

"Quiet," my attorney whispered back. "Talking can only hurt us."

"See, he's been using my place like it's his own playground now for so long I can't even remember otherwise," The Innkeeper continued.

"So please," the prosecutor said, walking over towards The Innkeeper. "Tell us how he's been conducting his business."

The Innkeeper: Well, for starters, he created some foundation, as he calls it, where he takes in money under the auspices of helping the inn and then just uses it like his own personal bank account. And he admitted to that too.

"I did no such thing," I whispered into my attorney's ear. "This is lunacy."

"Like this," the prosecutor said, again handing the judge a piece of paper. "Where he checked yes to."

Exhibit I-iii: "…'self-dealing.'" (33)

The Innkeeper: Sure. And buying things like a portrait of himself. And using the money to cover his personal expenses. All kinds of stuff like that.

"Objection," my attorney suddenly yelled again. "The fact that my client believes in charitable donations should not be used against him."

"Fine," the prosecutor simply said. "Let's just clarify the contention this man (and yes, he pointed at me again) has about being a successful business man. Can you please enlighten us about the number of businesses that you are aware of that this man has driven into bankruptcy?"

"Or worse," The Innkeeper simply answered. "Because half the time he doesn't even pay his bills. So he might stay in business, but someone else might go under."

"Like this," the prosecutor immediately interrupted.

Exhibit J-jjj: "If things don't work out, I renegotiate." (34)

The Innkeeper: Yeah, that's one, sure.

"And this."

Exhibit K-kkk: "I'll deduct from their contract, absolutely." (35)

The Innkeeper: A little out of context, but yes. And then there's that whole point he makes about debt.

"You mean this one?"

Exhibit L-lll: "I'm the king of debt." (36)

The Innkeeper: Yep.

"Good, but now please tell us about your failed business point," the prosecutor said, walking back over to his table.

The Innkeeper: Well, there's that whole fact about his going bankrupt four times.

"Only four?" the prosecutor immediately interrupted, shaking his head, clearly confused. "I heard it was six. And they were all his businesses. That's my understanding. But no matter, please continue."

The Innkeeper: Sure. And true. And a lot of them dealt with casinos, but there's his whole series of failed business enterprises like the steaks and the airline and the vodka and the mortgage company and the board game and the magazine and the university and the water and the football team and the bike race and the restaurant and the nutritional supplement and the radio show and the media outlet.

"Whoa, okay," the prosecutor suddenly said, waving his hands in the air, cutting her off. "Anything else."

The Innkeeper: His multiple violations and rental practices and his lawsuits. Something like 3,500 lawsuits. He's quite the litigious man.

Personal Note: Can that possibly be true?

Meanwhile, two people behind me (reporters I assumed), who the whole time during the proceedings were writing things down, suddenly started arguing—

No, it was 2500 lawsuits.

No, the second man replied, it was 3500 and the word was litigant.

Licentious, the first man said, that's certainly what he said.

Lascivious then, the second man continued.

Litigious, the first man roared.

"Alright, alright, fine," my attorney finally said. "We get it, his (and then my attorney actually pointed at me) character is in serious question. And he's not really the greatest businessman who ever lived. And most of his money came from his daddy. But so what? That doesn't prove anything."

"No," the prosecutor replied. "Perhaps it doesn't, but it certainly establishes a character who'd be willing to engage in all sorts of nefarious and scrupulous activities."

"Objection, You Honor," my attorney suddenly retorted, so excitedly that I still feel it was more on his behalf than mine. "That's conjecture."

"Of course," the prosecutor replied. "My bad."

"Agreed," the judge added. "We need facts and facts alone."

"Which is why I will now call my final witness."

"In five," the judge said. "I need a break."

Act Twenty-One

Cry at the Crown Performance

"What are we doing?"

"What are we going to do?"

"What is going on?"

"What should we do?"

"Why do I have to endure this?"

"Why is this happening?"

"Can I fire my counsel?"

"What will everyone think of me after this?"

Those thoughts and so many more simply thundered around in my head as I sat in the courtroom waiting for the prosecutor to call the last witness to the stand.

"Go ahead," the judge finally said, pounding his gavel back down on his bench top. "You've got the floor again."

"Why do I think it's going to be The Mayor," I whispered to my attorney.

"I doubt it," my attorney simply whispered back. "He doesn't stand by anything he says."

479

"Thanks," the prosecutor replied. "So, now, I call The Maestro."

"Who?" I said, turning around and suddenly seeing this guy, clearly deformed and oddly mangled, to clarify (who I'd never seen before anywhere—in my file or otherwise) slowly wander up to the witness stand.

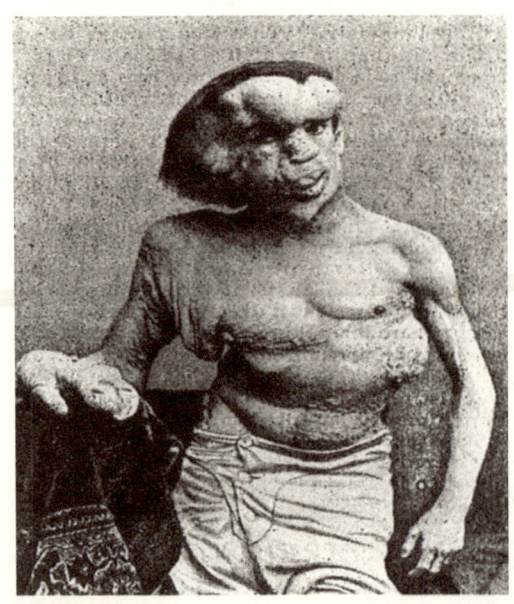

(A real close approximation)

"Who's that?" someone in the back of the courtroom yelled. "I've never seen him before."

"Me neither," someone else yelled. "But look at him?"

"Order," the judge roared, repeatedly pounding his gavel on his bench top. "Order in the court. This is the last witness, and then we can get out of here. So keep it quiet."

"Thanks," The Maestro said, continuing to slowly wander up towards the witness stand. "I really don't need these intrusions."

"Do you know who that is?" my attorney asked me (obviously unsure himself).

"No," I answered back, whispering into my attorney's ear. "Not at all. Does he even live here?"

"I don't know," my attorney replied. "I've never seen him before."

"Look at him," some lady behind me whispered, unconsciously it seemed. "What a sight."

"Your Honor," my attorney suddenly proclaimed, standing up from his seat. "Who is this? We were not aware that this witness would be called."

"Of course, of course," The Maestro simply interjected, continuing to slowly wander up to the witness stand, everyone in the courtroom staring at him. "I'm sure it is a surprise."

"This is my final witness," the prosecutor replied. "And it is our privilege to meet him."

"Your Honor," my attorney continued. "I object to this witness."

"Finally," The Maestro said huffing slightly, sitting down at the witness stand. "That's quite a walk. So let's get this on with. I've got many more important things to attend to today."

"This is my final witness," the prosecutor repeated, before turning and looking directly at the judge. "And after this we can all go home."

"Objection, Your Honor," my attorney proclaimed again, still standing at the table in front of me. "This witness isn't even on the docket."

"You and your little rules," The Maestro grunted, struggling to catch his breath. "How joyfully petty. Let's begin already."

"Overruled," the judge declared. "We can hear the witness. And then we can get back to our normal way of things."

Personal Note: Who is this guy?

"Of course," The Maestro simply said. "And then you can get back to your normal trifle things."

"Fine," my attorney replied, before sitting down next to me and muttering, "You're going to destroy my reputation around here forever. Do you hear me?"

"Thank you, Your Honor," the prosecutor replied. "Because of the nature of my final witness, and the sheer magnitude of his importance to all things regarding this Town, I simply couldn't bother him with the usual formalities. That simply wouldn't do."

"No it wouldn't," The Maestro interjected, oddly looking out at everyone in the courtroom, before adding, "So this is what I've come for."

"That's all you're going to do?" I whispered to my attorney.

"This man," the prosecutor said (again pointing at me). "Has been the ruin of this Town. We've shown you his character. And we've demonstrated his willingness to do anything to benefit himself. And so now I've asked my final witness to attest to his understanding of the situation. What will be our understanding of the situation," the prosecutor then seemed to clarify.

"Yes, for your gratification," the Maestro interrupted. "That's what you mean."

"What more can I do," my attorney answered. "So quiet. I want to hear this."

"Certainly," the prosecutor continued, walking over towards the jury booth. "And what you've told me about this man."

"As you will," The Maestro simply said, leaning back in his chair, before adding (seemingly to no one, quite honestly) "And I got stuck with this. Couldn't we have farmed this out to Abigail or something?"

"So now," the prosecutor thundered, walking even closer to the jury booth. "Is it not true that you've witnessed the various actions of this man?"

The Maestro: Yes. Of course. Haven't we all?

"And you have allowed for these things to continue?"

The Maestro: We all have, obviously. But so what? He's just our pressure value anyways. Just a tool to let off some steam. And isn't that evident?

"And you've witnessed his contempt for norms and his blatant disrespect for all things decent in this world?"

The Maestro: Well, yes, of course. And that's an odd peculiarity, for sure. But whatever, people seem to love it.

"They seem to love it?" the prosecutor asked. "Is that what you said?"

The Maestro: Sure, everyone needs someone to hate. Or love, for that matter. That's how things work. Just imagine a story without a villain. Or a tale without a hero. You don't really have a story now do you?

"No," the prosecutor answered. "No you don't."

"What is he talking about?" someone in the courtroom yelled. "And who is this guy?"

"Quiet," the judge nearly shouted, banging his gavel down several times on the top of his bench. "I will have no more interruptions in this courtroom today. And I want to hear him speak. So please continue," the judge then added, looking over at The Maestro.

The Maestro: They really are rude aren't they?

"And you've watched as this man (again pointing at me) simply undermined and destroyed all of our values."

The Maestro: I wouldn't say that. What has he actually done? But no matter, everyone needs a fall guy. We certainly know that.

"And you're aware of his tactics then?" the prosecutor asked, continuing to pace around the front of the courtroom like some lion in a cage.

The Maestro: Sure, and they're kind of funny actually. But we need to whip up contempt. And stir up outrage. That's just the nature of the beast.

"And he's done those things?"

The Maestro: Even better than we expected. Honestly, it's been amazing in that regard. And besides, we've got to either appease or scare everyone. Those really are our only two options.

"We do?" the prosecutor asked, suddenly turning and facing me. "All of us."

The Maestro: Sure. Just think of how scared you all are now.

"What is he talking about?" someone shouted out again. "I'm not scared."

The Maestro: Or satisfied.

"Villain," someone else screamed at me. "You're nothing but a villain."

"Order," the judge nearly shouted again, while repeatedly banging his gavel down on his bench top. "You've all been warned. I will have no more of these outbursts in my courtroom."

The Maestro: Thank you, Your Honor.

"Aren't you going to do anything?" I asked my attorney, looking over and noticing this hanging above the door to the side exit of the courtroom.

(A pretty good representation)

"I am," my attorney answered. "I'm trying to figure out how to save my career right now."

"And you've witnessed his grotesque and barbaric attacks and assaults on the people and institutions and practices and everything else regarding this Town?"

The Maestro: Regrettably, yes. And all of that's a little unsettling. His ability to simply relish in the despicable and the base and the petty and the cruel and the vile is almost amazing. Honestly, we couldn't even have imagined someone quite like that. But it was what was needed. We all agreed to that. Even with the odd peculiarities.

"We did?" the prosecutor asked, seemingly surprised by this point.

The Maestro: Sure. And it's what you expected.

"We did?" the prosecutor repeated, walking over towards the jury booth. "Really?"

Personal Note: Did we expect this?

The Maestro: See, and even you have to feign outrage.

"But these are real crimes this man has committed. And these are serious offenses to our Town. Don't you agree?"

The Maestro: We all agree. Every last one of us. But that's not the real question. This man (and then The Maestro actually pointed at me) he's not the issue, he's just some puppet, don't you see that? He's nothing more than some crazy fool acting any way he wants. And he knows exactly who he's working for. Obviously. He wouldn't be here otherwise. So no, that's not the real question.

"Then what's the real question?" the prosecutor asked, starting to pace around the courtroom again.

Personal Note: Who am I actually working for?

"You," The Maestro simply answered, pointing out across the courtroom. "And how you all fell for this?"

"How we all fell for this," someone yelled again from the back of the courtroom. "What are you talking about? I didn't fall for anything."

"Yeah, what is he talking about?" someone else yelled.

The Maestro: And accepted what we did.

Personal Note: Am I really just some puppet?

The Maestro: And all the lies.

"I didn't accept anything," someone else yelled from the far side of the courtroom. "Why do you think I'm here?"

Yet Another Personal Note: And who's the "you" he's talking about?

"Why do you think we're all here?" someone else yelled.

"Vindication," someone else yelled from the back of the room. "Just look at this place. That's why. And look at what's been done. It's total vindication."

"Order," the judge roared again, slamming his gavel down on his bench over and over and over. "I said order in this court."

"And to make this Town great," someone else yelled. "It needs to be The Greatest Place on Earth again."

"Order," the judge repeated. "You will all be held in contempt of court."

The Maestro: Thank you, Your Honor. Their disruptions really are shameful.

"Aren't you going to say anything?" I asked my attorney yet again, leaning over and talking into his ear.

The Maestro: And look, it's all our win.

"Quiet," my attorney simply answered. "You're killing me."

"Whose win?" some lady a few rows behind me roared. "Whose win would that be?"

"That's it," the judge said again, literally bashing his gavel down on the top of his bench. "We need a recess. This court is in recess. We will resume in fifteen minutes so that everyone can get their heads back on straight."

Personal Note: What just happened?

And then, before I could even think about things too long, my attorney rushed me out of the courtroom and into some small side room in order to talk with me about what we should do next.

"I'm never going to be able to work in this Town again," my lawyer nearly cried, sitting down at a table at the back of the room, banging his briefcase down on the table top. "Do you hear me?"

"You," I simply replied, looking at him, his face suddenly reminding me of a young boy's. "They're going to kill me out there."

"And I'll be nothing but a laughing stock."

"Did you hear what I just said?" I replied, nearly yelling, while standing at the table, hovering over him. "They're setting me up to take their fall. That's what's going on. Don't you see that? It's just a witch hunt. A total witch hunt, I tell you. Nothing but a conspiracy against my good name. That's all this is."

"And my wife probably won't even want to talk to me anymore," my attorney simply continued.

"And why didn't you ever cross examine anyone?" I then asked, nearly yanking my hair out of my head. "What kind of strategy is that?"

"And my kids will think I'm a joke."

"And where's my assistant?" I asked, straining not to hit my attorney. "Why don't we call him in as a witness? He can attest to my character and actions?"

"Look," my attorney said, staring up at me. "I don't know what's going on. And I don't know what to do. Alright? There's no rules for everything that you've done. Do you understand me? We're in no-man's land here."

"What I've done?" I replied, pushing myself away from the table. "I haven't done anything. And as far as I can tell, neither have you. You're supposed to defend me."

"I'm a lawyer," my attorney said, continuing to stare at me. "Not some magician."

"But you have an oath to defend me. So defend me."

"I'm not running the show," my attorney simply replied. "Can't you see that?"

Personal Note: Who is running the show?

"What are we going to do?" I asked, leaning back against the wall. "That's all I want to know."

491

"Write your final goodbyes," my attorney said, looking at me. "That's my advice. And pray for a miracle," he then added, before handing me this—

DISPATCH NUMBER TWENTY-FIVE: Remember, up is down. Down is up. Left it right. Right is Left. Etc. Etc. Etc. Disembowel the Researcher. ROGER & OUT.

"But none of this makes any sense," I said, throwing the note on the ground. "This is all just lunacy."

"You heard me," my attorney simply replied, shaking his head at me. "And I'm going to do the same."

And then, perhaps because I was so worked up I just couldn't think to do anything else or perhaps because I thought it really was something I should do, I simply sat down at the table next to my attorney and wrote several different letters—

Dear Ginny: (In calligraphy again)

> *I know what we need to do.*
> *I do.*
> *I really do.*

Bob

And then I paused for a moment, looked over at the far side of the room, and suddenly noticed another picture on the wall.

(A close approximation)

And then I simply turned my notebook to a new page, and wrote this note in really big letters (because it seemed necessary, for some reason)—

Dear Aaron:

Stand up for yourself more. You know better than this. I know you do. And so do you.

Dad

And then, I paused for yet another moment, simply sitting there thinking about how Aaron really needs to remember a basic lesson Ginny and I taught him years ago: "Don't expect anyone to do something for you that you need to do for yourself," when my attorney reached over and handed me yet another note—

Dear Bob:

I know I didn't expect much from you to begin with. But honestly, I thought you'd do a little more than this. We all did. And we're still here. Remember that. We didn't go anywhere.

The Gang (as we are now expected to call ourselves)

"Right, the gang," I thought, sitting there, looking at the note, before deciding to write Evelyn a quick letter (in handwriting I'd never even used before either)—

Dear Evelyn:
    EV
        ERY
            T
            H
            I

```
NG                    IS
        J     U      S      T
                     G            R      A
  N     D
```

Dad

And then I paused again for another moment, simply looking at the letter I wrote Evelyn (proud at the clarity and directness of it all, mind you), before my attorney suddenly interrupted me by handing me yet another note.

"Oh here," my attorney said, sliding the note over to me. "I almost forgot to give you this too."

"But aren't we going to work on my strategy?" I asked, looking at him. "Aren't we going to do anything at all?"

"I am," my attorney simply said. "I'm going to hope everyone just forgets that any of this ever happened."

Personal Note: Is that possible?

"But I can't forget, I can't forget at all," I replied.

"Sure," my attorney said. "And it will really be a mess for a while around here too. But no matter. I suppose that's the cost of belief."

"What?" I asked, looking at him, confused by his sudden statement.

"Nothing," my lawyer replied. "It was really nothing at all."

And then, before I could ponder that too long, my attorney simply directed my attention back to the letter he gave me—

Dear Bob: (It began, and from my assistant I immediately realized)

I know you're probably a little confused by all of this. Okay, you're probably a little more than a little confused by all of this. But what can you do? We all have to eat. And we all have to make sure things stay chummy, so to speak. And sure, you were probably hoping for a different ending. Some kind of redemption or something. Or perhaps, some kind of explanation even. But really, things don't work like that. You know? Fairy tales only have happy endings. And this isn't a fairy tale.

But all in all, you've got to admit it wasn't too bad. At least for us that is. We really got what we needed. And isn't that how things should be? Deserved.

And sorry about leaving you like that. I know that that probably seemed a little rude.

But it was the only prudent thing I could do. We all were going nuts, you know? Just bonkers. And we couldn't let that happen to The Greatest Place on Earth. This is our deal.

All of ours.

ROGER & OUT. (Known=Unknown.)

Your Assistant

And then, utterly baffled, my head simply spinning around from the weird words from my assistant, I looked up and noticed yet another picture on the wall.

(A real close approximation)

But then, before I could even ponder that too long, my attorney looked at me and said, "Let's go. I've got to start picking up the pieces."

"Okay," I answered, not sure what to think.

"Now."

And then I simply walked back out to the courtroom, my head slumped down, waiting for The Maestro to continue, while hoping to get on with the next chapter of things.

The End.

PS: Really, the end.

PPS: Really, the end?

Appendix 1—The Inn Guests

(Specifically described)

The Skywalker: Scott Pruitt

The Proctor: Betsy DeVos

The Constructor: Ben Carson

The Human Kow-Tow: Tom Price

The Horsemaster: Ryan Zinke

The Shill: Sean Spicer

The Sleeptalker: Wilbur Ross

The Escapologist: Steven Mnuchin

The Tongue Twister: Kellyanne Conway

The Gorilla-Faced Man: Rick Perry

The Concentric Circle Man: Carter Page

Long-Legged Lucy: Hope Hicks

Darth Doom: Steve Bannon

The Bait-Boy: Sam Nunberg

The Shallow Diver: Roger Stone

The Elixir Lad: George Papadopoulos

The Ever-Shrinking Man: Jeff Sessions

The Barn Burner: Mike Flynn

The High-Brow Suck-Up: Reince Priebus

The Wing Walker: Jared Kushner

The Snake Charmer: Ivanka Trump

The Mute Lady: Melania Trump

The Confectioner: Steven Miller

The Mouse Man: Anthony Scaramucci

The Dog Man: Rudy Giuliani

The Pantomime: Sarah Huckabee Sanders

The Giant Hat Man: Jim Jordan

The Prism Lady: Nikki Haley

The Eel Man: Paul Ryan

(With person in mind but not specifically described)

The Innkeeper: Mike Pence

The Innkeeper's Daughter: Stormy Daniels

The Noble Preacher: Jerry Falwell Jr. (or seemingly any other Evangelical leader)

The Mayor's Deputy: Mitch McConnell

The Mayor: Donald Trump

The Town Accountant: Larry Kudlow

The Enormous Man: Richard Blumenthal

Man from Resistance: Adam Schiff

Dinner Servant: Devin Nunes

His First Attorney: John Dowd or Ty Cobb (you pick)

His Second Attorney: Us (or at least most of us, quite honestly)

Judge John PQ Doe: Us again (or at least most of us again, quite honestly)

The Sword Swallower: Donald Trump Jr.

The World's Most Unfit Man: Sam Clovis

"The Greatest Place on Earth"

Count Von Creepy: Paul Manafort

The Human Cannonball: Rick Gates

The Fixer: Michael Cohen

The No-Brain Boy: Eric Trump

The Black Gold Albino: Rex Tillerson

Shady Davey: James Comey

Chief Spitfire: John Kelly

(The file photos)

The Seductress: Kellyanne Conway (yes, used again)

The Practitioner: Harold Bornstein

The Prospector: Donald Trump (obviously used again)

The Magistrate: Rod Rosenstein

The Pugilist: Every TV News Host (Chris Wallace, Chuck Todd, etc.)

The Administrator: Dina Powell (for lack of anyone better to choose from)

The Squawker: Boris Epshteyn

The Barrister: Jay Sekulow

The Strongman: Sean Hannity

The Pontificator: Hillary Clinton

The Purveyor: Ted Cruz

The Provocateur: Any high-profile Never-Trumper (John Kasich, Jeb Bush, etc.)

The Necromancer: Lindsey Graham

Jeff Weisman

(Mentioned but not specified—with suggestions here)

The Tightrope Walker: Nigel Farage

The Lion Tamer: Michael Caputo

The Belly Dancer: Richard Pinedo

The Trapeze Artist: Allen Weisselberg

The Contortionist: Erik Prince

The Glass Eater: Omarosa Manigault

The Fire Eater: Laura Ingraham

The Plate Spinner: Sam Patten

The Knife Thrower: Ann Coulter

The Antipode: Randy Credico or Jerome Corsi (you decide)

The Mime: Steve Doocy

The Pogo Sticker: Julian Assange

The Hook Suspender: Peter Smith

The Whistler: Tucker Carlson

The Saber Lady: Maria Butina

The Fortune Teller: _____(You fill in the blank here)

(Other characters of import but not specified)

First Bureau Employee

My Assistant (Jim)

Reggie

The Old Man (from the Opposition)

The Blue-Billed Man

"The Greatest Place on Earth"

Late Sixties Woman (from Banquet)

Ninety-or-so-year-old Man (from Banquet)

The Maestro

Appendix 2—Works Cited

Act Seven: Partake in the Midway

1. From the Republican presidential nomination acceptance speech at the Republican National Convention in Cleveland, Ohio, on July 21, 2016. www.politico.com/story/ 2016/07/full-transcript-donald-trump-nomination-acceptance-speech-at-rnc-225974.

Act Seventeen: Hear the Ringmaster

1. Taken from an email exchange written by Donald Trump Jr. on June, 3 2016, to Rob Goldstone. www.cnn.com/interactive/2017/07/politics/donald-trump-jr-full-emails/.
2. From the official plea agreement statement signed by Michael T. Flynn on November 30, 2017. www.lawfareblog.com/michael-flynn-plea-agreement-documents.
3. Attributed to Sam Clovis by Sarah N. Lynch and Mark Hosenball in "Former Trump Campaign Advisor Denies Encouraging Aide on Russia Dealings" from *Reuters* on October 31, 2017. This attribution was never actually disputed. www.reuters.com/article/ us-usa-trump-russia-

clovis/former-trump-campaign-adviser-denies-encouraging-aide-on-russia-dealings-idUSKBN1D02MT.

4. Taken from the official plea agreement signed by George Papadopoulos on October 5, 2017, characterizing an email written by him to the London Professor Joseph Mifsud. www.lawfareblog.com/george-papadopoulos-stipulation-and-plea-agreement.

5. From the job application written by Paul Manafort and sent to Donald J. Trump in February 2016. www.documentcloud.org/documents/4159063-MEMO-Manafort-JobPitchToTrump-02-2016.html.

6. From an email written by Paul Manafort to Konstantin Kilimnik as reported by Natasha Bertrand in "'Of Course We Discussed Trump': Russian-Ukrainian Operative Explains His Emails with Manafort" for *Business Insider* published on September 27, 2017. www. businessinsider. com/konstantin-kilimnik-explains-emails-with-paul-manafort-about-trump-2017-9.

7. Granted, as the time of this writing, this was not proven, but it was a key question the Mueller team was investigating according to a Justice Department lawyer as reported by Avery Anapol in "Justice Depart Lawyer Says Manafort May Have Served as 'Back Channel' to Russia: Report" on April, 19, 2018, in *The Hill*. thehill.com/homenews/administration/383985-justice-dept-lawyer-says-manafort-may-have-served-as-back-channel-to.

8. Taken from Paul Manafort's job application to Donald J. Trump from February 2016. Additionally, Manafort's work with the Pro-Russian Ukrainian President Viktor Yanukoviych cannot be overlooked. www.documentcloud.org/documents/4159063-MEMO-Manafort-JobPitchToTrump-02-2016.html.

9. From the hacked emails of Andrea Manafort written to her sister Jessica Manafort published in "In a Series of Text Messages, Paul Manafort's Daughter Implicates Her Father in Mass-Murder" from *The Intellectualist* on July 13, 2018. hmavenroundtable.io/ theintellectualist/news/in-series-of-text-messages-paul-manafort-s-daughter-implicates-her-father-in-mass-murder-3QYf7RjMh0a8yRWFEc-LsA/.

10. Ibid.

Act Eighteen: Witness the Aerial Ballet

1. From an email written by Carter Page to Trump campaign officials describing his July 2016 trip to Moscow, as reported in the story "Carter Page Sent Email Describing 'Private Conversation' with Russian Official" from *The Washington Post* on November 17, 2017, by Rosiland S. Helderman, Matt Zapotsky, and Karoun Demirjian. www. washingtonpost.com/politics/trump-adviser-sent-email-describing-private-conversation-with-russian-

official/2017/11/06/b39d4c84-c33b-11e7-84bc-5e285c7f4512_story.html? utm_term=.94686b187576.

2. From an interview with Chris Hayes on the "All In with Chris Hayes" show on MSNBC on October 30, 2017 as quoted in the article "Carter Page: I May Have Discussed Russia in Email with Papadopoulos" by Brent D. Griffiths from *Politico* on October 30, 2017. www.politico.com/story/2017/10/30/page-papadopoulos-russia-probe-244349.

3. From Roger Stone's tweet on Monday, October 3, 2016, about WikiLeaks founder Julian Assange as published in the story "The WikiLeaks Tweets Roger Stone Can't Explain" by Dan Friedman and David Corn from *Mother Jones* on September 26, 2017. www. motherjones.com/politics/2017/09/the-wikileaks-tweets-roger-stone-cant-explain-1/.

4. From "Roger Stone Claimed Contact with WikiLeaks Founder Julian Assange in 2016, According to Two Associates" by Tom Hamburger, Josh Dawsey, Carol D. Leonnig, and Shane Harris of *The Washington Post* on March 13, 2018, describing an interview Roger Stone had acknowledging a phone discussion with Sam Nunberg about Julian Assange. www.washingtonpost.com/politics/roger-stone-claimed-contact-with-wikileaks-founder-julian-assanage-in-2016-according-to-two-associates/2018/03/13/a263f842-2604-11e8-b79d-f3d931db7f68_story.html.

5. From a Roger Stone tweet written on Wednesday, October 5, 2016, about the then still unreleased emails regarding Hillary Clinton, as described in the story "Roger Stone Claimed to Know of WikiLeaks Email Release Date, Despite Saying Otherwise" by Andrew Kaczynski for CCN News on Saturday, April 7, 2018. www.cnn.com/2018/04/07/politics/kfile-roger-stone-wikileaks-comments/index.html.

6. Ibid. As transcribed from an October 2, 2016, InfoWars radio interview.

7. From the *Vanity Fair* article "Michael Cohen Would Take a Bullet for Donald Trump" by Emily Jane Fox from September 6, 2017. www.vanityfair.com/news/2017/09/michael-cohen-interview-donald-trump.

8. As reported in "NPR Publishes Audio of Cohen Threatening Reporter" by Aris Folley of *The Hill* on May 21, 2018. thehill.com/homenews/media/390134-audio-recordings-reveal-cohens-history-of-making-legal-threats-to-save-trump.

9. From Michael Cohen's own statement published in the article "Trump's Personal Lawyer Said He Paid Porn Star Stormy Daniels Out of His Own Pocket" written by Saheli Roy Choudhury for CNBC on February 14, 2018. www.cnbc.com/2018/02/14/trumps-lawyer-said-he-paid-adult-film-star-out-of-his-own-pocket.html.

Act Nineteen: Gawk at the Lion Tamer

1. Quoted directly from the released transcript of Kelleyanne Conway's interview on "Meet the Press" on January 22, 2017. www.nbcnews.com/meet-the-press/meet-press-01-22-17-n710491.

2. From the transcript of Sean Spicer's remarks published in "Transcript of White House Press Secretary Statement to the Media" in *Politico* on January 21, 2017. www.politico. com /story/2017/01/transcript-press-secretary-sean-spicer-media-233979.

3. As reported about Hope Hicks' testimony to a House intelligence panel in "Hope Hicks Admits She Tells 'White Lies' for Trump but Not about Russia Inquiry" from *The Guardian* on February 28, 2018. theguardian.com/us-news/2018/feb/28/hope-hicks-donald-trump-russia-investigation.

4. From Sarah Huckabee Sanders' daily press briefing on June 29, 2017 as reported in "Sarah Huckabee Sanders Raised Eyebrows with the Claim that Trump Has Never 'Encouraged Violence'" by Allen Smith in *Business Insider* on June 29, 2107. www. businessinsider.com/sarah-huckabee-sanders-trump-never-encouraged-violence-2017-6.

5. As reported in "The Worst Lies Sarah Huckabee Sanders Has Told" by Natalie Gontcharova for *Refinery29* on June

15, 2018. www.refinery29.com/2018/06/201952/ sarah-huckabee-sanders-worst-lies-trump-administration.

6. Quoted in "Anthony Scaramucci: I've Seen Trump 'Throw a Dead Spiral through a Tire'" by Anna Giaritelli for *The Washington Examiner* on July 21, 2017. www.washingtonexaminer.com/anthony-scaramucci-ive-seen-trump-throw-a-dead-spiral-through-a-tire.

7. What Donald Trump said on "The View" in 2006 as cited in "Donald Trump's Creepy Ogling of His Daughter Happened More Than You Think" by Paige Lavender from *The Huffington Post* on October 3, 2016. www.huffingtonpost.com/entry/donald-trump-ivanka-trump-comments_us_57f250d5e4b082aad9bbf2d7.

8. Donald Trump on "The Howard Stern Show" in 2003 as reported in "Donald Trump's Unsettling Record of Comments About His Daughter Ivanka" by Adam Withnall in *The Independent* on October 10, 2016. www.independent.co.uk/news/world/americas/us-elections/donald-trump-ivanka-trump-creepiest-most-unsettling-comments-a-roundup-a7353876.html.

9. From "'This Week' Transcript: Eric Trump, Joel Benenson, and Evan McMullin" published on October 23, 2016 by ABC News. abcnews.go.com/Politics/week-transcript-eric-trump-joel-benenson-evan-mcmullin/story?id=42988580.

10. From "Donald Trump's Cabinet Members, Ranked by Their Over-the-top Praise of Trump" by Chris Cillizza for

CNN News published on June 13, 2017, quoting Secretary of State Rex Tillerson during President Trump's Cabinet Meeting on Monday, June 12, 2017. www.cnn.com/ 2017/06/12/politics/trump-cabinet-ranked/index.html.

11. From "Cabinet Members Give Trump Unusual Tribute" by Kevin Liptak for CNN published on June 12, 2017, quoting Attorney General Jeff Sessions from President Trump's Cabinet Meeting on Monday, June 12, 2017. www.cnn. com/2017/06/12/ politics/trump-cabinet-tribute/index.html.

12. From "Donald Trump's Cabinet Members, Ranked by Their Over-the-top Praise of Trump" by Chris Cillizza for CNN published on June, 13, 2017, quoting Education Secretary Betsy DeVos during President Trump's Cabinet Meeting on Monday, June 12, 2017. www.cnn.com/2017/ 06/12/politics/trump-cabinet-ranked/index.html.

13. Ibid. Quoting UN Ambassador Nikki Haley during the same Monday, June 12, 2017, Cabinet Meeting.

14. Ibid. Quoting Health and Human Services Secretary Tom Price during the same Monday, June 12, 2017, Cabinet Meeting.

15. From "Cabinet Members Give Trump Unusual Tribute" by Kevin Liptak for CNN News published on June 12, 2017, quoting White House Chief of Staff Reince Priebus from President Trump's Cabinet Meeting on Monday, June. 12, 2017. www.cnn.com/2017 /06/12/ politics/trump-cabinet-tribute/index.html.

16. Taken from former FBI Director James Comey's opening statement to the Senate Select Committee on Intelligence on June 8, 2017, published in "Comey: 'Trump Asked for 'Loyalty,' Wanted Him to 'Let' Flynn Investigation 'Go'" by Jessica Taylor on June 7, 2017, for NPR. www.npr.org/2017/06/07/531927032/comey-trump-asked-for-loyalty-wanted-him-to-let-flynn-investigation-go.

17. Ibid.

18. From a transcript of a Fox News Sunday interview with Chris Wallace on December 11, 2016 as published in "Trump Broke 64 Promises in His First Month in Office" by Ryan Koronowski for *Think Progress* on February 24, 2017. thinkprogress.org/trump-broke-64-promises-in-his-first-month-in-office-5470f2c337e1/.

19. In "Trump: 'The President Can't Have a Conflict of Interest" by Issac Anrsdorf for *Politico* on November 22, 2016. www.politico.com/story/2016/11/trump-the-president-cant-have-a-conflict-of-interest-231760.

20. "The Trump Allegations" by Lucia Graves and Sam Morris of *The Guardian* from November 29, 2017, quoting Jessica Leads, originally sourced from *The New York Times*. www.theguardian.com/us-news/ng-interactive/2017/nov/30/donald-trump-sexual-misconduct-allegations-full-list.

21. Ibid. Ivana Trump in her divorce deposition, originally sourced from *Lost Tycoon: The Many Lives of Donald Trump*.

22. Ibid. Jill Harth, a former business partner, originally sourced from *The Guardian*.

23. Ibid. Kirsten Anderson, originally sourced from *The Washington Post*.

24. Ibid. Kathy Heller, originally sourced from *The Guardian*.

25. Ibid. Temple Taggart, originally sourced from *The New York Times*.

26. Ibid. Karena Virginia, from a Gloria Allred press event.

27. Ibid. Bridgette Sullivan, originally sourced from *Buzzfeed*.

28. Ibid. Melinda McGillivray, originally sourced from the *Palm Beach Post*.

29. Ibid. Jennifer Murphy, a former contestant on "The Apprentice."

30. Ibid. Rachael Crooks, originally sourced from *The New York Times*.

31. Ibid. Natasha Stoynoff, originally sourced from *People*.

32. Ibid. Ninni Laaksonen, originally sourced from the Finish newspaper *Ilta-Sanomat*.

33. Ibid. Jessica Drake, from a Gloria Allred press event.

34. Ibid. Samantha Holvey, originally sourced from CNN News.

35. Ibid. Summer Zervos, from a Gloria Allred press event.

36. Ibid. Cassandra Searles, from Facebook via *Yahoo News*.

37. Taken from the transcript of the 2005 recording of Donald Trump talking with "Access Hollywood" host Billy Bush, published in *The New York Times* on October 8, 2016.

www.nytimes.com/2016/10/08/us/donald-trump-tape-
transcript.html.

Act Twenty: Gasp at the Elephant Routine

1. Quoted from "Donald Trump Wrong Again That Recent
    Tax Bill Is Biggest Ever" by Louis Jacobson for PolitiFact
    on Tuesday, January 30, 2018. www.politifact.com/truth-o-
    meter/statements/2018/jan/30/donald-trump/donald-trump-
    wrong-again-recent-tax-bill-biggest-e/.
2. From "Fact Check: Trump Incorrectly Claims He's 'Signed
    More Legislation Than Anybody" by Ryan Struyk for CNN
    News published on Thursday, December 28, 2017. www.
    cnn.com/2017/12/28/politics/trump-more-legislation-fact-
    check/index.html.
3. Taken from a statement Donald Trump made at a rally in
    Pensacola, Florida, on December 8, 2017, as quoted in
    "Donald Trump Wrong That Black Homeownership Rate Is
    at a Record High" by Louis Jacobson for PolitiFact on
    Monday, December 11, 2017. www.politifact.com/truth-o-
    meter/statements/2017/dec/11/donald-trump/donald-trump-
    wrong-black-homeownership-rate-record/.
4. From an interview on E.W. Scripps Television as reported
    in "Once Again Trump Overstates U.S. Tax Ranking" by
    Jon Greenberg for PolitiFact on Wednesday, October 18,
    2017. www.politifact.com/truth-o-meter/statements/2017/

oct/18/donald-trump/once-again-trump-overstates-us-tax-ranking/.

5. Donald Trump at the Wisconsin tool company Snap-on on Tuesday, April 18, 2017, as reported in "Fact Check: Trump Ignores Presidents Who Were Higher-Achievers in White House" by CBS News on April 19, 2017, and originally published by *The Associated Press*. www.cbsnews.com/news/fact-check-trump-ignores-presidents-who-were-higher-achievers-in-white-house/.

6. Donald Trump at a rally in Cleveland, Ohio, on Saturday, October 22, 2016, as reported in "Donald Trump Wrongly Says 14 Percent of Noncitizens Are Registered to Vote" by Allison Graves for PolitiFact on Monday, October 24, 2016. www.politifact.com/truth-o-meter/statements/2016/oct/24/donald-trump/donald-trump-wrongly-says-14-percent-noncitizens-a/.

7. In an ABC News interview with David Muir on Tuesday, September 6, 2016, Donald Trump said this as reported in "Donald Trump Says His Financial Disclosures More Than Make Up for Lack of Releasing Tax Returns" by Louis Jacobson for PolitiFact on Wednesday, September 7, 2016. www.politifact.com/truth-o-meter/statements/2016/sep/07donald-trump/donald-trump-says-his-financial-disclosures-more-m/.

8. As reported on Donald Trump's social media response session by Eugene Mason in "Here's What Happened

During Donald Trump's Ask Me Anything on Reddit" for PBS NewsHour on July 28, 2016. www.pbs.org/ newshour/politics/heres-happened-donald-trumps-ask-anything-reddit.

9. From a May 8, 2013 Donald Trump Twitter Post as cited in "Donald Trump's IQ Obsession, in 22 Quotes" by Chris Cillizza for CNN News on Tuesday, October 10, 2017. www.cnn.com/2017/10/10/politics/donald-trump-tillerson-iq/index.html.

10. From a video clip of a Donald Trump rally as discussed with George Stephanopoulos and reported in "Trump's Outrageous Claim That 'Thousands' of New Jersey Muslims Celebrated the 9/11 Attacks" by Glenn Kessler for *The Washington Post* on November 22, 2015. www.washingtonpost.com/news/fact-checker/wp/2015/ 11/22/donald-trumps-outrageous-claim-that-thousands-of-new-jersey-muslims-celebrated-the-911-attacks/? utm_tern=.22c8f929e7dd.

11. From an August 6, 2012, Donald Trump tweet as reported in "67 Times Donald Trump Tweeted About the 'Birther' Movement" by Ryan Struyk for ABC News on September 16, 2016. abcnews.go.com/Politics/67-times-donald-trump-tweeted-birther-movement/ story?id=42145590.

12. Donald Trump at a rally in Florida on Wednesday, August 10, 2016, as reported in "Donald Trump's Pants on Fire Claim That Barack Obama 'Founded' ISIS, Hillary Clinton

was 'Cofounder'" by Louis Jacobson and Amy Sherman for PolitiFact on Thursday, August 11, 2016. www.politifact.com/truth-o-meter/statements/2016/aug/11/donald-trump/donald-trump-pants-fire-claim-obama-founded-isis-c/.

13. From a March 4, 2017, Donald Trump tweet as reported in "Donald Trump Just Flat-out Lied About Trump Tower Wiretapping" by Chris Cillizza for CNN News on September 5, 2017. www.cnn.com/2017/09/05/politics/trump-doj-wiretap/index.html.

14. Taken from the transcript of the Donald Trump news conference on August 12, 2017, published in the article "Trump's Comments on White Supremacists, 'Alt-left' in Charlottesville" by the Politico Staff for *Politico* on August 15, 2017. www.politico.com/ story/2017/08/15/full-text-trump-comments-white-supremacists-alt-left-transcript-241662.

15. Donald Trump in a 2012 tweet about Arianna Huffington as published in "Donald Trump's Long History of Disparaging Women's Appearances" by Andrew Kaczynski and Nathan McDermott for CNN News on June 29, 2017. www.cnn.com/2017/06/29/politics/kfile-trump-long-history-disparaging-comments/index.html.

16. From a Donald Trump tweet on February 6, 2016, about Cheri Jaccobus as reported in "Donald Trump Faces Defamation Lawsuit for Twitter Assault on Political

Consultant" by Douglas Perry on April 19, 2016, for *The Oregonian*. www.oregonlive.com/today/ index.ssf/ 2016/04/donald_trump_faces_defamation.html.

17. From a Donald Trump tweet about Rand Paul on August 10, 2015, as reported in "Trump: 'Weird' Rand Paul Is Like a 'Spoiled Brat Without a Properly Functioning Brain'" by Pete Kasperowicz on August 10, 2015, for the *Washington Examiner*. www. washingtonexaminer.com/trump-weird-rand-paul-is-like-a-spoiled-brat-without-a-properly-functioning-brain.

18. Donald Trump in an August 7, 2015, tweet about Karl Rove as reported in "Trump Goes After GOP Pollster for Being a 'Low Class Slob'" by Betsy Rothstein on August 7, 2015, for *The Daily Caller*. dailycaller.com/2015/08/ 07/trump-goes-after-gop-pollster-for-being-a-low-class-slob/.

19. Donald Trump in his presidential candidacy announcement speech on June 16, 2015, as reported in "Here Are all the Times Donald Trump Insulted Mexico" by Katie Reilly on August, 31, 2016, for *Time*. time.com/4473972/donald-trump-mexico-meeting-insult/.

20. From "Donald Trump Has Read a Lot of Books on China: 'I Understand the Chinese Mind'" by Tony Pierce in *The LA Times* on May 3, 2011. latimesblogs.latimes.com/ washington/2011/05/donald-trump-i-understand-the-chinese-mind.html.

21. From "Donald Trump: 'I Have a Great Relationship with the Blacks'" by Garance Franke-Ruta on April 14, 2011 for *The Atlantic*. www.theatlantic.com/politics/archive/2011/04/donald-trump-i-have-a-great-relationship-with-the-blacks/237332/.

22. Donald Trump at the Family Leadership Summit in Ames, Iowa, from "Trump Attacks McCain: 'I Like People Who Weren't Captured'" by Ben Schreckinger for *Politico* on July 19, 2015. www.politico.com/story/2015/07/trump-attacks-mccain-i-like-people-who-werent-captured-120317.

23. Donald Trump in an ABC News interview with George Stephanopoulos from "Donald Trump Responds to the Khan Family: 'Maybe She Wasn't Allowed to Have Anything to Say'" originally in *The Washington Post* and then published in *The Denver Post* on August 1, 2016. www.denverpost.com/2016/07/31/donald-trump-khizr-kahn-response-dnc/.

24. Donald Trump to CNN's Anderson Cooper as quoted in "Donald Trump: 'I Think Islam Hates Us'" by Theodore Schleifer for CNN News on March 10, 2016. www.cnn.com/2016/03/09/politics/donald-trump-islam-hates-us/index.html.

25. Donald Trump during a speech in Alabama regarding what NFL owners should to do NFL players kneeling during the National Anthem as quoted in "Donald Trump Blasts NFL Anthem Protesters: 'Get That Son of a Bitch Off the Field'"

by Bryan Armen Graham for *The Guardian* on September 23, 2017. www.theguardian.com/sport/2017/sep/22/donald-trump-nfl-national-anthem-protests.

26. Donald Trump during a CNN interview with Don Lemon as reported in "Donald Trump's 'Blood' Comment About Megyn Kelly Draws Outrage" by Holly Yan for CNN News on Saturday, August 5, 2015. www.cnn.com/2015/08/08/politics/donald-trump-cnn-megyn-kelly-comment/index.html.

27. Donald Trump in a January 13, 2014, tweet as reported in "10 of Donald Trump's Most Embarrassing and Contradictory Tweets" by Mark Molloy on October 8, 2016, for *The Telegraph.* www.telegraph.co.uk/women/politics/10-of-donald-trumps-most-embarrassing-and-contradictory-tweets/.

28. Donald Trump at a campaign rally in South Carolina in 2015 as reported in "Trump: 'I Know Words, I Have the Best Words'—Obama Is 'Stupid' [Video]" by Steve Guest on December 30, 2015, for *The Daily Caller.* dailycaller.com/2015/12/30/trump-i-know-words-i-have-the-best-words-obama-is-stupid-video/.

29. Donald Trump in an October 17, 2012, tweet as reported in "Here Are Some of the Most Ridiculous Things Donald Trump Has Ever Tweeted" by Aliza Chasan on June 16, 2015, for *The New York Daily News.* www.nydailynews.com/news/national/donald-trump-twitter-article-1.2259806.

30. Ibid. Donald Trump in a May 8, 2013, tweet.

31. Donald Trump as quoted in "Donald Trump's 10 Most Offensive Quotes of All Time" by Lynette Rice on June 19, 2015, for *Entertainment Weekly*. ew.com/article/2015/06/29/donald-trump-most-offensive-comments/.

32. Donald Trump in a 2011 ABC News interview with Ashleigh Banfield as reported in "Trump 'The Beauty of Me Is That I'm Very Rich' Has Lost $1 Billion Since the Election" by Bess Levin on October 8, 2018, for *Vanity Fair*. www.vanityfair.com/news/2018/10/trump-has-lost-dollar1-billion-since-the-election.

33. An admission made in a 2015 tax filing regarding the Donald J. Trump Foundation as reported in "Trump Foundation Admits to Violating Rule Against 'Self-Dealing'" by Katie Reilly on November 22, 2016, for *Fortune*. fortune.com/2016/11/22/donald-trump-foundation-self-dealing-irs/.

34. Donald Trump in an interview on "CBS This Morning" from "Trump Defends 'Brilliantly' Using Bankruptcy Laws" by David Wright for CNN News on Wednesday, June 22, 2016. www.cnn.com/2016/06/22/politics/donald-trump-defends-bankruptcy-history/index.html/.

35. Donald Trump in an interview for *USA Today* as cited in "Hundreds of Small Businesses and Employees Have Reportedly Accused Donald Trump of Not Paying Them" by Michelle Mark for *Business Insider* on June 9, 2016.

www.businessinsider.com/ businesses-and-employees-accuse-donald-trump-of-not-paying-them-2016-6.

36. Donald Trump in an interview with Norah O'Donnell that aired on "CBS This Morning" as reported in "Trump: 'I'm the King of Debt'" by Louis Nelson on June 22, 2016, for *Politico*. www.politico.com/story/2016/06/trump-king-of-debt-224642.

Appendix 3—Photo Credits

(listed in order of text inclusion)

Title Page: Barnum and Bailey Circus. Photoseum.com.

PT Barnum. Worldatlas.com.

Shackleton expedition. Themarysue.com.

Ghost drawing. (Author created).

Ticket booth: Library of Congress (Cropped).

Train. Railwaywondersoftheworld.com.

Clown. Thecircusblog.com.

Dust storm. National Archives.

Bulldog Cafe. Martinturnbull.com.

Girl. Imgur.com.

Schoolhouse. Wikimedia Commons.

Factories. Nydailynews.com

Circus tent entrance. Castinglux.com.

Circus cart. Classic.circushistory.org.

Civil War soldiers. Timetoast.com.

Automobile. Silodrome.com.

Boy. Thehumanmarvels.com.

Performers. (Cropped version in text.) Screendaily.com.

Hippopotamus. Change.org.

Zeppelin. Wikiwand.com.

Man. Librarie-tropiques.fr.

Men. Cctimesdemocrat.com.

Prison. Copteseurope.info.

Bike riding. (Cropped version in text.) Reddit.com.

Elephant balancing. Reddit.com.

Woman. Klyker.com.

Trapeze artist. Reddit.com.

Cojoined twins. Buffalo.edu.

Shoe House. Ogden Union Station. (Cropped).

Rollercoaster. Facinate.com.

City.

https://lh3.googleusercontent.com/6yvSKFhWTQ6gOgPuxL0HeE ukvvB40xV_HmT hxH2A6e71PJMAeHxn_Wfle8G_MeKQPGEP TdU=s170.

Parade. Wikiwand.com.

Klan march. Reddit.com.

Woman. Listreallife.com.

Shack.

https://lh3.googleusercontent.com/ODMSA81NF7RdKtCMypC7g gOvuV3R-QdVWO8vPgrWNpQgzdP6RzLrl8a1oUK9VtIyo CrDsZU=s151.

Women. Wikipedia.org.

Man. Sideshowcollectors.com.

Carousel. Showmensmuseum.org.

Women in carnival ride. Justcarguy.blogspot.com.

Amusement ride. Forestparkhighlands.com.

Man. 8 tracks.com.

Indians. Alexwestern.wordpress.com.

Slaves. Magazine.uconn.edu.

Immigrants. Library of Congress.

Family. Cpr.org.

Zebras. (Cropped version in text.) Vintag.es.

Polar bears. Thecircusblog.com.

Strongman. Quora.com.

Men. Immigrantexpereince.krystymoon.org.

Farmers. Timetoast.com.

Store. Pubwiki.co.uk.

Stilt walkers. Imgur.com.

Phonebooths. Anglophile.ru.

Man. Peoples.ru.

Woman on horse. Bygonely.com.

Mansion. Californiasun.co.

Civil War battlefield. Pbs.org.

Fort. Civilwartalk.com.

Circus scene.
https://lh3.googleusercontent.com/s9BA6CpuXSC9JWNBOQhQB
u3M5xFCEWA TaB6sfhuOSLcUrMiZ2B7A05mH5bz6sj3
YJNNHdw=s137.

Prisoners. Foursquare.com.

Child laborers. Wikipedia.org.

Man. Zazzle.co.nz.

Tank. www.tanks-encyclopedia.com.

Susan B. Anthony. Timetoast.com.

William Lloyd Garrison. Discover.hubpages.com.

Woman. (Cropped version in text.) Mediastorehouse.com.

Clowns. Szinhaz.org.

Plymouth Rock. Roadsideamerica.com.

Young man. Findadeath.com.

Political Cartoon. Wikimedia.org.

Civil War Cemetery. Unrememberedhistory.com.

Liberty Bell. (Cropped version in text.) Atthefair.homestead.com.

Crowd. Library of Congress.

Lincoln Funeral. Karibu-travels.com.

Company storefront. Seattletimes.com.

Trains meet. Rgusrail.com

Empire State Building. Fineartamerica.com.

Mickey Mouse. Dailymail.co.uk./Andrew Parsons/I-Images.

Washington Monument. Gettysburgdaily.com.

Mount Rushmore. Reddit.com.

Car. Mcginneschevy.com.

Man. Daylol.com.

White House. National Park Service. (No claim to original U.S. Government works).

Yellowstone. Takinginthesights.com.

Meat Packing. https://lh3.googleusercontent.com/cY-EPNlDy OC1hrlrelAF784Pzt-4_Ss5 FmswHXvdqi8BUIVaozW6s8qM_ 5ucY5QbDi25ATk=s134.

St. Louis Arch. Missouriartscouncil.org.

Golden Gate Bridge. Jimcanning.com.

Statue of Liberty. Statueofliberty.org.

Cornelius Vanderbilt. Timetoast.com.

Man. Thingssaidanddone.wordpresscom.

Pentagon. Wikipedia.org.

Fort Knox. 40tnfun.fortunecity.ws.

Circus Performers. Vintag.es.

A Checklist of JEF Titles

* Winners of the Kenneth Patchen Award for the Innovative Novel

- ☐ 0 *Projections* by Eckhard Gerdes
- ☐ 2 *Ring in a River* by Eckhard Gerdes
- ☐ 3 *The Darkness Starts Up Where You Stand* by Arthur Winfield Knight
- ☐ 4 *Belighted Fiction*
- ☐ 5 *Othello Blues* by Harold Jaffe
- ☐ 9 *Recto & Verso: A Work of Asemism and Pareidolia* by Dominic Ward & Eckhard Gerdes (Fridge Magnet Edition)
- ☐ 9B *Recto & Verso: A Work of Asemism and Pareidolia* by Dominic Ward & Eckhard Gerdes (Trade Edition)
- ☐ 11 *Sore Eel Cheese* by The Flakxus Group (Limited Edition of 25)
- ☐ 14 *Writing Pictures: Case Studies in Photographic Criticism 1983-2012* by James R. Hugunin
- ☐ 15 *Wreck and Ruin: Photography, Temporality, and World (Dis)order* by James R. Hugunin
- ☐ 17 *John Barth, Bearded Bards & Splitting Hairs*
- ☐ 18 *99 Waves* by Persis Gerdes
- ☐ 23 *The Laugh that Laughs at the Laugh: Writing from and about the Pen Man, Raymond Federman*
- ☐ 24 *A-Way with it!: Contemporary Innovative Fiction*
- ☐ 28 *Paris 60* by Harold Jaffe
- ☐ 29 *The Literary Terrorism of Harold Jaffe*
- ☐ 33 *Apostrophe/Parenthesis* by Frederick Mark Kramer
- ☐ 34 *Journal of Experimental Fiction 34: Foremost Fiction: A Report from the Front Lines*
- ☐ 35 *Journal of Experimental Fiction 35*
- ☐ 36 *Scuff Mud* (cd)
- ☐ 37 *Bizarro Fiction: Journal of Experimental Fiction 37*
- ☐ 38 *ATTOHO #1* (cd-r)
- ☐ 39 *Journal of Experimental Fiction 39*
- ☐ 40 *Ambiguity* by Frederick Mark Kramer
- ☐ 41 *Prism and Graded Monotony* by Dominic Ward
- ☐ 42 *Short Tails* by Yuriy Tarnawsky
- ☐ 43 *Something Is Crook in Middlebrook* by James R. Hugunin
- ☐ 44 *Xanthous Mermaid Mechanics* by Brion Poloncic
- ☐ 45 *OD: Docufictions* by Harold Jaffe
- ☐ 46 *How to Break Article Noun* by Carolyn Chun*
- ☐ 47 *Collected Stort Shories* by Eric Belgum
- ☐ 48 *What Is Art?* by Norman Conquest
- ☐ 49 *Don't Sing Aloha When I Go* by Robert Casella
- ☐ 50 *Journal of Experimental Fiction 50*
- ☐ 51 *Oppression for the Heaven of It* by Moore Bowen*
- ☐ 52 *Elder Physics* by James R. Hugunin
- ☐ 53.1 *Like Blood in Water: Five Mininovels (The Placebo Effect Trilogy #1)* by Yuriy Tarnawsky

JEF

Journal of
Experimental
Fiction

www.ingramcontent.com/pod-product-compliance
Lightning Source LLC
Chambersburg PA
CBHW030743030726
47497CB00001B/110